mys pepper

C

DATE DUE

PRINTED IN U.S.A.

CHAPTER 1

VOULA VARGA WOKE UP on New Year's Day and went about her usual morning routine, not knowing it would be the final day of her life.

As she stood in her kitchen, waiting for the coffee maker to release her coffee, she scowled and tapped her long, black-lacquered fingernails impatiently.

Soon, she told herself, she would live in luxury and have a maid to bring her coffee in bed and fix her manicure. When that day finally came, all of the drudgery of hustling for a living would be behind her. Her humiliation would be over.

She couldn't wait to see Misty Falls in her rear-view mirror. The postcard-pretty little town, nestled in a scenic mountain valley, was a nice enough place, except for the people. The residents all bored her to tears with their terrible, awful, horrible, tedious niceness. On top of that, they failed to recognize her as any different from the rest of them.

Voula Varga should have been a star. If those Hollywood casting agents knew how to spot genuine talent, they would have seen it. But they were fools. Instead of giving her the lead roles she deserved, they cast her in small parts. Some actresses would have been happy to get a few speaking lines and a regular paycheck, but for Voula, each assignment was a personal insult. She was always cast in the same pathetic role: fortune-teller.

By the time she left Los Angeles, Voula Varga had been credited as the gypsy fortune-teller or psychic or voodoo priestess in more than forty feature-length films and an equal number of television dramas. Her closest thing to a breakout role had been in a fantasy epic, playing an evil sorceress who summoned the dead. It was to be her big break. Unfortunately, the film tanked at the box office and went on to become a joke. There were regular viewing parties around the country now, where people gathered to watch the movie and make fun of it, yelling out Voula's lines of corny dialog at the screen.

Her movie career had flatlined after that film, along with the careers of all but a few people associated with the failed endeavor. She fled Los Angeles and wandered from town to town, working odd jobs here and there until she stumbled upon a way to use her particular curse for her own gain.

Voula Varga was utterly perfect at playing a fortune-teller.

So, instead of fighting it, she embraced her curse and *became* her typecast role. Even before she'd fully mastered the tricks of the trade, people who visited her booth to have their palms read thought she was the real thing. From her dark, curly hair to her golden eyes, Voula looked the part of a mystical psychic, and now she played the part for real. It was the role of a lifetime, and she would soon be wealthy and powerful.

She had a plan.

She'd moved to Misty Falls six months earlier, in the summer. It was the warmest day of the year for the little town, and she was overdressed in her layers of dark scarves and flowing dresses. People eyed her uneasily on her first walk through town, as though they could tell she had a plan to suck the life savings out of all the gullible townspeople before disappearing again.

On the first day of the new year, Voula Varga poured her morning coffee, unlocked her front door, walked upstairs, and stood at one of the windows that overlooked the entire unsuspecting town. She stood there and she cackled her evil, malicious laugh, not unlike a witch in a bad movie.

Two hours later, the doorbell rang. Voula quickly changed out of her silky nightie into one of her everyday long dresses. She pulled on her winter jacket, grabbed a box of bullets, and answered the door.

"I have a little treat for us," Voula told the visitor as she held up the bullets. "Give me a minute to gather up some old cans, and we'll see if that lovely antique still fires."

The visitor was surprised by this suggestion, but reluctantly agreed to go along with the plan.

Of course her visitor had agreed to her suggestion of target practice. Voula always got what she wanted from regular people who weren't as sophisticated or as smart as her.

Voula smiled as they walked through the snow, down the sloping hill of the backyard. The visitor fretted that people would hear the gunshots, but Voula said, "They'll think it's just illegal fireworks, left over from last night."

They put foam earplugs in their ears, loaded the old gun, and took turns firing at aluminum soda cans lined up on a fallen log. The shots were loud, but the house was secluded, just outside of town, so Voula didn't worry about the town's bumbling police force showing up to snoop around.

Voula laughed freely as she fired shots at the cans. She missed every shot, but liked the feeling of the gun's kick in her hands. She loved the power. She couldn't get enough of it.

The visitor, however, wasn't as excited by target practice and began to grumble about cold hands.

Voula stopped shooting and pulled out one of her earplugs to re-mold it. She tilted her ear toward the house. "Do you hear something? Like crying?"

They listened in silence for a moment, but the only sound was the whistle of a breeze that had just picked up.

"Never mind," Voula said. "Must have been a stray spirit whimpering in the wind. Sometimes they get shy and stop talking when you actually listen."

They walked back up to the house, made a second pot of coffee, and went upstairs to the room where Voula hosted the knitting club and did readings.

As they talked about how last night's performance had gone, Voula tried to focus on what her visitor was saying, but it was all so boring and beneath her. She nodded and pretended to be listening as she sorted through her basket of knitted dolls. These dolls were her own invention, and she'd learned to knit just so she could make these little voodoo dolls. Even before they were dressed in their clothes, they seemed to have their own personalities. Sometimes, when she was finishing a doll, she imagined that she really *was* a witch, and that these objects held magical powers.

She picked up the green and purple masquerade mask she'd been given the night before. With a few snips of her sharp scissors and a dab of glue, she would be able to create a miniature version of the mask.

She smiled, because out of everything, the crafts were probably her favorite part. While knitting or creating miniature outfits, the rest of the world disappeared.

"What about you?" asked the visitor.

Voula looked up and blinked as she tried to recall the last few seconds of conversation.

"Sorry," Voula said as she pushed away the basket of dolls and crafting materials. "The spirits were speaking to me, and I didn't hear you over their noises." She made an elaborate hand gesture and uttered a nonsense spell before hissing, "Hush, foul spirits. Hush and be still."

The visitor fixed her with a steady look and repeated the same question Voula hadn't heard the first time. "Are you dating anyone? Your cheeks have the glow of a woman in love."

Voula snorted with contempt. "A wise woman doesn't confuse a few moments of vigorous exercise for love." She let out a mean-spirited cackle. Firing the gun had unleashed something in Voula. She felt raw and energized, and for once she wanted to say what she really felt instead of uttering the lines from a script.

"Vigorous exercise? Do you mean… a lover?"

Still warm from her witchlike laughter, Voula continued, "Men are only useful for two things, and the most pathetic of the lot are only useful for *one* thing, and that's paying the bills. Of course, you have to make all the right noises to let them think they're competent at the other thing, or you'll have to deal with the sulking." She rolled her eyes and groaned.

"I'm sorry I asked." The visitor frowned and pushed back their chair. "Never mind."

Voula sensed her control over the situation evaporating and quickly went into damage-control mode. She shook and convulsed, pretending to be fighting an internal battle with spirits. Gasping, she gripped the edge of the table and said hoarsely, "That wasn't me. That was a man-hating spirit." She convulsed, then waved her hands as though shooing away ghosts. "That wasn't me," she repeated.

The visitor didn't push the chair away and leave, but didn't seem comfortable, either. They looked down at the gun on the table, equal distance between them. The box of bullets sat alongside.

"Voula, tell me the truth," the visitor said gently. "Were you really possessed by a spirit just now? Is any of the stuff you do real? Do you even believe in the power of love?"

"What does it matter?" Voula spat back. "Don't act like you're better than me. Who were you thinking about shooting in the eye when you fired off those bullets in the backyard just now?"

The visitor gasped. "Nobody! I'd never think about killing a person."

"What if you could make it look like an accident?" Voula grinned and tapped her long, black-lacquered fingernails on the table. "Don't act like you haven't been planning the perfect murder ever since that first night we shared a bottle of wine and I said too much."

The visitor reached for the gun on the table. "This was a bad idea."

Voula reached for the gun at the same time. "Don't you dare wimp out."

CHAPTER 2

THE DAY BEFORE
(NEW YEAR'S EVE)
STORMY DAY

I WAS DEALING with what felt like the biggest decision of my life when my friend showed up at my front door.

"You're not dressed yet," Jessica said.

I clutched the colorful robe closed at my neck and chuckled. "And to think… the people of Misty Falls say *I'm the one* with the keen powers of observation."

Jessica arched her delicate red eyebrows and smirked. "People say that? You mean when they're not clucking their tongues over that fancy car you drive?" She nodded toward my car, parked in the snowy driveway and added, "Speaking of which, I see you got the window fixed, but not the bullet holes."

"Bullet holes add character." I waved for her to come in, and shivered as the cold air swirled up the interior of my robe.

"Character, huh?" She looked for an instant like she might cry, but shrugged it away. "Better those bullet holes are in the car than my best friend, I suppose."

She wasn't moving fast enough, so I grabbed her arm and playfully yanked her in. It was snowy and cold that night, and she was letting out the heat, but more importantly, I didn't want my tenant to see me in the bathrobe. *Not again.*

Jessica narrowed her pretty blue eyes as she looked me up and down. "Stormy Day, what's going on here with this clown outfit? Are you having a meltdown because of the gift shop? Retail isn't for everyone, but you can tell me if you're not up for the party tonight. You *have* been through a lot lately."

"I'm fine," I said, and I meant it. Now that Christmas was done, I was almost looking forward to doing storewide inventory. *Almost.*

"You're not fine. You're wearing the bathrobe of a murderer, and it's not even a *nice* bathrobe." She leaned in to examine the fabric. "Are those smudgy things flowers or pink flamingos?"

"They might be fish." I smoothed out a section of the robe and used my finger to trace a shape that could have been a fish. "If you don't want to be staring at this magnificent work of art all night, help me pick out something better to wear. I've got three dresses, but they're all wrong."

"Then wear jeans."

"That's my backup plan!"

Jessica hung her jacket by the door and proceeded into the adjacent open-plan kitchen, where she stuffed groceries into the fridge, then followed me down the hallway to my bedroom, where the *real* owner of the house was relaxing on *his* bed.

"Jeffrey McFluffy Trousers," Jessica cooed as she jumped on the bed and smothered her face in his dark gray tummy.

I watched, smiling, as Jeffrey, my new Russian Blue cat, pretended not to enjoy the attention being lavished on him.

"Let's see your dresses," Jessica said, her voice muffled by Jeffrey's soft fur as she gave him what we called *schnerfles*. With the back of her head facing me, I got a good view of her fancy hairstyle. Her naturally red locks were gathered into a twist, with small braids of red hair woven through.

Seeing her cute braids made me miss my long hair, but only fleetingly. I didn't miss all the time I used to spend using a blow drier or flat iron to straighten my naturally curly hair. My short pixie cut was much more sensible and easy, which was perfect. Moving back to my hometown and giving up my executive lifestyle in the venture capital business was all about simplifying.

I gathered the dress options for Jessica's opinion. All three had been in the window of Blue Enchantment before I dropped in and bought them all. Undressing window display mannequins was becoming a guilty pleasure of mine.

Jessica tore herself away from her noisy *schnerfles* on the cat just long enough to say, "The black and white stripes."

"Won't I look like a zebra?"

"Sure, but I don't think there'll be any lions or tigers at the Fox and Hound. Steer clear of the watering hole, just in case."

I couldn't argue with her logic, so I slipped off the warm bathrobe and finished getting dressed. I went into the washroom to fluff up my hair, where I was surprised to hear a muffled woman's voice.

ANGELA PEPPER

"Jessica," I hissed from the bathroom doorway. "Come here. Quickly. I think Logan's got a woman over."

She came running, her blue eyes wide and her pale cheeks flushed. "Is he allowed?"

I smiled. Technically, yes, Logan Sanderson could have anyone he wanted over. He paid his rent on time, and whatever he did over there was his business, but I still felt like I'd caught him at something.

I held my finger up to my lips as I pressed my ear against the wall separating the two bathrooms.

"He can't do this to us," Jessica sputtered as her freckled cheeks became even redder. "I mean, he can't do this to you. He's supposed to be your date for tonight."

"He's not my date," I said softly. "I asked him to be our chauffeur."

Jessica shushed me and pressed her ear to the wall. The muffled sounds were a real woman's voice, and not the TV or radio. Unfortunately, the walls of my duplex were just thick enough to prevent me from making out any of the words she was saying.

"Maybe it's a client," I whispered. "Some after-hours legal emergency."

Jessica grabbed the water glass from my bathroom counter and held it between the wall and her ear. "Nope. Still can't hear what she's saying." She pulled away from the wall and set the glass back on the counter. "Stormy," she said slowly. "What did you mean, about Logan being our chauffeur?"

I used my hands to shoo her out of the bathroom and away from the shared wall. The rest of the house had better soundproofing, so I chased her all the way to the kitchen, where I offered her some of the fancy crackers and soft cheese I'd set out.

She crunched on the snacks, then demanded an answer. "Why doesn't Logan know he's your date tonight?"

"It's not a date. I can't exactly date my tenant."

"So, why take him to a New Year's Eve party? What happens at midnight when everyone's kissing?"

She had a good point, but now I was thinking about kissing Logan, feeling the tickle of his beard on my cheek. To stall, I stacked some delicious, creamy soft cheese between two different kinds of crackers and stuffed my mouth.

Jessica waited patiently for me to swallow and answer.

"We could kiss," I said. "But it's not a date, because dating my tenant would be a disaster. I've got a whole series of activities in mind. Come spring, we can work on the garden together. I was hoping that if things went well, neither of us would notice we were dating until we were already married." I let out a self-conscious giggle. "By the way, we're eating goat cheese."

"This is goat cheese? Who knew goats made such delicious cheese?"

"It's called chèvre."

"Great. We can serve chèvre at your wedding to Logan, when you surprise him with that. Just a tip, though. If you're wearing a big white dress, he might get suspicious."

"Good tip."

Something dark streaked by the edge of my vision. Jessica and I made jokes about surprise weddings for the next few minutes, not noticing that Jeffrey had jumped up to sample the goat cheese. We were oblivious to his forbidden feasting until he got too enthusiastic and knocked some cutlery off the counter.

I grabbed him and set him back down on the floor, laughing. "Nice try, little man. You nearly got away with the perfect crime, but you got greedy."

Jessica asked, in a serious tone, "Do you think it's possible to plan the perfect crime? To get away with murder?"

"Is your boss making you triple-wash the pre-washed spinach again?"

"Very funny." She smiled wanly and handed me a cracker sandwich that may or may not have been pre-licked by a gray cat.

"I just have a bad feeling," she said. "I lie awake in bed thinking about stuff. After what happened to Mr. Michaels, it's all everyone wants to talk about. Everybody's got their own theory about where the killer went wrong."

I snorted. "The killer went wrong by getting on my bad side."

"Then it's settled. You can never move out of Misty Falls again. We need you to scare away those would-be murderers."

"Who said I was thinking about leaving?"

"Sometimes you get that faraway look, like a kid who wants to run away from home."

"So, I'm a runaway?" I asked in a light tone.

She fixed me with her bright blue eyes, which were just as lively as I remembered from when we were little kids, bonding over loose teeth and favorite comic books.

"Jessica, I'm not going anywhere. I moved back here for a reason."

She kept giving me her skeptical look.

To change the topic, I opened the container of herbed olives. "These aren't garlic-stuffed," I assured her. "Just fresh herbs, in case *you* want to smooch someone at midnight."

She helped herself to the plump, glistening olives with a happy sigh. "Good. I'll crash here tonight, and I'll have decent breath for smooching Jeffrey McFluffy Trousers."

There was a knock at the door.

"Logan's here," I said. "Quick, refill the cheese tray and make it look like we haven't touched it."

"Of course," she said as she spread out more crackers. "We are *dainty ladies* and we'd never eat the guest food before the guests arrive."

I ran to the door, nearly tripping over Jeffrey, who seemed to think he was a dog sometimes, eager to see who was at to the door when someone knocked softly, but not if they knocked loudly. He pawed the door impatiently.

I opened the door, bracing myself for the possibility Logan would have his own date for the evening, the woman whose voice I'd heard through the bathroom wall.

To my relief, he was alone. To my disappointment, he wore jeans and a college sweatshirt, both well worn. I'd seen him in suits, so I knew he owned good clothes, but this casual attire didn't bode well.

"Stormy Day in a dress," he said gruffly. "For a kooky cat lady, you clean up real nice once the bathrobe comes off."

"Logan Sanderson, for a hotshot lawyer, you resemble an unemployed drummer on your days off."

He looked down my body. "Those are some nice stripes. Black and white. Very eye-catching."

13

Logan's blue eyes took a second and a third tour of my zebra stripes, and he flashed me his perfect teeth. His dark beard made his teeth look even brighter, and his lips redder.

Despite the cold air coming in the open door, I was feeling warmer and warmer.

He nodded down at Jeffrey, who was sniffing and rubbing his face on the frayed hem of Logan's jeans. "May I come in, or are we waiting for the cat to finish claiming me? You know, they rub their cheek glands on things they like. He's saying I'm *his* now."

"That would be funny if humans did that."

He laughed. "It would make life easier." He scooped up Jeffrey, gave him a manly kiss on the forehead, then handed him to me.

I stepped aside and nodded for Logan to come in. As I clutched the squirming cat to my chest, I noticed how rapidly my heart was beating. The night wasn't going as planned, but it did promise to be memorable.

CHAPTER 3

I INTRODUCED LOGAN to Jessica. She'd seen him around town, including one night in December that we'd all been at the Fox and Hound, but they hadn't met. She immediately showered him with praise for being such a hero the night I was nearly shot and killed.

"You're giving me too much credit," he protested. "Stormy took care of herself, and I didn't get involved in any of the action."

"Maybe next time," she said. "You look like you work out." She reached for his bicep, and he flexed for her, pursing his lips in that funny way guys do when they're focusing on their arm muscles. Jessica gave me a nod of approval. "Stormy, your boy here's got some muscles."

"Good. Come spring, he can help me move some of those big rocks around the front flowerbed."

Logan grunted, "Me. Break. Rocks. On. Head."

We laughed while Jessica grabbed the snacks and steered us toward the living room.

Jessica said to my tenant, "Any friend of Stormy's is a friend of mine, so you just let me know if you ever need anything."

"Like what?" He took a seat at the end of the sofa. His tone was friendly, but not flirtatious. He had been giving Jessica some admiring looks, glancing over her bright red hair and attractive figure, but his eyes didn't linger. His gaze kept returning to my black and white stripes, then he spotted Jeffrey circling the coffee table and cheese plate with bad intentions, and scooped the cat up into his lap. Jeffrey squawked, but didn't run away.

"Like what? Hmm." Jessica tapped her freckled chin and looked up at the ceiling. "Well, I'm the one to call if you need a deal on catering. The sandwich shop I manage specializes in retro party food. Have you ever had miniature cocktail wieners in aspic? It was all the rage in the sixties to put anything and everything into molded gelatin. Of course, we do regular food, too, but the retro showpiece dishes are mainly to get people talking."

"That does sound fun," he said. "Would you guys make ants on a log? That's a celery stick with peanut butter and raisins."

"I know all about ants on a log!" She punched him on the arm, her tomboy side coming out, in contrast to her princess-styled red hair.

"I've always wanted to have a fondue party," he said, and soon the two of them were engrossed in conversation about the best cheeses for melting, and whether or not raclette parties—the kind where guests cook their own skewered food on a tabletop grill—were the height of entertainment or just a goofy fad.

I watched, smiling, as the two of them chatted.

Jeffrey, who had lodged a verbal complaint when Logan scooped him onto his lap, seemed to have mixed feelings about his current predicament. He'd settled on one of Logan's thighs, and was being petted vigorously. Logan's hand looked so big on the cat's small head, bobbing up and down with the pats. Jeffrey lengthened his body and wrapped his front paws around Logan's knee, looking like a kid gripping the safety rail on a roller-coaster—having the time of his life, but also unsure about what might happen next.

I poured sparkling apple juice for everyone, then the three of us nibbled the snacks and debated how to host the perfect dinner party. We agreed that food was important, but not as important as having the right dinner guests. You wanted a few people who were polite, at least one to help you with serving, and maybe one or two bad seeds who would stir up a bit of trouble to keep things lively. The way Logan talked, I wondered if he saw himself as a bad seed who'd drink too much wine and cause a scene. That was probably a bad thing for someone trying to maintain a professional image.

Time flew, until the reminder on my phone beeped that it was time to get going to the party.

Jessica pointed to Logan's college-logo sweatshirt and said, "If you change that shirt, you can be more than just our chauffeur. They're still selling tickets at the door, so get yourself changed and join us for a night of dancing."

"Who has two thumbs and doesn't dance?" He used his thumbs to point to himself. "This lawyer."

I interjected, "You don't have to dance. Just come and hang out."

He stroked his neatly trimmed beard and looked around my living room like he was searching for an excuse. Jeffrey was still on his lap, eyeing the last chunk of cheese.

"I appreciate the offer, ladies, but I've got a full night of research ahead of me. Back in my old life, I specialized in a very narrow field of law, but now that I'm one of only a few lawyers in a small town, I'm training myself to become more of a generalist."

"On New Year's Eve?" Jessica squealed in disbelief. "You're not planning to ring in the new year studying. Tell us the truth. Have you got a girl coming over? Is she there right now? Is that who I heard through the bathroom wall?"

I shot Jessica a wide-eyed look, but it was too late. The question had been asked, and I was curious to hear his answer. Even Jeffrey looked interested, gazing up from his perch on Logan's knee.

Logan looked right at me. "My landlady never warned me about thin walls. Hear anything good lately?" He raised one dark eyebrow, turning his statement flirty.

"Anything good?" I gave him a bewildered look. "I wasn't spying, but the wall between the bathrooms is thin, apparently. This house is new to me, and you're my first tenant."

Jessica said, "We didn't hear anything interesting." She grabbed the last cracker and gave him a goofy grin. "Bring your friend along tonight. The more, the merrier."

"Yes, you're both welcome to come."

He smiled up at me. "I told you the truth. I'll be spending tonight alone, studying. And I don't dance."

I got to my feet and smoothed down the stripes of my new dress. Even if I did look like a zebra, I looked like the kind of zebra Logan couldn't take his eyes off.

"Have fun with your studying," I said with a smile. "We'll be sure to raise a toast to your new endeavors as a generalist."

"And save me a kiss," he said with an even bigger smile.

"A kiss?" I repeated.

Jessica, who'd just taken a sip of her sparkling apple juice, made a noise as she struggled to swallow her drink without choking.

Logan gently evicted Jeffrey from his lap, then got to his feet. "Sure. If you have any left over, it's a cheap and easy way to tip your chauffeur."

The three of us moved over to the door and started putting on our jackets. Jessica patted Logan on the shoulder and said, "Cool your jets, there, big guy. If you want a kiss, you need to take my friend Stormy on an official date before you even try."

He gazed down at me, still much taller than me even after I'd put my high heels on. "I'll take that under advisement," he said huskily.

"Thanks for driving us," I said. "It's such a busy night for the taxis, but you don't have to wait up. We'll get our own ride home. It's easier to share a ride when everyone's leaving the same place."

"It sounds like the whole town's going to be at this party," he said.

Jessica teased, "Everyone but you, Mr. Non-Dancing Lawyer Pants."

He opened the door and the three of us stepped out into the crisp night air. I walked toward Logan's mid-sized SUV in the shared driveway, carefully stepping where the snow had been flattened by tires so I didn't get snow inside my party shoes.

The yard was well lit by street lamps, and I noticed there was a set of tracks behind Logan's SUV that didn't match his tires. The tracks couldn't be from Jessica's little car turning around, because she'd parked on the street facing the way she would have been headed when coming from her apartment.

These tire tracks were from whoever had been at Logan's place, talking to him from his bathroom.

"Ooh, pictures," Jessica said. "By the snowy tree."

I backtracked and posed next to her, with a snow-covered tree as our backdrop.

"Gorgeous, ladies," he said as he clicked pictures using her phone, some with the flash and some without. "Now do the Charlie's Angels pose."

Jessica and I made finger guns and struck poses until we were laughing through chattering teeth. Then we piled into our chauffeur's vehicle and headed toward the Fox and Hound.

By the time we pulled into the parking lot for the pub, Logan still hadn't been convinced that dancing was something a real man could enjoy.

Jessica pointed to an unusual car in the parking lot —a hearse. "Look! The voodoo lady is here," she said. "I wonder if she's doing fortunes tonight."

"Voodoo lady?" Logan asked. "Is this some Misty Falls tradition I should know about?"

"Beats me." I reached for the door handle and let myself out of the vehicle. I'd gotten about six feet away when I suddenly remembered something troubling and turned around.

Logan lowered his window and leaned out. "Did you forget something?"

Jessica didn't notice me turning back, because she'd spotted some people she knew and started talking to them near the entrance.

I trotted back over to talk with Logan without having to yell across the parking lot. When I reached his door, the air around us crackled with a different energy now that it was just the two of us. He leaned out the window, his blue eyes level with mine.

"It's probably nothing," I said casually. "But remember when we were at the station together, giving my statement?"

"And you were in that fuzzy, splotchy housecoat? How could I forget?"

"Didn't that lady officer, Peggy Wiggles, say something about the police being busy with complaints about some voodoo lady?"

He nodded, his expression growing worried. "You're right. She did mention a voodoo lady. What are the odds this town would have two of 'em?"

"You should come in and meet her. A person like that might be needing a lawyer soon."

He frowned at the hearse, then turned back to me. "You should stay away from this person. It's not that I'm superstitious or believe in magic, because I don't, but some fortune-tellers can be dangerous. Just like all people, there are good ones and bad ones, but when it comes to something like this, the bad ones are… bad seeds, and not in the fun way."

We both looked over at the strange vehicle.

The woman's hearse was black, like most modern hearses, but had a swirling custom paint job on the sides. The lettering was purple and blue:

VIBRANT & VIVACIOUS!
~ VOULA VARGA ~
PSYCHIC EXTRAORDINAIRE

I chuckled, trying to lighten the mood. "Are you worried she's going to get a hex put on me? Logan, I've already survived one attempted murder—two, if you count the sleeping pills. I think I'll be okay dealing with some gypsy palm reader, or whatever she is."

Behind me, Jessica called for me to come join her.

Logan fidgeted with his seatbelt, like he was considering parking and coming in.

"They don't have a dress code," I said. "You look like a college kid on laundry day, but I'm not too ashamed to be seen with you."

"Just be careful," he said. "Have fun tonight, but keep your eyes open, okay?"

"I'm a big girl," I said cheerily. "Happy studying."

He leaned out, like he was expecting a kiss goodbye. I leaned toward him for the briefest of moments, then we both jerked back, catching ourselves.

"Thanks again for the lift," I said as I backed away, waving. "Don't wait up!"

He waved back, eyed the psychic's hearse one more time, then raised his window and drove away.

CHAPTER 4

I JOINED JESSICA and the two people she was talking to near the pub's entrance. Her friends were a couple, both with sandy brown hair, but I didn't know who they were because both wore masquerade ball masks.

Jessica had pulled on her disguise, too—a glittering red mask that made her look like an orange-haired, crime-fighting superhero. I quickly reached into my purse and donned mine so I would fit in. My costume mask, covered in glittering purple sequins and accented with green feathers, had been purchased from the town's costume shop earlier that month. I'd bought it as an excuse to do some snooping, and now I was happy to put it to use.

"Stormy Day, you don't recognize us," said the male of the couple.

"You sound disappointed," I said lightly. "But shouldn't you be glad your disguises are so good?"

I leaned in to admire the intricate beadwork on the couple's matching brown-gold masks.

"Those are lovely, by the way," I said.

"Marcy made them," he said.

I took two steps back in surprise. "Marvin and Marcy! I should have guessed it was you."

Marcy reached out to give me a hug. "So good to see you again, and in one piece, with no bullet holes." She squeezed me hard, like she really meant it.

Marvin and Marcy were a nice couple in their early forties who owned the local computer repair shop, Misty Microchips. The store was two blocks off the main retail strip, not far from my gift shop. I'd first met the couple through Jessica, and we'd all been out for Chinese food at the Golden Wok a few times, plus Marcy regularly popped into the gift shop to "soak in the cuteness." Marvin and Marcy had been married for ten years and didn't have kids, unless you counted the Labrador-Poodle cross they were seldom without.

"No wonder I didn't recognize you," I said. "You don't have Stanley with you."

Marcy pouted, her lips sticking out in an exaggerated duck-bill shape to compensate for her eyes not being visible.

"Poor Stanley-boo-boo had to stay home," she said. "We put his handsome tuxedo jacket on, though. That's what we call the compression vest we got from the dog therapist. It gives them a hug that calms them down. Poor guy gets so nervous about the fireworks, so we probably won't stay here too late."

"He'll be fine," Marvin said with a groan. "That poor dog wouldn't be such a neurotic wuss if you didn't coddle him so much."

Marcy sighed. "Says the man who feeds him bacon scraps."

Marvin cleared his throat, but didn't deny the allegations.

Considering the number of people-food treats that my cat had been enjoying, I couldn't judge either of them. I looked down at my feet and kicked a chunk of snow with the toe of my shoe.

Another group walked past us and opened the door of the pub, letting music and laughter spill out into the wintry night.

"Brrrrr," Marvin said. "Shall we, ladies? We didn't buy tickets to stand shivering in the parking lot."

"I should hope not," Marcy said huffily. "These tickets weren't cheap. I hope the midnight buffet is better than the one we had at your cousin's house last year."

The couple walked on ahead, their backs to us as they argued with each other.

"My cousin's buffet wasn't so bad," Marvin said.

"Marvin! It was nothing but a sad tray of pickles and a stack of rice cakes."

"Some people can't eat gluten or dairy. They were just trying to accommodate everyone's diet needs." He gripped her hand, leaned toward her ear, and said, "Marcy, please don't start complaining and picking everything apart the way you always do."

She yanked her hand out of his and pulled open the door to the pub. "If you don't want to hear me complain, you'd better stay away from the booze tonight."

He leaned closer to her and said something I couldn't hear. Marcy listened, frowning, then looked over her shoulder and offered us an apologetic smile. "Sorry for the bickering," she said. "I get cranky when I'm low blood sugar. I'm not diabetic or anything, but I've got that condition. What's it called? Oh, right, being human."

She let out a squeaky laugh, and Jessica and I joined in awkwardly.

Marcy said, "You'll still sit at our table, won't you? We promise to behave."

"Of course we will," Jessica said, with enough warmth to smooth out the discomfort.

We all walked into the cozy, noise-filled pub, and gave our tickets to the doorman. Marvin and Marcy went ahead to the upper level to scout for a table while Jessica and I left the group's winter jackets at the coat check.

"What's going on with those two?" I asked Jessica.

She raised her red eyebrows high above her glittering red masquerade mask. "They're always a bit edgy when they don't have the dog with them. He's some sort of relationship buffer. I'm sure everything's fine."

We finished at the coat check and made our way through the crowded bar. Less than a third of the people in attendance wore masquerade masks, but I was surprised at the effect. I hadn't been back in Misty Falls long enough to know everyone, but as I glanced around, I didn't see a single familiar face. I felt unsettled and surrounded by strangers, some of whom could be dangerous.

I followed Jessica up the stairs to the upper level of the pub, paying minimal attention to where I was going. I'd heard the words "voodoo lady" buzzing around in me in conversations, and now I was curious about this Voula Varga person. I scanned the pub for someone who looked like a "psychic extraordinaire."

It didn't take long to spot someone who fit the name and title. A regal figure with billowing, curly, dark hair sat near the upper level's railing, the wall to her back and the entire place within her view. She wore dark, iridescent layers of deep purple and green. My own mask would have been a perfect match for her outfit, if she'd needed one, which she didn't. Instead of a mask made of fabric, glue, and sequins, like the rest of us had, she wore a makeup mask of dark paint around her eyes. The edges were defined with glued-on sequins, and she wore long false eyelashes that glittered and caught the light. She saw me looking her way and caught me in her gaze, her gold-hued eyes practically glowing.

I nearly tripped over nothing. Voula Varga had the theatrical aura of a circus performer and the hungry eyes of a tiger.

I broke away from her visual grip on me and elbowed Jessica, saying, "If that woman over there isn't the one with the hearse parked outside, this town has two voodoo ladies."

Jessica snickered. "That's Voula, all right. She's just sitting there with some friends, though. It doesn't look like she's telling fortunes tonight, but who knows. The night is young. Hey, she might be able to help you with Logan."

"Hah! In what way? A love potion?"

"Something like that. She makes these knitted dolls that are magical. You dress them up like the person you want to fall in love with you."

"That's adorable, yet disturbing. Wait. Jessica, how do you know about this? Don't tell me you have one of these voodoo dolls hidden in your apartment."

"I certainly don't have one… hidden under my pillow."

I let out an exaggerated gasp. "You wicked girl! Who's the guy? I mean, who is the voodoo doll supposed to be?"

"Can't say. But if it works, you'll find out soon enough."

"Um… okay." I racked my brain to think of who her top crush might be. She liked a few guys, including a banker from the credit union, who ate lunch at the sandwich shop several times a week, plus there was her on-again-off-again former boyfriend, the professional skateboarder, who "chilled" in Misty Falls when he wasn't touring, and then there was the new guy, a driver who delivered lunch meats to the cafe. It could have been any of those guys, or someone new. I got so wrapped up in trying to figure it out, I came to a standstill.

Jessica caught my hand and tugged me to keep walking. She kept me close as we squeezed our way through the crowd. I finally spotted a few familiar faces—people I knew from school days, from before I left town, as well as some people I'd gotten to know recently, thanks to owning a busy retail store.

We reached our table, where Marvin and Marcy were already seated, and took our spots across from them. They seemed to have gotten over their tiff, and were helping each other put on pointed party hats. Theirs were gold, the same as their masks, and as I was commenting on how perfectly everything matched, our waitress appeared and handed me and Jessica a purple hat and a red one, respectively.

"Good evening, darlings," the waitress said. "Aren't we all looking gorgeous tonight!"

"You're Dharma, right?" I said to the waitress. We'd only met once before, but she'd made quite an impression on me. With her snowy white hair, she had to be in her sixties, but moved like she could work a shift slinging drinks and then go home and bake a pie or two before sunrise.

Her eyes twinkled as she smiled, revealing teeth as pearly white as her downy hair. "That's right, honey. My name's Dharma, which rhymes with karma, and I live a charmed life because I help others as much as I can."

"It's nice to see you again," I said.

"You too, dear."

We were interrupted by loud laughter that sounded like cackling, cutting through the din. Everyone at the table, plus our waitress, turned to look for the source of the noise. It was Voula's table making all the racket, and she was the loudest one, laughing with her head thrown back in a theatrical way.

Dharma turned back to us with a sour look on her face. "You know that woman is a witch, right? She practices powerful magic. You young folks should steer clear of her, do you hear me? She's going to make some people in this town very rich, but nothing comes without a cost." She pulled out a notepad and tapped her pen to it. "Now what can I bring you to drink?"

The four of us exchanged looks, but with the masquerade masks on, it was hard to see each other's expressions. I finally raised my hand and ordered a bottle of Chardonnay for us to share.

Dharma nodded, turned her head to cast a dirty look toward Voula's table, then left to get our order.

Jessica leaned in over the table. "What was *that* all about?"

Marcy nodded and answered, "Professional rivalry. Dharma Lake thinks *she* should be the only matchmaker in town."

"That's right," I said as a memory came back clearly. "That Dharma lady is totally a matchmaker.

29

The first time I met her, she tried to set me up with someone. But it seemed more like a hobby than her profession. Are you guys saying she charges for setting people up?"

"Dharma doesn't charge," Marvin answered. "She does good deeds for karma, remember?" He let out a disapproving chuckle. "What a sucker," he muttered under his breath.

Marcy smacked him on the arm. "Don't be nasty. Some people really are nice."

The two of them bickered for a few minutes, then Marvin said to the group, "Dharma Lake isn't as sweet and innocent as she pretends to be. I've heard things."

Jessica and I asked, in unison, "Like what?"

Marvin just smiled and tilted his chin up to alert us that Dharma had returned with our wine and four glasses. We all sat in rigid silence as she set up the stemware and poured our first round. I studied her finely wrinkled face and tried to find any sign of malice, but all I found were a few sunspots and some white hairs on her chin. I'd pulled a few stray hairs out of my own chin recently, so I knew chin hairs were evil, but evil in a grooming and aging sort of way, and not a sign of *repressed evil.*

Dharma finished pouring the wine, took our order for chicken wings and other appetizers, then went to tend the other tables in the area.

I watched out of the corner of my eye as she approached the table where Voula was sitting. Sure enough, I could see Dharma's body language changing when she talked to her so-called rival. She was clearly on edge, her movements jerky and her posture defensive.

My friends complimented the wine and chatted amongst themselves while I kept my gaze riveted on Dharma and Voula.

It was hard for me to estimate Voula's age because of her masquerade makeup. She sat with three other women, and the two I could see clearly appeared to be dark-haired sisters in their sixties. Voula seemed younger, either early forties or a well-preserved fifty. Her dark, curly hair looked thick, like the mane of an exotic jungle cat.

She and Dharma were clearly arguing about something. The voodoo lady's voice was rising in volume, but I couldn't hear her words over the music and chatter in the crowded pub. I felt sorry for Dharma, and had a difficult time keeping my butt glued to my chair and not jumping up to defend the white-haired waitress.

Suddenly, Dharma lunged for the pitcher of ice water that had been sitting on the table. She tossed the entire thing on Voula, who jumped to her feet in a sputtering rage.

The whole section now noticed the fight between the two women and went quiet, waiting to see what would happen next.

Voula howled, "You dare call me a WITCH? I'll SHOW YOU a witch!"

"It's not fair!" Dharma yelled back. "You can't use your black magic for gain. It's not fair. Using magic isn't fair."

Voula stood glowering, an imposing figure at nearly a foot taller than the senior waitress. She plucked an ice cube from her plunging neckline like she was pulling out a dagger, and tossed the ice to the floor. She drew back her dripping wet arm, like she was about to hurl something at the waitress, but then she stopped.

Around me, people murmured about spells and curses and getting on the wrong side of scary people.

Voula seemed to feed off the energy of the crowd, getting bigger, or so it seemed. It was possible the tossed water was making her curls frizz up.

She tipped her head from side to side nonchalantly, shook out her arm and said, "You're not worth it. I'll save my magic for the paying customers, who appreciate my talents for making them rich."

Dharma bowed her head, turned, and walked away briskly. Even in the dim light of the pub, I could see her cheeks flushing with rage or shame.

Across the table from me, Marvin began to clap.

"Wonderful performance," he said, still clapping.

People around us let out sounds of relief and joined in the applause. Some of them were already inebriated enough to believe they'd just witnessed dinner theater, by the sound of it.

"Now, that's entertainment!" Marvin kept clapping while Marcy looked like she wanted to crawl under the table and pretend she didn't know him.

I leaned over to Jessica and whispered, "We can't say our first New Year's Eve together in a decade was boring, can we?"

She whispered back, "I'm sorry about Marvin. He's not usually so obnoxious. Something's gotten into him lately."

I nodded toward the bottle of wine, which was being emptied into Marvin's empty glass by Marvin. "Some Chardonnay is getting into him tonight."

"That man is a hero," she said in a low voice. "He's heroically saving all of us from a wicked hangover."

"You look thirsty, though. I'm not sure if our waitress will be back, so I'm going to head over to the bar and get another bottle."

Jessica reached for her purse. "It's my turn. Let me get this one."

I pushed my chair back and got up quickly. The wine hadn't been expensive, even by Misty Falls standards, but I knew Jessica's accounts were at their limits.

"This next one's actually on the house," I lied.

"Really?" Even with the red glittering mask over her eyes, she gave me a skeptical look.

"Yes, that bottle was on the two-for-one list."

Jessica grinned. "Oh, Stormy, you're so brilliant at getting deals! I didn't even know there was a two-for-one list. And it was nice wine, too, from what I tasted." She licked her lips in anticipation of a second glass, assuming we could keep it away from Marvin's thirsty lips long enough to liberate a serving.

I grabbed my purse from the back of my chair. Jessica's gaze went to my purse, and I anticipated her thoughts: *If the second bottle was free, what did I need my wallet for?*

"Just going to freshen up in the washroom," I explained. "If the food shows up, don't wait for me to dig in."

I left the table and wove my way through the crowd, stopping at the bar to prepay for another bottle of wine, then making my way to the ladies' room.

The washroom was relatively quiet and chilly compared to the rest of the bar. A tiny window was open for fresh air. The doors for all the stalls were open, and there was only one other person in there with me: the voodoo lady.

The front of her dark clothes were black from the tossed pitcher of water, but she didn't seem as concerned about that as she was her face.

Facing the mirror, she scrubbed at the smeared dark makeup around her eyes. She did not look happy. The water had caused her beautiful mask to melt down her cheeks. I couldn't help but flinch when she looked my way, because the sopping-wet, bedraggled woman looked like something from a horror movie—something that might crawl out of a dark lagoon.

"Don't be frightened," she said. "I don't bite."

"Here, let me help you with that," I said as I dug around in my purse. I could feel her eyes on me, which caused me to nervously start a dialog with the contents of my bag. "Hello, purse guts, hello, breath mints and things I forgot I had in here."

She didn't say anything in response to my rambling chatter, so I kept going, even while I told myself to shut up. It was like a case of nervous giggles, only without the giggles.

"Darn you, purse, I know you have tissues. Don't hold out. Soft tissues are so much nicer than those awful brown paper towels. Those darn things are scratchier than tree bark, aren't they? And when you get them damp, they have that weird pulpy smell. Why is that, do you suppose? How can freshly cut wood smell so good, yet the smell of damp cardboard is the epitome of revolting?"

I looked straight at Voula, pretending I'd been talking to her the whole time, and not talking to my purse like a weirdo.

"Damp cardboard?" She sniffed the wadded brown paper towels she'd been using on her smeared makeup. "You are right. That smell is revolting." She turned to meet her own golden tigress eyes in the mirror, and frowned at her black-streaked face. "I am revolting."

"No, don't say that." I finally located my pack of tissues, plus a travel-sized bottle of moisturizer. "Here, try this." I set the items on the counter between us, carefully avoiding hand-to-hand contact.

Maybe it was the fact that the waitress had called Voula a witch and accused her of practicing black magic, or maybe it was the terrifying effect of her smeared dark makeup, but I felt apprehension toward the alleged psychic. I also felt pity, but not as strongly as the apprehension.

She tentatively applied some of my moisturizer to one dark-streaked cheek to loosen up the makeup, then stroked it off with a clean, soft tissue. The darkness came off—not perfectly, but at least she wasn't scrubbing her cheek raw.

"Thank you," she said. Her voice had an accent to it, maybe Eastern European, but it could have been an affectation—all part of her branding or image, like driving a hearse around town.

What next? I couldn't leave without using the washroom in some way. I'm not usually the superstitious type, but I worried she would put a curse on me for being rude if I did. So, I carefully removed my glittering masquerade mask, lifting my cone-shaped party hat so I didn't tangle the elastics. I set the mask on the counter and started fixing my eye makeup. My eyeliner was a little smudged from the mask, but not bad. Unlike the specter next to me, at least I didn't look like a ghoul from a horror movie.

"You have pretty eyes," Voula commented with her exotic, yet non-specific accent. "Why are you not married?"

I laughed at her direct approach. "Beats me. I was engaged once, but it didn't work out."

She arched one thick eyebrow, urging me to continue. "Why did it not work out, this engagement? It was because of you, your temper, no?"

"Long story short, he was afraid of a little spider."

She clucked her tongue. "If this is true, that is not the man for you. A woman like you, a woman with courage and fire, you need a real man. Like a horse and a tiger, but in a man."

"That's a good idea. I should put up an internet dating profile. *Courageous woman seeks horse-tiger-man.*"

Voula held up one manicured finger, catching my attention with her black-lacquered nail, which tapered at the tip like a claw.

"Be careful what you dream of," she said. "The fates enjoy twisting your desires into your nightmares. Do not ask for anything in jest, or you will not like what happens."

I powdered my nose and cheeks, keeping an eye on her and those black claws via the mirror. "I'll keep that in mind."

She kept wiping at her face until the tissue packet was empty, and then she pouted at her reflection. "I look like what the cat spits up."

"No, you don't," I said with a smirk. "I've seen what my cat Jeffrey hacks up, usually into one of my shoes if he can make it there in time, and you look much nicer than what I had to rinse out of my penny loafers yesterday."

"I will go home," she announced with a sadness that tore at my heart. The scrubbed-red streaks around her eyes made her look like she'd been crying.

I picked up my masquerade mask and held it out to her. "You can't go home before midnight. Not on New Year's Eve. I'm not really a mask person, so I'm actually done with this for the night."

She held her hands to her chest, hesitant to accept my gift.

"This practically belongs on you," I said. "The purple and green match your outfit perfectly, and look at me—I'm dressed like a zebra. Take it. I insist."

She fixed her golden eyes on mine. "We will trade. I take your gift, and you take mine."

"Sure," I said, because it was easier to accept whatever trinket she had than continue to stand in the washroom of the Fox and Hound arguing with her.

She accepted my mask and slipped it on. It fit her perfectly and made her whole multilayered purple and green outfit come to life.

I started backing away, toward the door. It struck me as strange that, on the busiest night of the year, not another soul had come in to use the washroom. Had Voula cast some witchy spell to give us this moment? Just as I was puzzling over the idea, the door banged open and a cluster of women came in all at once, laughing as they made beelines for the stalls.

Voula was suddenly in front of me, pressing something into my hand—a business card.

"You will come see me tomorrow at noon," she said. "I will return your beautiful favor."

"No, you don't need to do that. The mask was only a few dollars, and I was done with it anyway. You don't need to give me a free… um… whatever it is you do."

"Tomorrow is New Year's Day. All the stores are closed. You have no plans for noon. Don't argue with Voula Varga. You will come see me, and I will help your heart."

"My heart?"

She leaned in close, filling my nostrils with her spicy perfume, and whispered in my ear, "I will help your heart, yes. To take away your anger, for you to get over Christopher."

My breath caught in my throat.

Voula pulled away, and with a swirl of her layered skirts and shawls, she was gone, leaving me standing in the washroom of the Fox and Hound with my mouth open, wondering how the heck she knew that my spider-phobic ex-fiancé was named Christopher.

CHAPTER 5
JANUARY 1

THE FIRST MORNING of the new year, I awoke with a weight on my chest. It wasn't anxiety, though. Just a gray cat, lightly touching his wet nose to my chin and mouth.

"Good morning," I said with a crackly voice.

He pulled his head back in reaction to my morning breath and quickly retreated, flicking his long gray tail as he jumped off the bed.

"Let that be a lesson to you," I called after him. "Stick your nose where it doesn't belong and you might get something you don't want, like halitosis."

He slipped out the partly open bedroom door just as Jessica appeared. She had her long red hair plaited into a single braid resting on one shoulder, and she looked crisp and casual in dark jeans and a blue turtleneck that matched her eyes.

"Want your breakfast in here?" she asked. "Maybe on a tray?"

I sniffed the air, detecting cinnamon and fresh coffee.

"Breakfast in bed? Jessica, you should sleep over more often." I sniffed again, detecting something else —bacon. "Is that bacon?" She nodded. "Forget sleeping over. You should move in."

She laughed and shook her head. "I'm an early riser during the winter months, and that's when I bake. I drive roommates crazy. I won't live with someone again unless we're already married, so they can't back out when they realize what I'm all about."

I climbed out of bed, pulled my housecoat on over my nightie, then got down on one knee in front of Jessica. "Marry me."

She patted me on the head. "Come have some breakfast."

"I'll be there in a sec." I headed down to the washroom to freshen up before eating. The room was quiet, with no sounds coming from Logan's side. My cat followed me in and supervised, as usual, looking curious about my toothpaste, then disgusted that I would willingly splash water onto my face.

Out in the kitchen, the setup on the table looked as wonderful as it smelled. I took a moment to dish out Jeffrey's breakfast on his kitty plate, then sat down to enjoy the spread.

My phone, which was in its usual charging spot by the front door, began to ring.

Jessica jumped up and grabbed it for me. "I gave Marcy your number," she said, wincing as she handed the phone to me. "She wants to apologize for last night, and she wants to ask you something."

"Ask me what?" I looked down at the phone in Jessica's hand like it was a ticking bomb, or a coffee cake made with broccoli.

"She wouldn't tell me. It's probably something crazy. Marcy has been so paranoid lately."

"Drama," I said with a groan as I reluctantly accepted the phone. As soon as it touched my hand, the phone stopped ringing. It didn't beep with a new message, though. Marcy hadn't wanted to talk bad enough to wait for voicemail.

"She hung up? Probably for the best," Jessica said as she filled my coffee cup. "Who needs more drama in the new year? Not me. I slept great last night. How about you? Got any resolutions?"

"Not really. How about you? Maybe we'll both get some ideas after this afternoon's meeting with…" I grabbed the card from my purse and read off the business card she'd given me the night before: "*Vibrant and Vivacious, Voula Varga, Psychic Extraordinaire.*"

"What do you mean, *we*? I'd love to meet with Voula again, but I've got a date with a half-frozen lake. I'm doing the Polar Bear Dip, same as I do every year."

"Sounds fun," I lied.

"So much fun," she said with a smile, oblivious to my sarcasm. "The cold water is amazing for your circulation and pores. My mother swears the Polar Bear Dip is basically a fountain of youth."

Jessica's mother did have perfect skin, but I wasn't so easily swayed. I pulled my warm bathrobe tighter against the mere idea of plunging into the chilly waters at the foot of Misty Falls.

The waterfall the town was named for had a rocky outcropping midway down that served as a perfect jumping-off point for locals. The drop from the ledge was about fifteen feet, and I'd jumped off plenty of times, both clothed and unclothed, but never in the middle of winter. It was the perfect location for the town's annual Polar Bear Dip because the moving waters kept ice from forming, unless the weather was extraordinarily cold.

"It's my tenth year," Jessica said proudly. "I get my ten-time pin."

"If I go and jump in ten times in a row, do I get a pin?"

She pursed her lips in mock outrage and handed me a hot-from-the-oven cinnamon bun to go with my scrambled eggs and bacon.

We ate our breakfast and gossiped about the previous evening's events. Marvin and Marcy had gotten drunk enough to stop bickering around the third bottle of wine, and the mood lightened once our friend Harper arrived with some other young twenty-something friends in tow, straight from another party.

Marvin had heroically saved me from a hangover by drinking most of the wine, so the new year was off to a good start. I hoped my noon appointment with the psychic would bring more positive things into my life.

I'd puzzled over what Voula Varga had said to me about my ex-fiancé, and had come up with a reasonable explanation. If she was a con artist, as Logan had suggested, she would have researched local residents with money. A quick internet search would reveal plenty of information on me, including the name of my former business partner and spider-phobic fiancé.

You're just a con artist, I thought as I tapped the edge of her business card on the table. *Voula Varga, I'm onto your so-called magic tricks. You may have sold my gullible friend Jessica a voodoo love doll, but you'd better not try to pull one over on me, or you'll be in for trouble.*

CHAPTER 6

As I DROVE to Voula Varga's house, I rehearsed what I would say to get out of any mumbo jumbo she might try to pull on me.

First, I would casually mention that my father was a retired police officer, and that I'd inherited his skepticism about all things mystical.

Secondly, if the cop thing alone didn't kill her interest in scamming me, I would cut the visit short by claiming I had something else scheduled—like getting started on counting the inventory at my gift shop while it was closed for the day.

Voula's house was just outside of town, perched high on its own hill. The house itself was famous, by Misty Falls standards. It had been used for a horror movie filming location back when I was in high school. The Hollywood people had modified the windows on the front to look even more like eyes on a face.

I'd seen the glowing eyes of the house countless times, but I'd never been to the house before today— the day I'd been *summoned* there by Voula the Psychic Extraordinaire.

I didn't spot the turnoff for the road leading up the hill the first time I passed by it, so I pulled a U-turn and drove back slower. The weather that day was overcast, so between the blanket of snow on everything, plus the lack of shadows, everything looked flat and featureless. It was the kind of murky day where things can hide in plain sight, right in front of you.

Finally, I spotted the turnoff for the road—which wasn't much more than a goat trail—and steered my car onto it. As I bumped over the snowy ruts, hoping the scraping sound coming from the undercarriage wasn't anything to worry about, the idea of trading my fancy car for something more practical, like a Jeep, became more appealing.

As I rounded what was a blind corner due to a thick stand of evergreen trees, another vehicle sprang up in front of me, bright headlights gleaming through the murky daylight as it came right at me.

The narrow road barely had enough room for one vehicle, let alone two, so I slammed on my brakes, expecting the other vehicle to do the same.

The other vehicle didn't stop, though. Either the driver didn't see me, or they did, and *wanted* to have a head-on collision. My car was equipped with the finest in safety features, but I didn't want to test my air bags that day, so I hastily cranked the wheel to the right, took my foot off the brake pedal, and hit the gas. My car graciously obeyed my command and sailed off the road and down the slope into a ravine.

A horrific crunching came from below, as trees whizzed by left and right. I hit the brakes, but I was sledding, not rolling, so it made no difference. I used the steering wheel and the magic power of curse words to nudge the car left, narrowly avoiding impact with a tree. The vehicle eventually came to a halt in fluffy snow, deep enough to cover the headlights.

Behind me, the road was clear. The driver didn't even have the decency to stop and check on me, let alone take responsibility for the accident.

After letting out a few unladylike epithets, I put the car in reverse and attempted to get back onto the road. My car tried to obey, bless her precision-crafted engine, but the slippery snow and the steep incline were too much. I would need a tow truck, unless I could figure out another route.

I shut off the engine and stepped out to survey the situation. My tire tracks down the edge of the ravine showed me how lucky I'd been to squeeze between the many trees without hitting any, except...

I walked along the tire tracks and scooped up something familiar. It was my passenger-side mirror. I had hit a tree after all, clipping it with my mirror.

"Could be worse," I said to myself as I tossed the loose mirror into my trunk.

I slammed the trunk shut, which startled the birds in the tree branches above me. They took flight with alarmed squawks, shaking loose snow down on me. The snow fell down the back of my jacket, inside my shirt, and down my pants. I let out another unladylike epithet and did the snow-in-my-pants dance as I tried to shake it out of my pant legs with a minimum of melting. A total of maybe three individual snowflakes made it out, while the rest turned to water.

"Could be worse," I repeated, tempting fate further as I looked around.

Through the trees, I could see Voula's house up ahead, beckoning me with its bright eye-windows. Since I could call a tow truck just as easily from a warm house as from a snowy ditch, I made my way up the snowy bank and then on to the house.

As I stepped onto the creaky porch, I shuddered. It wasn't just the melted snow in my clothes giving me a creepy, shivery feeling. The wide, covered veranda, which should have felt welcoming, was anything but. Instead of seasonal Christmas lights or cheery wreaths, it was still decorated for Halloween, with creepy stuffed ravens—the kind with the shiny eyes that seem to be watching you.

"Nice touch, witch lady," I muttered under my breath as I rang the doorbell.

A full minute passed, and nobody seemed to be coming to the door, not even after I rang it a few more times.

Somewhere nearby, a dog barked, and then whimpered.

I turned around and called out, "Hello? Voula, are you out walking your dog? It's me. Stormy Day. I'm here for our noon appointment."

"What?" answered a female voice, also outside.

"I'm on the porch!" I yelled back.

A moment later, a woman emerged from the woods near the side of the house. She wasn't Voula, though. She was a tall, willowy young woman with long, poker-straight hair as black as the stuffed ravens staring at us from the porch. The girl was walking a brown and white Corgi who looked eager to be my new friend.

"We're allowed to cut through here," the raven-haired girl said defensively. "It's city land all around, and we're just passing through, so it's not like we're trespassing."

"I'm just here for an appointment," I said. "Do you know if the lady who lives here is around? There's no answer."

"Are you a witch, too?"

"No." I looked over her clothes, noting that every single item she wore was black, including the studded choker around her neck. "Why? Are you a witch?"

She cracked a grin, seemingly against her will, then quickly shut it off again.

"Whatever." She rolled her eyes, then turned to leave, and tugged the leash for her dog to follow. The Corgi, who was wearing a matching studded choker, gave me a happy, tongue-lolling parting look, as if to say, *She's not so bad, really, and she spoils me rotten.*

I could tell by the minimal clearance between the Corgi's belly and the snow line that the Corgi did, indeed, have a charmed and treat-filled life.

Alone again, I returned to Voula's door and rang the doorbell again, then knocked on the door. The lock must have been unlatched, because the door creaked open under my knuckles.

"Hello?" I stepped inside the psychic's ominous house, my ears straining to hear a response.

There was only the ticking of a clock.

I stamped the snow off my boots on the entryway mat, then proceeded into the house slowly. A kitchen lay to the left, and I checked there first.

It was a modest kitchen, probably original to the date of the home's construction about forty years ago. The room smelled of coffee, and the half-empty carafe was still warm, but not hot. Two mugs, both with lipstick imprints, sat in the sink.

I left the kitchen and passed through a dining room, which held a table but not much else. The lack of decoration told me this wasn't the room where Voula did her readings. A woman wouldn't put so much effort into her appearance and then meet clients in a boring room with cardboard filing boxes stacked in the corner.

The dining room led to a living room, which was a shocking vision in red. The claustrophobic room held reproduction-antique furniture, upholstered in crushed red velvet. The walls were a deep burgundy, and even the rug was predominantly red. Seeing all that red made me shiver, while a combination of melted snow and nervous sweat trickled down my back.

Were the walls actually closing in on me, or was it just the effect of all the red? I'd expected grander rooms from the look of the house on the outside.

"Hello?" I called out again.

The only answer was the ticking of a grandfather clock standing in the corner. At the instant I looked at the face of the clock, the minute hand clicked into place at the topmost position and the clock began to gong.

GONG!

It kept gonging, presumably counting to twelve. I'd been early for the appointment, but now Voula was late.

GONG!

The sound was so unpleasantly loud that it drove me up the stairs to the home's upper level.

At five gongs, I opened the washroom door and found the room empty.

At eight gongs, I found Voula's bedroom, with a queen-sized bed, but no Voula.

At eleven gongs, I reached for the door handle of the only room I hadn't checked.

I turned the handle and pushed the door open a crack.

"Hello? Am I interrupting?"

No answer.

Something on the dark wood floor caught my eye —a knitted doll, about six inches tall. The doll wore dark clothing, and had black button eyes and a tiny pink mouth.

GONG!

The clock downstairs let out its twelfth gong, and I relaxed, glad to be done with that noise. Antique clocks were beautiful, but why people would want such a noisy thing in their home mystified me.

I stepped into the room, which smelled pleasantly of smoky incense, and scanned from left to right. This room had sucked up the whole decorating budget, with tapestries on the walls, comfortable chairs, and warm glowing lamps dotting the perimeter. Surely this was where Voula would be reading my fortune today, if she decided to show up.

My eyes went back to the curious little doll on the floor, next to a pile of dark clothes. I knelt down to examine the doll.

The back of my neck tickled, and I heard a static buzz in my head, telling me something was wrong.

I froze, barely able to move my eyes. The dark shape on the floor to the right of the doll was a pile of clothes, but it was also something else.

From beneath a fringed, dark purple shawl extended a pale hand, tipped in pointed, black-lacquered nails.

My first thought was, *That's an unusual place for Voula to take a nap.*

And then I saw the pool of blood surrounding her body.

I stood quickly and took a step back, followed by more stumbling steps, until I bumped into the room's pedestal table. The table rattled, and something fell from its surface with a clunk.

I wheeled around to see what had fallen. A pistol lay gleaming on the floor, pointing right at me.

My hand flew to my mouth as I choked back a scream. Either Voula was very devious in setting up a terrifying prank just for my benefit, or the woman had been shot.

I ran to the woman's side, to see if she was still alive and there was anything I could do for her. She wasn't yet room temperature, but she was already gone.

As I held her cooling fingers in one hand, and the knitted doll in the other, I thought angrily of the vehicle that had driven me off the road moments ago.

I should have held my ground and let the vehicle smash into me.

I shouldn't have let Voula's killer get away.

CHAPTER 7

DOWNSTAIRS IN THE dead woman's kitchen, I used her vintage wall-mounted phone to call the police. With the heavy headset cradled to my ear using my shoulder, I used one hand to hold my cell phone while I scrolled through my contacts.

I wanted to call Jessica, to hear her soothing voice, but I didn't want to upset her. Besides, right about then she would be jumping into a near-freezing lake, with her phone tucked into her waiting clothes.

My finger paused over the contact for Logan Sanderson. Did I need a lawyer? His friendly face and smirking blue eyes came to mind. No, I didn't need a lawyer. Needing wasn't the same as wanting.

I pressed the option for my father, Finnegan Day. As a retired police officer, he was the best choice.

When he answered, I said, "Dad, hang on and listen. I'm just on the other line with 9-1-1 dispatch."

He made a concerned noise, but listened. A woman with a Southern accent had answered my 9-1-1 call. I gave all the pertinent details to the dispatcher, the words tumbling from my mouth.

"Ma'am, did you say voodoo doll?" she asked. "Are there any human beings involved in this emergency?"

I groaned and started over. After repeating everything a second time, this time with most of the words in the right order, I finally got the information through.

"The authorities are on their way," the woman said. "What did you say your name was?"

I spelled out my name, finished the call, and hung up the heavy receiver with a clunk. I switched my cell phone to my other ear and asked my father if he'd gotten everything.

"Did you secure the premises?" he asked. "Are you absolutely sure you're alone in the house?"

"I didn't check all the closets, but I'm pretty sure it's just me and the voodoo lady. I wandered around looking for her for a bit, and then she was… well, in the last room I checked. Dead."

"Secure the premises now," he said sternly. "I'll hold the line. Better to be prepared, though. You said the gun was in the room? I'd say grab it for protection, but you've got no training in handling a weapon, so there's no sense in you supplying it to your attacker."

"Maybe I should wait outside."

"But the attacker could be outside, and you don't have access to your car. You can secure the house, but you can't secure the whole outdoors."

I couldn't argue with his logic, so I retraced my original steps through the house. I started at the front door and locked it, then moved on to a thorough inspection of possible hiding places. There were no closets on the lower floor. I checked behind the tall grandfather clock in the red living room, then walked up the stairs again. My body felt numb, almost weightless, like the air around me was water.

I checked the bathroom, and then the bedroom, including the closet and the underside of Voula's bed.

"That's weird," I said into the phone.

"Don't say *weird*. That tells me nothing. What do you see?"

"Just that there's hardly anything in her closet except for more of the same dresses, and nothing underneath her bed, not even dust bunnies."

"So, she's a neat freak, and not sentimental. That's not weird, Stormy, it's a personality profile. Keep going and tell me what else you see, and what you smell."

I stopped in the hallway. Why did he have to mention smell? Now I was painfully aware of the smell coming from the room with the body. It wasn't just smoky incense, but the coppery scent of blood, and it stopped me at the doorway.

"It stinks," I said, and I described the smell, and then the appearance of the room. The sky was still overcast, but the two large windows made the room feel bright and airy. It would have been a nice place to visit a friend for coffee, except for the dead body on the floor.

At least the gun was still there, right where it had landed when I'd backed into the table. Barring any strange coincidence, that gun had to be the murder weapon, and it was accounted for. This room didn't have a closet, and I could see under the leggy furniture from the doorway, so I didn't need to enter the room.

"All clear," I told my father as I hurried down the stairs and back into the relative comfort of the kitchen. "Even if it hadn't been the killer who tried to run me off the road on my way here, I rang the doorbell more than enough times to give them fair warning."

"Tell me more about this vehicle that ran you off the road. Start with the make and model."

"Didn't you hear all that during my 9-1-1 call? All I saw was headlights and danger, then snow, and trees whizzing past."

"What made you think that was connected to the shooting?"

"If you were here with me, you'd understand. The house is outside of town, and there's just the driveway leading in and out. You probably know the house—it's the one with the face. The windows look like eyes. They used it for that movie a while back."

"That was a good movie. I was there doing security for the filming, and you can see the corner of my hat in one scene." I heard the beep of his ancient computer booting up. "Did you get a look at the driver of the vehicle? Could you describe them to a sketch artist?"

"Dad, I don't even know if it was a man or a woman. They had their high beams on, I think. It's such an overcast day, and it was dark there in the trees."

"You didn't think to get a good look, even after they ran you off the road?" He sounded incredulous.

Flatly, I said, "Gee, what a great idea. I guess I was sort of busy not hitting trees."

I heard keys tapping.

"What are you doing?" I asked.

"Damn this hip," he said, his voice thick and gravelly.

With a stony voice, I said, "I'm okay, Dad. Thanks for asking."

"Of course you are, Stormy. I'd drive over there and investigate the crime scene with you, but I can't drive yet. Damn hip."

There was more typing, then he groaned, like he was pushing his home office chair back and getting to his feet.

"Are you okay? How's your pain level?"

He mumbled about needing to take his medicine.

"Keep taking those pain pills every four hours," I said. "Take it easy. I'm sure you'll be back up to speed faster if you let yourself heal now."

He mumbled something else I didn't hear. I smiled, my chest feeling lighter with the switching of my concern over to him. I was still inside a creepy house with a body, but I had other things keeping me tethered to my regular life.

There was the whacking of his cane on the floor, then the sound of running water. I could see him in my mind, pouring a glass of water in his kitchen, glaring out the window over the sink, wishing he'd recovered enough from his hip surgery to be able to drive his truck. I listened to him gulp the water, which made me realize I was lightheaded and could use something to drink.

I opened the cupboard next to Voula's sink and grabbed a glass. Again, something struck me as noteworthy.

"Dad, there are only four glasses in this woman's cupboard. Does that seem odd to you? It's a big cupboard, but it's practically empty. There are two coffee cups in the sink, but I don't see any more."

"What does that tell you?"

"Either she was a minimalist, or she wasn't planning to settle here in Misty Falls."

"Odd but not surprising." His voice twitched up, betraying his interest. "This psychic woman... I've heard a few things about her around town, but I've been too busy with other matters to look into the situation." He let out an irritated sigh. "This is all my fault."

"No, it's not your fault. You're retired now. And even if you weren't, it's not the job of the local police to *prevent* crimes. You're not psychics."

He let out a chortle. "Nobody's a psychic, because there's no such thing. Now, how far are you from the room with the body? Send me some pictures. You said she had some sort of doll in her hands? That's definitely a clue. Either she was trying to tell us something and grabbed it before she expired, or the killer put it there as a message."

I swallowed hard. "A message?"

"Try to get a few different angles, wide and close up. We need to know more about this doll."

"We do?" I poured myself a glass of water from the tap, careful not to disturb the two lipstick-marked coffee cups in the sink, and drank it down. I'd learned from my father that people in shock always need water. Most victims and witnesses don't realize it, but the adrenaline makes you sweat all over, and you lose moisture rapidly.

He explained, "For example, was it the only doll in the room? And if it wasn't, what's different about this doll? Why would she reach for it with her last dying breath?"

"I'm already back downstairs," I said. "The house is secure, like you asked. I'm not going to disturb the crime scene any more than I already have. Besides, wouldn't it be illegal for me to take pictures and send them to you?"

"We're just concerned citizens, Stormy. We can do anything we want." He chuckled. "Your father, Finnegan Day, is just a regular citizen, like anyone else."

I frowned as I faced the window overlooking the snowy driveway in front of the house. How long would it take for the police to arrive, so I could leave? And why was my father sounding so excited about being a *regular citizen*?

"The killer is probably the boyfriend," my father said. "It's usually the boyfriend. Do you have a name?"

"Calm down and put your service revolver away," I joked.

"Oh," he said excitedly. "I should clean my gun."

"I thought the police had your gun for evidence."

"Right." He sounded dejected. "Hey, when you're done taking the photos there, can you swing by here and drive me to the gun store?"

I thought of the gun on the floor upstairs and got a wave of nausea. "Can you call one of your other friends? I've had enough of guns for today."

"Never mind. It's a holiday. Everything will be closed today."

"That's right. Happy New Year, by the way. It's sure to be an interesting year, starting off like this. You know, I should be at home with Jeffrey Blue, relaxing. I've got some nice yarn and I was going to try knitting a scarf, but then I had to go and be nice last night and loan Voula my masquerade mask. Then she made me take her card and tricked me into coming out here today. No good deed goes unpunished, right?"

Ignoring my rant, he said, "How about those crime scene photos?"

"Let me think about it."

"What's there to think about?" He sounded mystified and annoyed. "Why'd you phone me if you didn't want me to take on the case?"

My phone chirped to let me know I had another call. The number showed, but I didn't have a name programmed in.

"Dad, can we continue this conversation later? Maybe when I'm not standing in a creepy murder house with windows that look like eyes and a dead body upstairs?"

"Come straight over here when you're done. Don't forget the photos."

My phone chirped again.

"I will. Can you do me a favor and call a tow truck for my car? Hopefully it's still in driving condition, but I will need a winch to get it out of the ravine."

"Did you say *witch*?"

"Winch."

"Doesn't matter. Have a look around for signs of witchcraft. She might be part of a coven. We'll have to canvass for other witches if she is."

"Sure," I said, even though I didn't know what constituted signs of witchcraft. There was the knitted doll, but that seemed more like voodoo to me. "Gotta go. I've got another call."

We said goodbye, and I switched to the other line and said hello.

"Stormy, are you okay?" The male voice was familiar and reassuring. It was Tony Milano, an old friend who'd been more than just a friend in the past, but was now married, with three kids.

"The premises are secure, and I didn't even throw up," I quickly assured Tony. "But I did get my fingerprints all over a water glass just now. I'm okay, but I can't say the same for the psychic." I kept staring out the kitchen window, expecting to see

Tony's police car emerging from the snow-covered trees at any moment.

"She probably had it coming," he said.

"Tony!" Even if it was true, that wasn't something I wanted to hear a police officer saying.

He said, "I don't know what she was up to, but it didn't sound good. We had a few complaints about her, but nothing to warrant an investigation."

"Complaints?"

"Hang on." I heard a static sound as Tony covered the receiver of his phone and barked an order at someone. There were sirens as well, and then they switched off abruptly. In the relative silence, I heard the clicking of something—his turn signal.

"Tony, you should focus on your driving. I'll let you go."

"I just need to know you're okay."

"Sure. I'll talk to you when you get here. My car's in the ditch, as you'll see when you drive up. Our prime suspect tried to run me off the road, but I didn't get a look at him or her."

"You stay put."

"I swear I'm not going to take off on you this time."

"Good," he said gruffly. "The fire department just got here with the equipment, so we shouldn't be long now, because I don't think we need it."

"Equipment? Oh, no. Was anyone hurt?"

"Not too much. Don't worry about this."

I wanted to ask him for more details, but the line was dead. The Misty Falls Fire Department were the ones with the hydraulic rescue tools, commonly known as the Jaws of Life. A vehicle accident in town explained why the police hadn't arrived at the murder scene yet.

That left me alone, with nothing else to do but look around, like a regular concerned citizen.

"A few pictures can't hurt," I muttered to myself as I switched my phone over to the camera function.

I had no doubt my father was serious about wanting pictures of the crime scene. He joked around about plenty of things, but not about murder, especially lately.

Normally, I might not have indulged him, but he'd been depressed. His recent hip surgery had made him realize he wasn't a superhero, and then there'd been the death of his neighbor, which would have been disturbing enough without him feeling partly responsible.

If photos of a crime scene would cheer him up, then—as weird as it was—I would get him photos of a crime scene.

I started with the lipstick-smudged cups in the sink, taking a few angles of photos without disturbing the objects. Then I retraced my steps once again, this time collecting photographic evidence.

The blood-red sitting room made me feel even uneasier, the color quickening my pulse as it reminded me of what lay upstairs. The single bookshelf held only the most generic items—the inoffensive balls of twigs and such, that you would use to stage a home for sale—so none of it gave me clues into the life of the home's resident.

I walked upstairs, giving the doorway to the room with the body a wide berth by tiptoeing along the far edge of the hallway.

Inside Voula's bedroom, I took my first breath since I'd started climbing the stairs. I exhaled and said to the room, "If I had secrets, where would I keep them?"

The bedroom was almost as sparsely decorated as the downstairs, so it wouldn't take long to check it.

My father had suggested the killer was a boyfriend, so I looked for signs of one. The laundry hamper contained only women's clothes, including some silky slips and more skirts and shawls. I snapped some photos, feeling a little nauseated at myself for photographing a dead woman's dirty clothes.

Next, I went to the dresser drawers. I pulled the sleeve of my coat over my fingers, but opened the drawers by gripping the edges, not the handles, just in case the police wanted to check for prints. I found the expected assortment of clothes and underwear, along with a number of biography books.

Why would someone keep their books hidden in a drawer, yet place balls made of twigs on their bookshelves?

I had a closer look at the spines of the books. Several of the biographies were about famous con artists. She'd been learning the tricks of the trade.

I took photos of all the books, because even though they didn't tell me much about whoever'd pulled the trigger, they told me plenty about Voula. My father always said that getting to know the victim was the path to solving the crime. If she had been successful in previous frauds, she likely had more than one enemy.

The books looked new enough, the pages not yellowed with age, but that didn't mean she hadn't been ripping people off in other towns for years.

Over on her nightstand was a notepad with some scribbled doodles. The notepad itself was one of those freebie promotional things, with a company logo printed on every page in the bottom corner. The business was one I knew: Misty Microchips, the computer business owned by Marvin and Marcy, the couple who'd nearly ruined my previous evening with their bickering.

I turned the notepad left and right as I tried to decipher the inky swirls. In between the looping and nonsensical shapes, there were numbers. It looked like long division—a six-figure number divided by the number twelve. The resulting number had a dollar sign in front of it.

"That's a hefty salary," I muttered to the empty room. Because of my business background, I had automatically considered that the number twelve stood for the twelve months in a year, and these were calculations for a CEO's monthly salary. I quickly dismissed this idea, though, because we didn't have any CEOs in Misty Falls, let alone ones that would earn that much. I snapped another photo, then moved on to the drawers of the nightstand.

The top drawer contained hand lotion, two empty boxes of chocolates, and a packet of birth control pills with the previous day's pill popped out, but not today's. Did Voula have a boyfriend, as my father had suggested? The lingerie in the hamper could have just been her regular nightgown. The night before, she'd been at the party with other women, which was something only single people did on such a special night.

That didn't mean she didn't have a man in her life. Then again, the existence of her birth control didn't mean she did, either. I knew some women took monthly hormones for other reasons.

I took a photo of the drawer contents without disturbing anything, then pulled open the lower drawer. This one contained a rolled-up extension cord and a charger that looked like the one I had for my own laptop. I took a photo, then checked the room for her computer. I wouldn't be able to do anything if it was password-protected, like most people's laptops, but it would be helpful to the police if I pointed it out for them.

I searched the entire bedroom, but didn't find the laptop. It hadn't been downstairs, which left only the room with the body.

I reluctantly entered the room slowly. The pool of blood seemed like it had spread out from the body, but it could have been my imagination. I noted the current border with a disconnected sense of curiosity, the way an experienced investigator might view the scene. I took several pictures inside the room, including shots of the knitted doll near her hand, and the gun, which looked old and somewhat fancy, with inlaid mother-of-pearl. I avoided looking directly at the body as I backed out of the room and pulled the door closed.

I stood there, unable to walk away. I don't believe in ghosts, but I felt her presence. She'd given me the creeps at the pub, but first impressions weren't everything. The woman had been alive and now she wasn't, because something terrible had happened. I felt like I needed to say something, even if it was more for my benefit than Voula's.

"I'm sorry this happened to you," I said to the closed door. "I don't know what you planned to do in Misty Falls, but I'm sure it wasn't this. On behalf of the town, I'm sorry. Wherever you are, I hope you're at peace. We're going to find who did this to you."

As I finished my speech, the air in the house changed. A cold breeze rushed along the hallway, putting a chill up my spine and raising the hairs on my arms, even under my sweater and jacket.

My breath caught in my throat. Was it a ghost? Voula's spirit passing by me?

Something thumped downstairs. I pressed my back against the wall of the hallway and froze, waiting for more sounds.

CHAPTER 8

THE THUMPS SOUNDED again. It was a familiar sound, almost homey: snowy boots being stamped on the porch.

Someone rapped on the door loudly.

"Police!" A man's voice came through the door.

"Tony?" I squeaked.

"I'm going to break down the door!" The house trembled at the threat.

"Coming!" I warbled as I ran down the stairs and toward the door. "Coming! Hold your horses!" I sounded ridiculous, like someone fresh from the shower running to get their parcel from UPS. "Almost there!"

"Stand back!"

I'd been reaching for the deadbolt, but jumped back instead of opening the door.

Two solid kicks later, the old wood door cracked away from its hinges and fell on the floor with a horrific clatter.

Tony Milano stood in the doorway, one hand ready to draw his gun. He didn't relax when he saw me, but kept scanning the entryway.

"Officer Milano," I said by way of greeting.

"It's actually *captain* now," he said. "Did you lock this door?"

"Yes, because you can't secure the whole outdoors." I could feel the big smile on my face, and

I knew it wasn't appropriate to look happy at that moment, but I was just so relieved to see *Captain* Tony Milano and no longer be alone in the house with a gun and a body.

My happiness faded, along with my smile, when I saw there was a stranger standing at the door with him. I'd been hoping to talk to Tony, alone, and then quickly leave, but now there were two male police officers stamping the snow off their boots and stepping inside over the fallen door.

"Stand aside," Tony said as he walked past me, moving toward the kitchen, his dark winter uniform jacket rustling with his movements. He looked more rested than the last time I'd seen him, with smaller bags under his dark brown eyes. I guessed that he and his wife's newest addition—their third child—was now sleeping through the night.

The other police officer was younger than Tony, in his twenties—his *early* twenties—and he was cute. His hair was as fair as Tony's was dark, and he had bright aquamarine-blue eyes that darted around eagerly, avoiding me. I didn't know him by name, but he looked awfully familiar.

Tony seemed satisfied we weren't in immediate danger and was shaking out his arms, burning off the adrenaline from kicking down the door.

"Where's Peggy?" I asked.

Before Tony could answer, the fair-haired young officer answered, "You mean Wiggles?"

Tony flicked his attention to the younger man and gave him a stern look.

"Sorry," the other officer said. He gave me a big grin, revealing youthful dimples in his cheeks. "Officer Peggy Wiggles is attending other matters, ma'am."

I raised my eyebrows and said to Tony, "Did your partner just call me ma'am? When did I stop being a *miss*? I can understand over the phone, but this is getting ridiculous. Is it my short hair?"

Tony looked at my hair, considering without comment, then said, "Stormy Day, meet my newest rookie, Officer Kyle Dempsey. If he keeps calling you ma'am, you have my permission to call him Dimples. That's what everyone at the station calls him."

Officer Kyle Dempsey offered me his hand, so I shook it.

"*Dempsey*," I said, and the familiarity of his face clicked into place. "Are you related to Julian?"

"He's my older brother."

"I went to school with Julian. In fact, I remember when you were born. Julian didn't appreciate having a new baby in the family and went through... a phase. He burned down the groundskeeper's shed behind the school, didn't he?"

Kyle gave me a knowing look. "My brother went through a few troubled phases, and more than one groundskeeper sheds."

"The third one was definitely a copycat pyromaniac, though. I think Julian was out of town at the time, so it couldn't have been him."

Kyle nodded. "He did eventually figure out the alibi thing."

"What's Julian up to these days?"

"Blowing up buildings," Kyle answered flatly.

My hand went to my mouth. "I'm so sorry." Julian had been a troubled kid, but he had a sweet spirit, and wasn't cut out for prison.

"Don't be sorry." Kyle's dimples got deeper as his amusement grew. "He's making great money in Hollywood as a pyrotechnics expert."

I laughed. "You're so bad!" I resisted the urge to punch him playfully in the shoulder, because it's not a good idea to hit someone carrying a gun.

Kyle caught my eyes with his baby blues and held them. Despite the circumstances, I felt my insides getting gooey, the way I used to feel when a cute boy —like Kyle's big brother Julian Dempsey, for example—talked to me in school.

"You and I should catch up some time," Kyle said. "We don't have to talk about my brother." He'd stuck his chest out further while talking to me. Now he looked me up and down, and I didn't get the feeling he was looking for concealed weapons.

I was about to answer in the affirmative, but Tony caught our attention by clearing his throat.

"You two should *definitely* catch up," Tony said through a smirk. "I'm sure a lot has changed since Stormy last saw your little winkie, Kyle."

We both turned to Tony. Did he say what I thought he said? *Little winkie?*

Tony's brown eyes gleamed with amusement. "Stormy, don't you remember? You used to babysit Kyle. I think you would have been twelve back he was one or two. Between you and your sister, you must have babysat every kid in Kyle's generation." He rubbed his chin dramatically. "Your father and I enjoyed all your funny babysitting anecdotes."

"I babysat…" I pointed to him. "Kyle?"

"You sure did." Tony chuckled. "Of course, it was much funnier to hear stories about babies back before getting peed on during diaper changes was part of my daily routine." He said, as an aside to Kyle, "This isn't the first shirt I put on this morning."

"Sorry I didn't recognize you, Kyle. I used to sit for a lot of families, and it all runs together." As I looked at his face, though, memories rushed back. Had those chiseled cheeks of his once been chubby-wubby cheeks I playfully pinched? Had I held a small version of Kyle in my arms and told him stories about genies living in bottles, then rocked him to sleep?

Kyle took the news in stride. "A lot of things have grown since then," he said cheekily.

"Yes. You're such a big boy now."

"We should still get that drink sometime."

"You used to love apple juice," I replied, the memories coming back. "In juice boxes."

He grinned, hitting me with a full visual onslaught of dimples. So many dimples.

"Juice boxes," Tony scoffed.

"About this crime scene," Kyle said. "We're not exactly following procedures, and I don't want to get in trouble from the captain, here. Ma'am, I mean Stormy, you wait here while we secure the premises."

"How about I shadow you guys? I'll behave." I tucked my hands into my coat's pockets, the way a little kid does when promising they won't touch anything inside a store.

Kyle and Tony exchanged a look, then Tony said, "Fine, but stand back behind us, and if anything happens, you drop to your knees or run for the exit."

"What about screaming?"

Kyle grinned my way. "Screaming is fine, but don't grab my shooting arm. I might need it." He unlatched the holster for his gun so it was ready to draw, and then followed Tony out of the entryway.

In the kitchen, Kyle said over his shoulder to me, "So, your father is Finnegan Day. He's quite the man. I'm surprised he didn't meet us here today."

"Sounds like you know my father. He asked me to take photos of this crime scene. I have a feeling you're going to get some help on this case, whether you want it or not."

At that, Tony, who was up ahead, groaned. "Tell me you didn't take any photos. I'll have to confiscate your phone."

I jerked my head up and eyed the ceiling. "Did you just hear a creak upstairs? Like the house was shifting, or someone was walking around? Maybe you should go up there, Tony Baloney. Let me and Dimples secure the main floor."

"I know you're changing the topic." Tony gave me a warning glance, then left to check the rest of the house. His boots clomped up the wooden staircase.

"This isn't my first murder," Kyle said once we were alone. "I did most of my training in the city, where I got a lot of experience."

"How old are you, twenty-three? I'm sure you have tons of experience, for twenty-three."

He glanced over his shoulder with a flirty look. "Trust me, I have enough experience to know what I'm doing when I'm doing it."

His comment left me temporarily speechless, which is saying a lot for Kyle and his dimples, because I usually have two or three things to say for every one thing that comes out.

We moved into the house's formal dining room, where he glanced around at the undecorated walls, face pinched in concentration.

"What is it?" I asked. "See something *weird*?"

"The resident wasn't much of a nester. This is the home of someone on the run. I'd guess she was hiding out here in Misty Falls, but you don't drive a hearse with your name painted on the side if you're keeping a low profile. She was up to something."

"Voodoo, I think."

"That never ends well."

"Really? Do you believe in magic?"

He quirked one light brown eyebrow at me. "Do you?"

"Of course not. I wasn't friends with the lady, and I wasn't a client, either. Not really. I met her last night at the Fox and Hound, very briefly. I helped her out in the bathroom with her makeup, and she gave me her card and insisted I come see her today so she could thank me." I started to shrug, but it turned into a shudder. "Discovering a dead body isn't much of a thank you. It reminds me of that saying, *no good deed goes unpunished.*"

He wrinkled his nose. "I don't like that saying. It's counter to what we do." He walked to the corner of the room and lifted the lid off the top filing box. Inside was an assortment of objects associated with the mystical: feathers of various colors, crystals, silver jewelry, polished stones, incense, and bundles of herbs, tied with colored ribbons.

Kyle picked up one of the bundles. "Do you think this is for cooking?" He sniffed it. "Smells incense."

"I think it's white sage for smudging. That's where you burn stuff to clear out bad spirits. I had a friend who'd burn those whenever she moved into a new apartment. There are two good reasons for a smudging ceremony."

I waited for him to ask for the two reasons, and he did.

"Number one, it clears out any pesky ghosts," I said, grinning. "Number two, you find out if the smoke detector's working."

He laughed. "I can see you're not a believer in the mystical, which is good." He dug around in the box. "This junk isn't dangerous, but the people who believe in it are." He got a solemn expression. "It might have been a dissatisfied customer who shot her."

"I think you're right. She was shot in the room where she did readings. I guess your top priority is looking for her appointment book, to see who she met with this morning before I showed up."

"That's a start," he said, nodding in agreement.

He pulled a crumpled newspaper from the box and examined the corner. "I'm guessing she came here from this small town in Florida. The date's from last summer."

"Good detective work," I said.

He grinned, all eagerness, like a puppy with dimples. "Do I get a juice box?"

"Only if you solve the case before nap time."

"Watch me." He nodded for me to follow him into the all-red sitting room. Kyle looked around with big eyes, taking it all in as he checked everywhere, including behind the grandfather clock and the drapes.

He went to the bottom of the stairs and called up, "Captain, we're all clear down here. Do you need a hand up there?"

As he waited to hear the answer from Tony, I studied Kyle's face in profile. The muscles in his cheek pulsed, like he was tapping his molars nervously. He was putting on a brave face for my benefit, and wasn't eager to see the dead body. Or maybe he was afraid he'd throw up in front of me. It's a normal human response to be ill after seeing death. I was surprised I'd held on to my own breakfast. Perhaps the stories from my father had made me more resilient than most people. Without a mother in the house to create a barrier between me and my sister and our father's work, we'd gotten a full induction in the ways of the world from a young age.

Kyle's parents, if I recalled correctly, didn't even have a television. And now their sons both had exciting, action-packed, dangerous careers. The irony wasn't lost on me.

Tony answered from an upstairs room, his voice clear even though he was unseen, "Anything noteworthy down there? Don't let Stormy distract you."

Kyle replied, "There's a clock down here that's going to start chiming on the hour. Don't shoot anything when it does."

Tony called down, "I won't if you won't."

Right on cue, the clock let out one GONG to signal that it was one o'clock. I'd been inside the house for a full hour—an hour that had felt like nothing, and also like an eternity.

Kyle grimaced at the post-GONG noise still echoing in the red room. "Now, did you see an appointment book around here?"

We looked, and talked through what we were thinking. Voula probably kept her appointment book on her phone or laptop, but we still hoped to catch a break and find something on paper that would tell us who her morning appointment had been with.

Kyle Dempsey's blue eyes didn't linger on anything for long, until he looked at me, and then it seemed like he couldn't look away.

"I'm distracting you," I said. "As soon as the tow truck gets here with my car, I'll go."

"No, you can keep helping me. Tony doesn't like to think out loud."

"He thinks he's the strong, silent type."

"And he's my captain." Kyle cleared his throat. "So, who do you think killed her? You saw the dustup with the waitress at the Fox and Hound last night."

"You saw me last night?" I could feel my cheeks blushing. "I mean, you were there, too? You saw that waitress woman—her name is Dharma Lake—throw a drink on Voula?"

"I saw. And I noticed that not one of those women at her table went with her to the washroom. Just you."

"I was only in there by coincidence. That was the first time I met Voula Varga, Psychic Extraordinaire, I swear. And right before I came here, I was at my house with Jessica. I'll give you her number."

He smirked and raised his light brown eyebrows. "Guilty conscience? Don't worry. You don't need an alibi. You're not a suspect."

I made a sniffing laugh sound, almost a snort. "I should be. I keep turning up dead bodies. If I'm not a suspect, I'm certainly a bad omen."

"No way. There's nothing pretty about a bad omen, and you are the prettiest girl in this whole town. I can see why Tony's so possessive of you."

"Tony?" I turned my head to give him a sidelong look. "We're just old friends. What do you mean, *possessive*?"

Kyle glanced toward the stairwell, then changed the topic, asking me what sort of music I liked. I named off a few bands and was surprised when Kyle was familiar with them. Hearing that we had similar taste in music almost made me consider accepting a date with him.

Almost.

Unfortunately, there was still the ten-year age difference. Plus I couldn't stop thinking about how I'd once put baby powder on his little red butt.

"What are you thinking about?" he asked. "You keep frowning and shaking your head, like you're wrestling with something."

"Just this murder case," I lied. "I wish I could remember something about the vehicle that ran me off the road, but it was dark in that grove of trees, and all I saw was headlights and my life flashing before my eyes."

"Don't be hard on yourself. You're doing great."

Kyle led me over to the red room's sofa. It was a tufted couch with tight upholstery—the kind of couch you perch on rather than sink into. We both sat on the edge, turned toward each other. A foot of space remained between our knees.

Kyle had his notepad and pen out, and asked me to start at the beginning. I walked him through my drive to the house, and the accident that sent my car into the ditch. This time through my story, I remembered the dark-haired girl I spoke to before I entered the house.

"Very good," Kyle said. "There aren't that many Corgis in town. If we don't round up an ex-boyfriend or a disgruntled client and this case drags out, I could call the local vets and get the girl's name."

"I could make some calls, if you'd like."

Kyle smiled up from his notepad. "We could trade jobs for the day. What is it you do? Besides run around town looking pretty and stumbling over bodies?"

Ignoring his compliment again, I answered, "I run a gift shop downtown. Glorious Gifts."

"And is the store as glorious as… your smile?"

Just then, Tony came down the stairs noisily.

"What's going on?" he demanded gruffly. "You two look awfully comfortable on that love seat."

"I believe it's a fainting couch," Kyle said. "Not a love seat. Technically."

Kyle's correct identification of the furniture didn't take the dirty look off Tony's face—the dirty look that implied I'd invited a known axe murderer to be my prom date.

"I'm just giving your rookie my statement," I said. "Save the monster-dad face for when your daughter starts dating."

"Your tow truck is here." Tony nodded to the window at the corner of the room, overlooking the front driveway. Sure enough, a tow truck was unhooking my rescued car at that moment. I hadn't noticed the flashing lights.

Kyle let out a low whistle. "Nice wheels."

"That one comes with real bullet holes," I said nonchalantly.

"I'll walk you out," Tony said firmly, nodding for me to follow him to the front door.

"Not yet. I'm helping with the case." I turned to Kyle. "There's a laptop charger inside her bedside table, but no laptop in the house. I'd bet you good money the killer took it. If she did internet backups, there will be mirror images of the files dating back at least a few months. Even if the killer got her laptop and deleted everything on the hard drive and current backup, we can still get access to those mirrored files, and there might be a clue—"

I didn't get to finish my thought, because Tony had grabbed me by the elbow and practically lifted me to my feet.

"Tony Baloney," I protested, using the nickname he hated.

"Witnesses can't be wandering around the crime scene willy-nilly." He hauled me toward the front door.

"I wasn't wandering, I was sitting. On a fainting couch. And I was helping."

He grunted a disagreeable noise.

We got to the front door, alone because Kyle hadn't followed. Tony picked up the kicked-down door and moved it out of the way, onto the porch. In addition to the tow truck, more police cars were parking in the front yard.

The open door had been cooling the house, but I was still warm in my zipped-up jacket, and the fresh air felt good. I stepped out onto the porch, where Tony stopped me by grabbing me at the waist.

"What do you think you're doing?" he asked as he pulled me to face him.

"Getting my car. Do I have to pay, or is the department going to pick up the tab?"

"I meant what were you doing with my rookie?"

Softly, I said, "I used to play *This Little Piggy* with your rookie's toes. I'm not going to date the boy, okay? Not that it's any of your business."

He gave me a stern look, but the softness in his dark brown eyes betrayed his true feelings.

"I'm seven years older than you," he said.

"Exactly. And nothing happened between us."

He took a step back. "Nothing?"

"Except for a few days, nothing."

"Stormy."

His tone when he said my name felt too intimate. I pushed past him and walked down the steps to solid ground. The heads of everyone standing in the snowy front yard turned our way. The cold air was bracing, bringing the situation into crisp focus.

What was I doing?

A woman had been murdered today. It was the first of January, and now all of this was happening. So much for the new year.

I turned back to Tony. "Good luck with your investigation. I look forward to hearing about it on the news when you catch the killer. I just hope you figure out the whole mess before someone else gets hurt or shot at."

"Mind your own business and you won't get shot at, Stormy."

I clenched my fists. "Are you saying it's my fault I've got those bullet holes in car?"

"I'm saying maybe you should stick to running your gift shop, and let us, the police, do our jobs."

I glared at him. He used to love getting my perspective on cases when he first started working with my father. What had changed since then? Oh, right. I was no longer a dewy-eyed teen girl with an adoring crush on him.

Tony nodded, dismissing me. "Thank you for your assistance, ma'am."

Ma'am? Oh, no, he didn't. *He did not just call me ma'am.*

Except he had.

The world was a blur. I walked over to the tow truck driver and paid him for the work. He rattled off estimate quotes for repairing the smashed-off side mirror, but I didn't stick around for auto shop recommendations. I couldn't get out of there fast enough. After Tony's rudeness, I couldn't even think straight.

Noise.

Blur.

Anger.

I was in my car, putting the house in my rear-view mirror.

CHAPTER 9

THE DRIVE AWAY from the crime scene was a blur, and soon I found myself on the road leaving town.

I kept on driving, ten miles over the speed limit, just to see how it felt to leave everything and everyone behind me. If I disappeared now, Tony would feel lousy about being such a jerk.

Speeding away from my life felt good, at first, but then I remembered my cat, all my stuff at the house, plus the fact that even if I did swing back for Jeffrey, we didn't have anywhere else to go.

I slowed down and watched for an exit.

By the time I reached a side road to turn the car around, I'd calmed down enough to sing along with the radio. It was the song I'd been singing to Jeffrey a few days ago, only my lyrics were, "I'm all about that mouse, about that mouse, no catnip."

I drove back toward Misty Falls, my confidence improving with each mile, thanks to the upbeat singing. Sure, I'd gotten dragged into another crime, but I'd survived the previous one, and I would get through this.

As for Tony being a jerk, that mystery had more than enough clues.

I still had feelings for him, clearly. His marital status informed my actions, but not my heart. Since our brief relationship, we hadn't been living in the same town and bumping into each other, creating new memories to wash over the old ones like a fresh coat of paint. Now when I looked into his eyes, which hadn't changed at all, the tender, intimate memories were as fresh as if they'd happened yesterday. He might not have admitted it, but the same thing had to be happening to him.

Where did we go from here? Tony was playing the role of the jealous protector, so where did that leave me? I could ignore him, and let more time pass, or I could accelerate the healing process by moving on. Right in front of him. Where he couldn't miss it.

I imagined dating his new, blond rookie, and found it was a little *too easy* to daydream about the hunky twenty-three-year-old. In fact, I was so caught up in the idea, I sailed by the Misty Falls turnoff from the highway and had to turn the car around yet again.

AT JUST AFTER four o'clock, I arrived at my father's house with a quarter tank of gas.

He'd been expecting me, perhaps watching from the front room window, and was holding the front door open before I'd even walked up the steps to the porch.

"You shaved," I said by way of greeting.

"Of course I shaved." He rubbed his chin. "Only a fool would frame a masterpiece in knotty pine."

I stamped my boots on the outdoor mat, then squeezed past him into the warm house. I was on my way to the back porch when he called after me, "Since you're heading to the kitchen anyway, I guess I'll have a beer. Use a mug from the freezer."

I smiled as I hung up my coat in the back mud room, as I'd been trained to do. It wasn't the first time he'd used this trick. In fact, kitchen errands were likely the main reason my sister and I hadn't been allowed to use the guest hooks by the front door.

I pulled open the fridge, taking comfort in the familiarity of these movements. It seemed really full for one person. The beer was on the bottom shelf, and to my surprise, he'd sprung for expensive beer, from a microbrewery.

Finnegan Day's usual choice of beverage was the rock-bottom cheapest. He could afford top-shelf beer, but seemed to take pride in his lowbrow taste, especially when he entertained and all his buddies complained about his choice of "swill."

My sister and I referred to this trait of his as Hobo Pride. My father grew up poor, and although it had been many years since he'd suffered hardship, he was occasionally obstinate about one thing or another, just to prove he *could* do without. He'd accept new wool socks for Christmas, but if I wanted him to actually wear them, I had to sneak into his room and confiscate the old ones with the holes.

Hobo Pride.

You had to laugh, of course, because that was one of the reasons he did it.

I selected two frosty glass mugs from the freezer and replaced them with fresh ones from the cupboard. Unlike Voula Varga, my father had too many glasses and mugs for the kitchen, unless you kept a few in the freezer.

I poured beer for both of us, tossed the bottles in the recycling bin under the sink, and proceeded toward the living room with both hands full plus a bag of pretzels tucked under my chin.

He was already in his easy chair, so I set his beer next to him, atop the coaster he had ready and waiting.

"Service with a smile." I took a seat on the sofa and looked around. There was something different about the room, but I couldn't put my finger on it.

He eyed my beer.

"That's why I don't keep the fancy stuff in the house," he said. "You'd drink it all."

I took a sip, smiling. After the day I'd had, the cold beer felt like the perfect solution, cheaper than therapy. I would have to start keeping frosty mugs in my own freezer. I'd put tiny bowls in there as well, so I could pour Jeffrey a saucer of cream and never drink alone.

"Go easy on that," my father said. "You'll give yourself the hiccups. Just like that young pup who brought me the beer."

"I should have known you wouldn't spring for anything with more than one color of ink on the label. Who bought these? The real estate guy selling the house next door?"

He tented his fingers, letting me know he had information and was going to mete it out slowly.

"Guess," he said. "Not the realtor."

This was just like him to make me work for information. If the beer wasn't from the real estate agent, that stumped me. Dad wasn't dating anyone— at least not that I knew of. He'd recently been involved with a younger woman, a physical therapist, but after some unfortunate events, she'd been scared away from Misty Falls.

Was there a new woman? I wouldn't have been surprised if Finnegan Day already had a new girlfriend. Or two. He was in his sixties, but other than the gray in his buzz-cut hair and a few laugh lines on his face, he hadn't changed much over the years. He'd always been a handsome devil, with movie-star looks—a square jaw and gold-flecked brown eyes that *smoldered*.

The *smoldering* of his eyes was something I'd been unfortunate enough to overhear about from a teacher at my high school. The worst part was, the lady who'd said it wasn't even single. I'd been horrified enough to drop out of her art class and transfer into a career prep class about business math.

I wondered how my father would feel if he knew my start in the business world came courtesy of his smoldering eyes and the wagging tongues of the women of Misty Falls.

Now, where had this beer come from? I gave it a swirl, imagining I was a psychic, waiting to see something in my crystal ball. Besides dating, my father had an active social life, from his time at the shooting range to fundraising for the local veterans' association. The swirling beer bubbles were golden… like a certain rookie cop's hair.

"Dimples," I guessed. "This beer came from Dimples. Also known as Officer Kyle Dempsey."

Finnegan Day slapped his knee in surprise. "He told you. Kyle must have been there today at the crime scene."

"He didn't tell me you knew each other. Face it, Dad. Your daughter is a little bit psychic."

"Not psychic. You *deduced*. Just like a good detective."

"You called him a young pup. There's definitely a puppy dog quality to him. He reminds me of a Golden Retriever."

Talking about Kyle reminded me of the photos, so I took out my phone, opened the folder, and handed it over to my father. "What was Dimples doing here at the house?"

"He had some questions about a cold case."

I raised my eyebrows as I took another long sip of the beer. The drink was going to my head, right where I needed it. My father, meanwhile, was diving into the crime scene, studying the photos on my phone with a look of determination on his face.

I asked, "How does Tony feel about the young pup digging up cold cases?"

"Tony doesn't know." He shot me a warning look. "And we won't be mentioning it to him."

"Fine by me. I don't want to talk to Tony, anyway. He was super arrogant today, acting like I was going to mess up his crime scene." I sniffed. "He's lucky I had that appointment, or the body might not have been called in for days."

"You did them a favor," he said without looking up from the screen of my phone.

"Tony sure has changed. He rushed me out of there like I was going to make him look bad."

"Cops don't like civilians getting involved. We'll have to keep a low profile."

"We?" I reached for my phone. "Gimme that back. I shouldn't have taken those pictures. I'm going to delete them."

He let me take the phone. "Delete away. I already emailed them to myself."

"Oh, really?" I gave him a dirty look. "So, you know how to use modern phones when you want something, but you can't reply to one of my text messages?"

"I sent you one of those picture things."

"On my birthday, you sent the icon of the little red devil, plus a fork, and a dog, and some other stuff. It made no sense."

"That was a story. Your old man, making hotdogs on the grill for your birthday. You weren't here, but I still made them in your honor."

I pulled up the message in question. There'd been no new texts from him since my birthday last summer, because he preferred voice calls.

I studied the bizarre combination of icons. "Fine. The dog is a hotdog. But what's with the diamond ring? Our trips to Ruby's?"

"That means you're my little jewel, Stormy." He cocked his head. "Did you hear that? Someone's breaking in the back door."

"What?" I got up and ran through the kitchen to investigate. The back door was locked, the sky out the window a dark gray as evening approached, and there wasn't a living soul in sight.

He called back, "Since you're in the kitchen, I could use a refill."

He got me again. I grabbed two more bottles, and was about to start a lecture about *The Boy Who Cried Wolf* when some papers on the kitchen table caught my eye.

The top sheet was the first page of an application for a private investigator's license. None of the fields had been filled in with my father's handwriting, but a pen sat nearby.

Rather than asking him about the papers, and having to play one of his guessing games, I returned to the living room with my mouth shut. If my father wanted to get his PI license, that was his business.

However, it bothered me he hadn't said anything about the PI application. Had he discussed it with Kyle, a.k.a. my father's new favorite person, and the son he'd never had?

My father flicked on the television, oblivious to the jealous, stormy mood coming over me, and started hunting around for something to watch.

After ten minutes, he clicked it off again with a heavy sigh. The living room was surprisingly quiet, and in that stillness, I finally noticed the blank spots in the room. Gone were all of his former girlfriend's photos and furniture, but that wasn't all. The room had less than half of what had been there the last time I'd been over.

"Dad, where'd all the furniture go? I see you got rid of Pam's stuff, but it looks like you got carried away. Where's the antique sewing table? Were you robbed?"

"Nobody steals those old iron tables. Most folks pass them along with the sale of a house, along with half-empty paint cans."

"You're not selling the house, are you?"

Instead of answering, he grabbed his cane from next to his chair and pointed the tip at the bare corner of the room, like a wizard pointing his staff. I half expected a puff of smoke to appear at the end.

"What's going on?" I asked. Something was very wrong, judging by the weary look on his face.

"That empty space is where your old man does his physical therapy exercises," he spat out. "He grunts and groans, and on a good day he can lift his knee all the way up without soaking through his shirt."

Oh. He was having a tough time recovering from his hip surgery. I'd asked him about it a dozen times, but he hadn't said a word. This was so like him to let his emotions bottle up until they exploded.

Gently, I said, "That sounds rough, Dad. Is there anything I can do to help? Say the word and I'm here. Twice a day, every day, if that's what you need."

He let out a long, audible breath, and sank back into his chair.

"Is that why you came back to town?" he asked. "To take care of the sad, old man in his twilight years?"

I snorted. "Don't be ridiculous. You know I'm only back in this town because nowhere else will have me."

"Yeah?" He lifted one white-flecked eyebrow.

"Yeah. And I'm only over here at your house to steal your beer. We both know Finnegan Day doesn't need anyone to take care of him."

A bit of his twinkle returned to his eyes. "Way to rain on my pity parade."

"Don't throw a pity parade and I won't have to rain on it." I nodded at the empty corner of the living room. "Your therapy corner needs some color. You've got room for one of those big exercise balls that are good for stretches."

"You must be psychic. I've actually got one of the darn things. In teal. Just haven't blown it up yet."

"No time like the present." I jumped up.

REARRANGING THE LIVING ROOM took about forty minutes, and by the end, we were sweating, but smiling. We'd moved the sofa and chair for better balance, and we'd set up a whole station for his therapy exercises. A checkered rug borrowed from the spare bedroom made the corner cheery.

We sat and admired our hard work.

"Happy New Year," he said.

"Oh, no! I totally forgot. We're supposed to be having a big dinner, and the oven's not even switched on." I jumped up. I'd seen the roasting pan and the defrosted turkey in the fridge when I'd gone for the beer, but must have completely blocked it out.

"Canceled," he said. "I called everyone already."

I stood, swaying. If I cranked up the oven, we could have turkey by midnight. It wouldn't be the latest we'd served dinner.

"Sit back down," he said.

"But the turkey…"

"Do you want to spend the next several hours peeling potatoes, then entertaining some shirt-tail relatives, or do you want to go over those crime scene photos, make some phone calls, and do up a list of suspects?"

I looked up at the ceiling, pretending to wrestle with the decision.

"Well?" he prompted.

"Can the first phone call be to a pizza place? I haven't eaten anything but those pretzels since breakfast. We'll do pizza, then crime scene photos, like the good ol' days."

The twinkle had fully returned to his eyes. "That's my girl," he said. "You want deep dish? Let me call Romeo's."

CHAPTER 10

I GOT HOME from my father's just after midnight, and walked right into a three-ring circus happening inside my living room.

The star of this circus, the ferocious wildcat, was performing an acrobatic routine that involved leaping from the back of a chair to the back of my sofa, *through* the branches of a ficus tree that had been dropping leaves since its purchase.

"Nice moves," I said.

Jeffrey gripped the sofa back with outstretched paws and whipped his sleek gray head from side to side, mouth wide open, trying to convince me he was crazy.

"Oh, dear. It must be the rabies."

His dark tail swished wildly from side to side, then he leaped from the sofa, hit the ground running, and skittered past me, his claws adding even more character to the old wood floor. His energetic activity wasn't much of a surprise—my human bedtime often coincided with Kitty Play Time Hour. If I'd dropped a twist tie on the floor during the day, he'd find it the minute I closed my eyes.

I took off my boots, hung up my coat, and put on the kettle. My mind was still actively chewing on information about the psychic's murder, so it would do me some good to have a cup of chamomile and let Jeffrey's playful kitty antics distract me.

My father and I had gone over the crime scene photos together over pizza—not Romeo's, because they weren't open on holidays—and he'd made several calls to his contacts. According to his source, the police hadn't issued any warrants yet, so we knew they didn't have an open-and-shut case.

I'd listened quietly as my father told more than one person, "C'mon, humor the old man who's been put out to pasture. I'm stuck at home with a bum hip, the literal personification of an armchair sleuth. C'mon, gimme something."

His ploy for sympathy worked, and he'd gotten an impressive amount of information. I had a feeling we were well ahead of the official police investigation.

Dad's contact at the real estate board confirmed that the creepy-faced house was owned by a commercial leasing division, so Voula had been renting it at market rates. His next call was to the property manager. He fed that woman the same lines about being put out to pasture, this time with an added layer of flirtation.

According to the property manager, who was not immune to my father's wily charms, Voula had been there six months so far, on a one-year fixed-term lease. If she chose to renew, she'd go month-to-month, but she'd told the property manager she'd be long gone by then. The notes in the file said something about moving to Greece. The last name of Varga is Hungarian in origin, but that didn't rule out her having connections in Greece.

As far as family went, she had no immediate kin, according to her rental application. She'd been forty-eight, which made her old enough to have adult children interested in an inheritance or insurance policy, but since she had no kids, they couldn't be suspects.

Around the fifth or sixth phone call, right after the thin-crust pizza arrived, my father had whooped for joy. He had a solid lead, in the form of a restraining order. For a few minutes, we thought the crime as good as solved.

Unfortunately, for our investigation, and also for a Mr. Harold Goldstein, the subject of the restraining order, Harold Goldstein was deceased.

Voula's stalker had suffered a misadventure five years earlier, on an unrelated matter, as he attempted to sneak onto the set of a popular spy movie franchise to inform the leading lady of his undying love for her. His love may not have died, but Mr. Harold Goldstein did. It wasn't the fall from the five-story building he was attempting to infiltrate that killed him. It was, as my father declared while slapping his knee, "the landing."

That information led us to what we should have begun our investigation with—a simple internet search. Within seconds, we found Voula Varga in the popular movie databases, linked to her roles in several films and TV series.

She'd never been what anyone would call a "star," but she booked roles regularly. She'd played witches and psychics, gypsy fortune-tellers, and even a one-eyed sorceress. I commented to my father that Voula must have been disappointed to always get typecast like that. He had a different point of view, and said she was lucky to have such a strong look that made her an obvious casting choice for those roles. Then he went on a ten-minute rant about all the entitled young people these days on the talent shows, and how everyone wants to be the big star overnight without any hard work.

I let him carry on while I scanned through movie stills and video clips. Voula Varga wasn't the worst actor—she was better at pretending to tell fortunes than I'd ever be—but I could see why she didn't get cast in meatier roles. She had an aura of *desperation* about her, in the way she drew out her few spoken lines, attempting to keep the spotlight on herself just a few seconds longer.

My father asked me to replay the clip of her as a half-naked evil siren, luring sailors to their deaths on the rocks. He said it was a shame she was gone, as she'd been "easy on the eyes." That was when I pointed out Voula was the curly-haired woman in the background, and he was looking at someone else entirely. He made a face and took back his compliment, which made me laugh, but also feel sad for her.

The woman I'd only spoken to in the women's washroom at the Fox and Hound had not been warm, but I felt pity for her anyway. According to her bio, she'd never been married, and it seemed that perhaps Mr. Harold Goldstein, her short-term stalker, had been the only man to see something special in her.

Without any obvious suspects from her life before moving to our town, that left only the residents of Misty Falls.

My father promised he would try to get access to her client list, even if it meant kissing some frogs at the police department—his words, not mine—but in the meantime I had an assignment. He wanted me to go undercover and *join a knitting club.*

According to the property manager, the knitting club had been meeting once a week at Voula's house.

Now that the home was a crime scene, my father figured the group would be looking for a new venue. He suggested I volunteer my house.

After I stopped laughing, he told me to give it some thought. "You're the one who wanted to fit into Misty Falls better," he'd said.

"I'm not taking over a dead lady's knitting club. No. Just no."

That night at home, as I sat on my sofa sipping a cup of chamomile tea, I giggled out loud at the mere idea of *being* in a knitting club, let alone hosting one.

Jeffrey whizzed into the living room, darted to the topmost perch in the room, which was a lamp, and gave me a quizzical look. The standing lamp quivered with the steadying movements of his legs and tail.

"Jeffrey, that lamp is not a tree. Off!"

His body tensed, but he didn't jump. He gave me a wide-eyed look, as if to say he was no physics major, but even he knew that leaping off the lamp could result in a broken something and a less-than-graceful landing. He kept staring at me, his tea-green eyes as round as billiard balls, until I finally got up and carefully extricated him from his predicament.

As my thanks for the rescue, I received a lick on the cheek. I had a quick look at the lamp while I held him, noting by the number of cat-claw-sized holes in the perimeter of the linen shade that this was not the first time Jeffrey had been to the peak of Mount Lampshade.

"Why don't you climb your cat-scratching post with the same zeal, hmm?"

He lolled his head around, making crazy eyes, then gave me another communicative look. *The cat post? So boring!*

Ah, yes, the cat post was only four and a half feet tall. Mr. Jeffrey Blue preferred more of a challenge. I could relate to that. I thought I'd be content running my gift shop, but now that it was operating smoothly, I was looking for my own Mount Lampshade.

"What do you think of me becoming a private investigator?"

I returned to my seat on the sofa, and Jeffrey stuck to me, settling on my thighs. He made crazy eyes at the paper tag swinging from the edge of my teacup, but soon his eyes became dozy as he curled into the warmth of my lap.

"My father's applying to get his license," I explained. "He hasn't told me yet, but I think it's because he wants me to be his partner, and he wants to wait and drop a few hints before he asks." As I talked, my theories became more concrete. It had only been a hunch, but telling Jeffrey about my father's possible intentions made them seem not just real, but obvious. The more I thought about it, there could be no other possible explanation. Finnegan Day wanted to start a father-daughter detective agency.

I reached over to the side table, careful not to disturb Jeffrey, grabbed a notepad and pen, then jotted down some possible names and slogans.

Day Detectives
We work day and night for you.

Day & Day
Investigating around the clock, no job too big or small.

Two Days Detective Agency

Father and daughter team, with youth plus experience.

I had a tough time being serious and coming up with a pun-free combination. Would people hiring a detective duo appreciate a bit of humor? I had no idea. I didn't know that much about the business, other than the fact it wasn't all glamor. My father had befriended a few private investigators over the years, and most of their stories were about tailing cheating spouses and finding increasingly inventive ways to relieve one's bladder while on stakeout.

I started to get panicky, thinking about hiding somewhere in wait for someone while needing to use the washroom. Maybe it was because I'd finished a huge mug of tea and I'd ignored my bladder's early requests because I didn't want to disturb the cat on my lap.

"No big mugs of tea on stakeouts," I said. "That'll be my first rule. And the second rule is that my father has to treat me like a partner, and not just his lackey. I bring a lot to the table. I've got… um… deductive skills."

Jeffrey gave me a sleepy look as I gently transferred him to a pillow that was warm from being behind my back. I went down the hall to use the washroom and got ready for bed. Was I sleepy yet? Not really. My face looked oily where it wasn't flaking from winter dryness—the joy of combination skin—so I gave myself a mask treatment and read a magazine.

I'd rinsed off the mask and was climbing into my bed when I realized I'd left the living room lights on and the curtains wide open. Ordinarily, I wouldn't have cared, but I'd stumbled upon a murder scene today, and the killer was still at large. I wasn't going to live my life in fear, but I could do a few sensible things.

With the warm, fuzzy bathrobe over my nightie, I walked out to the living room. Jeffrey struck an irresistible pose, front paws stretched out, begging to have his armpits tickled. Naturally, I gave in to temptation.

I was leaning over, teasing Jeffrey in his sleepy state, when I heard a man's voice outside, barking orders. By now it was nearly two, well past the time people took their dogs out for walks.

I couldn't make out the man's words, but his tone was angry. The hairs on my forearms stood up, and I self-consciously tightened my robe. With the bright lamp on, and the curtains for the picture window wide open, I might as well have been standing in a stage spotlight.

A second man answered the first, and they argued. I felt relief that it wasn't one man trying to get my attention, but then I grew worried. The voices sounded close by, like the two were fighting in my front yard.

I glanced over to make note of where my cell phone was—on the table by the door—and then clicked off the lamp so I could see out the front window.

CHAPTER 11

I SQUINTED AS my eyes adjusted to the light spilling into my snowy front yard from the nearby street lamp.

Two shapes, men of about the same size, were grappling, each with one foot on my shoveled pathway and one foot in the deeper snow.

I would have crossed the room for my phone, to call the police, but the car parked directly in front of my house was a police car. One of the dark-haired men wrestling on my front lawn was Captain Tony Milano.

Just as I was identifying Tony, he got the upper hand on his assailant, swiftly pushing him down, face-first into the snow. I let out a small cry of elation as Tony began handcuffing the other guy.

Through the double-paned glass of the window, I could hear Tony's voice fall into a familiar rhythm—he was making an arrest and informing the man of his rights.

I tapped on the window to let Tony know I was there, in case he needed anything. He whipped his head around, distracted, and loosened his hold.

The other man, craning his neck from his facedown position on the ground, spat out a mouthful of snow and yelled, very clearly, "Stormy!"

He was my tenant, Logan Sanderson.

I didn't even think about what I was doing. I slipped on the shoes closest to the front door and ran out to stop whatever was happening.

"Tony!" That didn't get his attention, so I yelled, "Police brutality!"

Tony kept his knee on Logan's back while he gave me an angry, confused look. "How long has this man been stalking you?"

"He's not a stalker." I crossed my arms, as much to prevent myself from pilfering the handcuff keys from Tony as to keep the chilly air from infiltrating my bathrobe.

"You know this man?" Tony demanded.

Logan groaned. "I told you, man, I'm—" He didn't finish, because Tony shoved his face into the snow again.

Now Tony had gone too far. This kind of casual violence was the sort of thing that gave some small-town cops a bad reputation.

I uncrossed my arms, strode forward purposefully, and shoved Tony off Logan. He wasn't expecting it, and landed awkwardly in the snow. His dark brown eyes blazed at me with fury.

"Uncuff him." I pointed to Logan's wrists.

"Stormy, I'm just trying to protect you," Tony said. "I was driving by and saw this guy prowling around your house."

"I wasn't prowling," Logan protested.

"You were prowling," Tony growled.

"Prowling isn't a crime," I said. "And what does that mean, anyway? My cat prowls around with a stuffed mouse in his mouth. Is that what Logan was doing out here? Was he on his hands and knees, prowling around in the snow? What are you arresting him for?"

"I'll think of something," Tony said.

"Just let him go," I said forcefully. "Let him go or you'll have to cuff me as well, because I *will* come at you." I held my fists up in what I hoped was a menacing fashion. "Prepare to be... prowled on."

Tony winced at my efforts, then righted himself and reached into his pocket for his keys. He was in no apparent hurry to uncuff Logan, moving just fast enough to keep me from shoving him again.

"Captain Milano, you do realize Logan lives here, right? You can't be a prowler or a stalker at your own house."

Tony flashed his eyes at me while slowly going through his ring of keys.

Had Logan been prowling? A moment earlier, I'd been standing in my brightly lit living room, wearing little more than a robe, at two in the morning. Tony must have been driving by when he spotted a man standing in my yard, watching me.

How long had Logan been watching me? Despite a few jerky comments when we'd first met, he didn't seem creepy, but now I wondered if I'd been blind to something. I wanted my tenant to be a good guy, so had I overlooked negative traits? Was he spying on me through my windows regularly? Were there rooms in the house where he could hear me, the way I'd heard someone in his bathroom?

Logan was wearing boots, fully laced up, and a winter jacket. The jacket was zipped up, which made me think he'd been coming back from a walk, and not on his way out. Not every guy is the same, but in my experience, men run a bit warm and wait until they've been outside for a while before they zip their jackets.

While Tony ever so slowly uncuffed Logan, I leaned over and placed my hand on the back of Logan's boot. It was cold; he'd been outside for more than a few minutes. I'd been in my washroom for at least twenty minutes, doing a fifteen-minute face mask. If Logan had been watching me while I sat with the cat, he would have assumed I'd gone off to bed when I disappeared down the hallway.

Therefore, Logan was not a creepy stalker, and had been coming home from a walk when he spotted me in the window. Maybe he thought I could see him, and stopped to wave hello. That would be the neighborly thing to do.

The handcuffs clicked as they released, and Logan got to his knees with a groan. He moved slowly, his eyes darting to Tony's gun holster and then sheepishly to my face, then down at the ground again before repeating the pattern.

"I'm so sorry," I said to Logan. "Tony's my friend, and he was just looking out for me. He's like a brother to me." I turned to Tony and gave him a pointed look. "Tony's sort of like an uncle."

Or a jealous ex-boyfriend, but we're still ignoring that giant elephant in the room, even when it eats all the food and makes its business on the coffee table.

Right about then would have been a good time for *Uncle Tony* to apologize for tackling my tenant, but he kept his lips pinched shut.

"Sorry," I said again, because I felt bad.

"Don't be," Logan said. "It's my fault. He yelled for me to identify myself, and I didn't." He gave me an adorably sheepish look. "I got embarrassed and didn't want you to know I was standing out here like an idiot, staring at you."

"But you weren't stalking me. You were just getting back from a walk, weren't you?"

"Yes. Walking clears my head, but sometimes I get lost in my thoughts. When I got back here and saw you in the window, I was thinking—"

"That's enough out of you," Tony barked, like Logan was about to describe some twisted stalker fantasy. "Next time an officer of the law asks you to identify yourself, you'll know what to do."

"I sure will." Logan had gotten to his feet and now squared his shoulders, facing Tony. Logan was taller, and he tilted his head back, making it clear he was looking down. They looked like brothers, with their similar dark hair and rugged good looks. Logan was younger, but looked older because of the height and beard.

They were barely moving, locked in a macho staring contest, their chests swelling and getting dangerously close to touching.

"Just kiss already," I said.

They broke eye contact and gave me annoyed looks.

"Oops." I brought my hand up to my mouth. "Did I say that out loud? Don't mind me, really. Keep going. I love a good bro-mance. Or a bro-mantic comedy."

"You're not funny," Tony said.

"Ouch," Logan said. "Burn."

"I suppose formal introductions are in order," I said. "Captain Tony Milano, I'd like you to meet my tenant and friend, Logan Sanderson. How about you two shake hands, now that nobody's in cuffs?"

The two moved hesitantly, shaking hands mechanically.

"You two have something in common," I said. "You're both involved in the justice system. Logan is a lawyer."

Tony gave him a surly look. "Not with that beard, you aren't."

Logan took a step back and pointed at Tony. "I remember you now. We met once before, at the veterinarian clinic. You said the same thing about my beard."

Something buzzed—Tony's phone, rattling in his belt holster.

"Excuse me a moment," he said, walking away from us to take the call in private.

Once he was across the yard, his low voice barely audible, I turned to Logan. "It's been a long day. Happy New Year, by the way."

He brushed the remaining snow off his clothes, but made no move to go back into the house.

I asked, "What were you thinking about on your walk?"

"Lots of stuff. I can't remember. But when I got back and saw you, I had the strangest thought. I was wishing we both were smokers."

"Smokers?" I let out a laugh, because laughter lubricates awkward social situations, and with Logan fresh from being tackled for alleged prowling, and me in my crazy bathrobe, the only thing that would make this more difficult would be my father turning up and asking when I planned to pop out some kids, while giving Logan meaningful glances. The last part of that wasn't just my overactive imagination—he'd done it to my former fiancé, Christopher.

For the second time in as many days, I was thinking about Christopher. What was he doing now, at two in the morning? Probably guzzling energy drinks at his computer keyboard, on his second or third wind of the day.

"Hey." I felt a warm hand on my shoulder, and looked up into Logan's blue eyes. "There you are," he said. "Did you hear a word of what I just said?"

I gave him an apologetic smile. "I'm tired. It's been a long day." I thought about telling him about my discovery at Voula Varga's house, but it was all too much information for words—let alone words that wouldn't lead to me sobbing in his nice, strong arms.

He gave my shoulder a respectful squeeze, then dropped his hand away. "About the smoking," he said. "I saw you talking to your cat, and I felt jealous of him, because he gets to live here without paying rent."

"You wish you were a freeloader who claws my furniture? I don't need two of those."

He chuckled and looked at the dark window. "Then I was thinking about how it would be nice if we both smoked, because we could meet on the front lawn for smoke breaks, and casually talk about our day."

"That would be nice," I said. "For two people who live together, we don't bump into each other much. Plus you don't dance, or so you say."

"Have you given any thought to vegetables?"

I laughed. He was good at changing the topic away from dancing.

He expanded on his vegetables comment, talking about putting in raised garden beds in the backyard. He described a method of multiple platforms stacked in a pyramid. It didn't gain you any space, but it made weeding a breeze and picking strawberries easier, because you didn't have to stoop down so far to spot the red berries under the leaves.

I nodded in agreement, my mouth watering at the idea of fresh summer strawberries. Logan's voice had such a rich, comforting timbre, like someone who could have his own gardening show on the radio. For a recent transplant to small-town life, Logan had such an earthy, woodsman vibe. I could imagine him in a log cabin, chopping his own wood for a potbelly stove.

He had snow in his beard, from his tousle with Tony. Without thinking, I began tidying up his beard, pulling chunks of icy snow from the dark hairs on his chin and jaw. He kept talking about gardening while I pulled away the ice chunks.

"…and fresh spinach to go with the tomatoes. Hey, thanks for grooming me."

I realized what I was doing and yanked my hands back. "Sorry. Jeffrey gets snow clumps between his toes. Force of habit for me to help pull them out."

Logan gazed at me calmly. His blue eyes looked dark gray under the thin light of the street lamp. "I got my wish," he said, his voice a low rumble in his chest. "I got to be your cat for a few minutes."

"You're a big cat. Don't start using Jeffrey's litter box."

"Somebody's jealous."

I thought he meant Tony, but then followed his gaze and saw Jeffrey on the windowsill, his dark gray body barely visible with the interior lights off. He saw me looking and feigned a yawn.

Something occurred to me out of nowhere. "Logan, you don't have a cat, or a dog. Why were you at the vet's the day we met? Don't tell me you have lizards or snakes in your place. You're not a reptile person, are you? I mean, why? Why would someone *own* reptiles?"

"Snakes are beautiful," he said with a neutral tone and expression. "Magnificent, even."

"No!"

"The snakes enjoy our shared laundry room, actually. If you see them in there, don't panic. They like to get up in the ceiling and then surprise you."

"Ugh," I said, playing along. "How many snakes?"

He shrugged. "They're so hard to keep track of once they start multiplying. I really should count up hatched eggshells."

"You're a big tease."

He held up both hands. "Guilty. If you must know, and it seems like you're the type of person who can't leave any mystery unsolved, I was waiting to get a fax."

"That makes sense."

His blue eyes twinkled. "The best alibis always do."

Captain Tony Milano cleared his throat to let us know he was approaching. "You two can be on your way."

"Why were you driving by?" I asked. "Did you want to talk to me about… that thing, from today?"

"It's late," he replied gruffly.

"But you drove here for a reason."

"It's late," he repeated, looking at Logan. "I'll drop by tomorrow morning. Around ten."

"I'll have the coffee on," I said cheerily.

He almost smiled. "I'll bring the donuts." He gave Logan a stiff nod, then started walking back to his car.

Logan watched him leave. "I'm glad he roughed me up. It might come in handy, to have a cop owing me a favor. I'm sure *the captain* doesn't want a complaint filed against him."

"Please don't file a complaint. Tony's a good cop. His heart's in the right place."

"For you, I'll drop the issue," Logan said. "But could you put in a good word for me?"

"Sure. I'll tell him how helpful you were last month, with the whole snowman thing. Plus you pay your rent on time, don't have parties, and probably don't own any snakes."

Logan looked down at my crossed arms. "Someone's teeth are chattering, and they don't sound like mine." He unzipped his jacket and tried to hand it to me.

I stepped back. "I should head inside this perfectly warm house."

He folded his jacket over his forearm and turned toward his own front door, on the other side of the house. "Sounds like a plan. See you around, landlady."

"See you around, tenant. Keep your scary reptiles out of the laundry room."

"No promises."

CHAPTER 12
JANUARY 2

IN THE MORNING, I left a voicemail for my employee to let her know our plans for doing storewide inventory were delayed, and she should open the store and run it as usual.

I didn't expect my meeting with Tony would last very long, but even if he got to my house right at ten, it could be noon by the time I got to the gift store, and counting inventory seemed like the sort of gargantuan task that was wrong to start mid-day.

It wasn't at all like me to procrastinate an important job, so perhaps this was the positive influence of small-town life. My father wasn't wrong about me moving back to town to keep an eye on him as he got older, but I'd also moved back for myself. There'd been days, working my old job in venture capital, where I felt like I was aging two days for every twenty-four hours.

Luckily, it hadn't shown on my face. One good thing about being a workaholic in an office is you don't get much sun damage. At thirty-three, I hadn't seen any crow's feet yet, *knock wood.*

Jeffrey sat on the bathroom counter and watched me put on eyeliner. He tilted his head and continued to watch as I put makeup remover on a cotton ball and swiped the eyeliner back off again, after deciding it was too sexy for a 10:00 a.m. coffee meeting with a married man.

TONY FINALLY SHOWED up at 11:15 a.m., with apologies, and donuts. For the last hour, I'd been reading a magazine, checking email on my laptop, and watching a daytime talk show. I would have done more, but I only have two hands.

I tidied up and put on a fresh pot of coffee as I told Tony to make himself at home.

He was in uniform, on duty. He kept his boots and coat on, and took a seat at the dining table, which was next to the island portion of the kitchen counter bar in my open-plan space.

"Donuts, as promised." He gave the donut box a shake before setting it on the table and flipping open the lid. The sweet smell of sugared frosting and vanilla wafted up.

"You're the worst," I said teasingly as I took a seat across from him and looked over the donuts. "It's January, and I should be making a resolution to eat more cruciferous vegetables." He gave me a confused look, so I explained, "That's the fancy word for broccoli and cauliflower, and we should all be eating more of those things."

"Cheese sauce," he said. "You learn all the tricks as a parent. Put cheese sauce on it, and they'll eat anything."

I was quiet, letting it sink in that Tony was somebody's dad. And not just one somebody, but three of them. Times like these, I was aware of how long I'd been away, and how everyone's lives had kept on going. Sure, I'd only been a few hours' drive away, but I still felt like an astronaut returning to earth at times.

Tony and I talked about cheese sauce and vegetables. I was curious about whether or not his eldest son, Tony Junior, looked exactly like him, but it seemed rude to ask to see photos. He seemed to be in a chipper mood, so I didn't mention anything about the incident from the night before.

The coffee maker let out a happy sizzle to announce the successful completion of its job.

Tony nudged the untouched box of pastries toward me, then got up to pour us two cups. He hadn't been inside my house before, but he was making himself at home, the way he had at my father's house.

"What do you think of the donuts?" he asked.

"These aren't the typical cheap cop-shop donuts. These are all different flavors, aren't they? So, now I've seen it all. *Artisan donuts* have reached Misty Falls. What's this one with the red-brown chunks?"

"Maple bacon. And there's only one, so you know what to do." He set the mugs of coffee on the table and grinned as he met my gaze, his brown eyes crinkling at the corners. Tony had a few crow's-feet, but they looked so good on him that I almost wanted some.

I licked my index finger and poked the maple-bacon donut, leaving a light imprint. "Dibs."

He licked his finger and poked the edge of the chocolate one next to it. "Dibs," he said with a laugh.

Dibs by licked-finger-pokes was a trick we'd learned from my father. Thinking of him reminded me of the private investigator's license application, and I might have mentioned something to Tony, but after yesterday's rudeness at the crime scene, I'd decided I wanted more distance between us.

The canvas of Tony's department-issued jacket rustled with even the smallest of gestures, and I found myself annoyed that he hadn't taken it off. He was in my home, but keeping me at a distance, drawing a line between officer and civilian. My feelings were very confusing. I wanted distance, but I didn't.

I put the maple-bacon donut on my plate and used a fork and knife to cut pie-shaped wedges.

Tony shook his head, amused. "Some things never change. You and your fork and knife. And that grin on your face."

"I'm only smiling because of the donuts," I said. "I'm still mad at you. Yesterday, at the crime scene, you were so rude to me. Then last night you attacked my innocent tenant. And I haven't heard an apology out of you yet."

"That's what the donuts are for."

"Hmm," I said through a mouthful of donut. The bacon bits added a smoky flavor, yet the donut didn't taste meaty. The maple in the icing was the real stuff, not imitation.

"I am sorry," he said, and his words, combined with the genuine respect in his voice, were even sweeter than the maple frosting.

"It's fine," I said hurriedly, feeling bad about forcing his hand. "Crime scenes are stressful places, and I know you meant well last night. My tenant is a bit macho. He should have identified himself when you asked."

I stuffed another wedge of donut into my mouth to quiet myself. *Why is it always like this?* You want a man to apologize, and then when he does, you feel the need to cover his embarrassment with apologies of your own.

Sometimes, I'd rather they didn't say sorry.

As crazy as it makes me, there's something pleasingly black and white about men refusing to apologize, and it throws everything off when they do. Where can you put the anger you still feel? The outrage doesn't just dissipate, or at least mine doesn't.

I pondered this as I sipped my coffee, the taste cutting through the maple syrup on my tongue perfectly.

Tony hadn't brought up the reason for his visit yet, and the curiosity was overwhelming.

"How's the case?" I asked.

"Fine."

I waited for more, but it didn't come.

"Your rookie, Dimples, claims to have experience in these things. Is he the lead on the investigation? Do you have any suspects?"

Tony avoided my eyes. "Something's bound to turn up."

"Was there a boyfriend? Did you find the laptop that went with the charger?"

"I'm not so sure she had either of those things. We've asked around, and it sounds like she didn't have any use for men, or technology."

"But she had email. There was an email address on her business card."

"She probably checked her email at the library. She had an account there, and checked out books regularly."

"Non-fiction or fiction? Were they biographies about con artists?"

Tony eyed me with suspicion. "How do you know about the books the victim checked out? Do I have a mole at the station?"

I reached for my coffee instead of lying. My father was getting information from someone at the station, but surely there wasn't any harm in it. He was just bored, and the details from a real crime case were more interesting than the ones on TV.

"It was Kyle," he said. "He's up to something, I can feel it."

"Who?" I paused before adding, "Oh, you mean your rookie. The Dempsey kid."

"You're not the first one to fall for Dimples. I'm just glad he's not a firefighter, or we'd have all the desperate housewives of Misty Falls setting their drapes on fire."

"Or putting kittens in trees."

Tony snorted. "That would be a nightmare. It's bad enough I've got you running around like Nancy Drew meets Veronica Mars, taking photos at crime scenes and cracking jokes during a murder investigation."

"Pardon me?" I pushed my plate away, my appetite gone. I glared at Tony, the storm clouds brewing.

"I kicked you out because you were in the way."

"In the way? I've done nothing but *help you* do your job. If it wasn't for me, you'd have two murderers running around, but you wouldn't even know about the second one if I hadn't found the body for you."

He leaned back in his chair, balancing on the back legs like a fidgeting teenager. The old wood creaked in protest. *That's how you break a chair*, I wanted to warn him, but instead, I silently wished the chair would break, so he'd land right on his butt.

"Why are you here, Tony?"

He kept rocking the chair on its back legs, giving me a look that was surprisingly insolent for a man of forty, with silver hair at his temples.

"Stay out of the way," he said. "Mine and Officer Dempsey's."

Now the pieces were falling into place. He wasn't here about the investigation at all. This was about Kyle asking me on a date.

I turned in my chair to look out the big window of the adjoining living room. "Speaking of Kyle Dempsey, where is he? Don't tell me you made him sit in the car." I spotted Tony's car across the street, and a shadow in the passenger seat. Tony hadn't taken off his jacket because Kyle was waiting out in the car.

The clunk of chair legs returning to the floor made me whip around, back to Tony.

"Stormy, don't turn this into a big deal. Just steer clear of this one. It doesn't concern you. Don't ask me about the case, and don't go around talking about it, especially not to Kyle."

He straightened up, looking tall in his chair, the canvas of his jacket rustling with authority.

"Playing detective is dangerous," he said.

"Whatever," I said. "I've already forgotten the whole thing. Voula who? I don't care. And I'm *not* trying to *play detective*."

Technically, that would be a lie if I joined my father's private investigation firm, but as of that moment, it was true enough to hurl at Tony's face. And with the way he was looking at me and diminishing my helpfulness, I did want to hurl things at his face.

"Good," he said. "I'm glad we had this discussion."

"Good," I said with equal finality. "I'll manage my gift shop, and you put away the murderers. How many suspects did you say you have? Was it zero? *Good job locating the victim's public library account.* I'm sure your big lead is right around the corner. *Maybe a librarian killed her for overdue fines.*"

His nostrils flared with the effort it took him to not take the bait. He got to his feet and headed toward the door.

"Wait!" I dashed into the kitchen, where I hurriedly transferred Tony's barely touched coffee into a plastic travel mug. "Take your coffee to go," I said sweetly.

He grunted his acquiescence and waited, shuffling by the door.

"Big plans for today?" I asked with fake cheer. "I swear I'm not playing detective, prying for details. Answer as vaguely as you like."

"I'll be talking to the waitress who allegedly tossed a drink on the victim New Year's Eve."

"Not allegedly. She definitely threw the drink on Voula Varga. I hope you have backup. That sweet little white-haired lady is a vicious criminal. If you back her into a corner, she's liable to grab the nearest knitting needle and skewer you."

Tony's nostrils were still flared. "We have to follow up on all the leads."

"All the leads? Did you trace the gun already? I bet the waitress stole it, cat-burglar style. Pat her down for weapons before you start the interrogation."

Tony didn't even smile. He twitched impatiently by the door. I finished the coffee preparations. I'd poured not one, but two travel mugs, and handed them to him.

"That one's for your rookie," I said sweetly. "I don't know if young Kyle takes cream or sugar, but you can send him in and I'll fix his up just how he likes it."

"You're too kind," he said flatly.

"I hope you don't think I'm interfering in police business." I batted my eyelashes. "It's just coffee. Us womenfolk are allowed to make you big, strong men coffee, aren't we? That is, when we're not setting the furniture on fire to get the sexy firemen to come over."

He slowly turned his gaze down to the floor and nodded, conceding that I'd won this particular round. Then he left, closing the door gently.

I went to the window and watched him walk away, a dark blue figure against the dazzling white snow. Unlike the murky gray day before, the second day of January was as gorgeous as a winter day could be.

Tony glanced back over his shoulder, his face neutral. His pace slowed, and I expected him to dump the coffee into the snow right in front of me, but he didn't. He kept walking, got into the police car on the driver's side, and drove off.

Something behind me made a plopping sound. Jeffrey had returned from wherever His Regal Grayness had been hiding, scared by the sound of Tony's boots inside the house. The plop was him calling dibs on the remainder of my maple-bacon donut by knocking it to the floor.

"You act like I don't feed you." I confiscated the donut and cleaned up the mess. He gave me an innocent look, then sauntered away.

A few minutes later, I was sipping my coffee and grump-eating another one of the donuts—chocolate with pink frosting—when a ball of yarn rolled past the table. The yarn was followed by a cat, tackling the ball like it was a dangerous foe. The yarn fought back surprisingly well for an inanimate object. It began to unravel, and after a few wrestling rolls, the yarn was winning, restricting Jeffrey's movements with loops and knots.

"This is not a cat toy," I said as I disentangled the embarrassed-looking cat.

I wound the ball back up and set it on the table before me. Jeffrey must have found it in my closet, with a half-dozen other objects I kept around to make myself feel guilty. Along with the yarn, there was a beaded-jewelry-making kit, various art supplies, and a yoga mat, still in its bag. My workaholic tendencies hadn't transferred to arts and crafts—at least not yet.

"Maybe you finding this ball of yarn is a sign," I said. "Dad wants me to infiltrate Voula's knitting club, but Tony wants me to be a good little Misty Falls housewife and stay out of trouble. Hmm. What to do, what to do…"

I grabbed my cell phone and scrolled through my local contacts. They say everyone in Hollywood is connected to actor Kevin Bacon by six degrees of separation. Small towns are even more connected. I could find that knitting group in three phone calls or fewer, especially if I started with the right person.

I clicked the contact number for Ruby Sparkes.

When she answered, she didn't even say hello.

"Stormy, it's about time you called. We have so much to talk about. I'm putting on the Earl Grey now, but I'm afraid I don't have any cupcakes."

I chuckled softly. Ruby did not waste any time. I hadn't planned more than a phone call with her, but the day was too gorgeous to spend inside anyway. Like Jeffrey, I enjoyed the comforts of home even more after some fresh air. Unlike Jeffrey, I preferred doing things other than sitting under the winter bird feeder and wishing it wasn't so high off the ground.

"How do you feel about fancy artisanal donuts?" I asked Ruby.

"Honey, do you even have to ask?" I heard the sound of running water—the kettle being filled. "I'm at the store. We're closed the rest of the week, and the lights are off in the showroom, but you can let yourself in. You know where to find me."

CHAPTER 13

RUBY SPARKES WASN'T just the energetic and friendly owner of a jewelry store called Ruby's Treasure Trove. She was a bit of a treasure herself, a sparkling jewel in the crown of Misty Falls. Not only did she have a knack for knowing practically everyone in town by name, but she was also part of the Secret Tearoom Ladies, a group that—as far as I'd figured out so far—kept an eye out for residents in trouble and tried to help them.

Last month, she drove her teen employee crazy with endless cleaning and make-work chores. Some people would chalk that up to Ruby being a tough boss—cruel, even—but there was kindness in her actions. She felt the girl, who was a dropout, would be better off in high school, and so Ruby tried to make schoolwork look more fun by comparison. Her plan worked, thanks to a little nudge from other parties, including yours truly.

As I entered Ruby's Treasure Trove and made my way back to the secret tearoom hidden behind the storage area, I hoped Ruby's invitation to drop by meant I was now part of her inner circle. I'd gotten the impression I was too young to be a member of the Secret Tearoom Ladies, but that only made me more curious about their activities.

I found Ruby humming to herself in the jewelry store's staff kitchen, setting up a serving tray with dainty teacups, milk, and chunks of sugar in the shapes of rocks. By the sound and feel of the space, we were the only two people there, yet others had been back there recently. In addition to the scent of Ruby's perfume and the lavender in her favorite blend of creamy Earl Grey, I also detected a rose perfume, in addition to that classic, Chanel No. 5.

"You're here because the ladies had a meeting," I guessed. "I can smell their perfumes."

"And hello to you, too," she said with a light laugh. "Aren't we a clever detective."

I looked down and pointed my toes together, embarrassed. Maybe Tony wasn't entirely wrong about me running around town spouting theories like some sassy teen detective.

I didn't feel awkward for long, because Ruby grabbed me for a friendly hug and crushed my face to her bosom. Her leopard-print blouse was soft, either silk or a silk blend, and was as soft on my cheek as talcum powder. When she released me, I took an admiring look at her from head to toe—curly hair colored a shade of red that was far from natural, but perfect nonetheless; bright eyes and beautiful wrinkles from sixty-six years of laughter; two thick gold serpentine necklaces around her neck, and no shortage of matching rings; the smartly tailored leopard-printed blouse; pleated trousers in Ruby's favorite color, purple; and dark brown leather dress boots that I would bet matched a nearby purse perfectly.

By comparison, I felt underdressed in my dark jeans and teal-blue cotton sweater with a mock turtleneck. I told Ruby as much, and she just laughed and said, "With those lovely earrings bringing everyone's attention to your beautiful face, you've got nothing to be worried about. Say, wherever did you get those earrings? They're breathtaking."

I grinned and reached up to twist one of the earrings. They were petite and daisy-shaped, with a tiny pearl in the center.

"These little flowers?" I asked, playing along. "A gift from my father for Christmas. Can you believe he picked them out all by himself?"

Her eyes widened meaningfully and she said, "Did he, now? All by himself, you say?"

She winked as she grabbed the serving tray and led me toward the windowed nook with the table. We both knew Finnegan Day had gotten help from Ruby, and that only made the gift even more special. He'd sent a matching pair to my sister, who was traveling and couldn't make it home for the holidays, but swore she was wearing her earrings every day and missing us.

We took a seat at the table, and Ruby apologized as she tidied away her laptop and assortment of other digital devices. I gazed out the window at the street and went silent in reverence for the view.

Misty Falls is truly a postcard town, with all its colorful locally owned storefronts, backed by snow-dusted mountains. The only neon in town is the red boot over the shoe repair shop. We do have some of the usual fast-food chains in town, but years ago the city passed bylaws restricting the signage and appearance of those businesses. If you come looking for Chicken McNuggets in Misty Falls, you'll have to know where to look or who to ask.

My view on that sparkling winter day was marred only by a young mother with kids in tow, stopping to lean in toward me and pluck a poppy seed from between her teeth. People don't normally behave that way around me, but part of the secret surrounding Ruby's tearoom is the window itself, which is a mirror on the other side, surrounded by a title mosaic decorated with uplifting words and phrases.

"Always the poppy seeds," Ruby said.

When I turned to her, she gave me a sympathetic look and asked how I was feeling, in light of my discovery the day before. The news was out.

We sipped our tea and sampled the donuts, and I filled her in on my experience at the crime scene. She was such a good listener, so I didn't hold back. I told her about young Kyle Dempsey flirting with me, and Tony's reaction.

"Men," she said with an eye roll. "Don't let my lack of a wedding ring fool you. I've been around the merry-go-round more times than a crop-duster pilot with an empty plane does loop-de-loops to show off." She looked away shyly as her cheeks colored. "I dated a pilot for a while," she explained, then waved for me to continue.

After some consideration of my father's privacy, I backtracked and told her about the information he'd gathered on Voula Varga: no family, no live stalkers, no obvious enemies, besides one waitress.

"It's a shame your father's retired now," she said. "He was a real asset to this town."

We locked gazes. Did she know about his plans to become a private investigator? Was she trying to determine if I also knew? I kept my face neutral and studied hers, but she didn't have any *tells* that I could distinguish. Finally, she drew herself up with a breath, and said, "I have very little to add, and, like your father, I can't reveal my sources, but I do have a name."

"A name?" A tingle went down my spine.

She glanced at the window, as though someone might be listening. During a previous visit, she'd told me it was triple-paned and nearly as soundproof as the adjoining wall, but I could understand her nervousness. A woman had been killed, and the murderer could walk by that window at any moment. With a start, I remembered that the front door had been unlocked when I'd arrived.

"Wait, Ruby. I didn't lock the door when I got here."

"There's a chime on the entry, but you make a good point, honey. Wait a minute, I'll be right back."

She left to lock the door, and I realized how tense with suspense I was. In my hands lay a damp, twisted white thing that had once been a napkin. I stretched my neck from side to side and reminded myself I'd come here for a purpose: to get contact information for the knitting club.

Of course, getting this name from Ruby would be a huge bonus. I had to assume the name was a suspect.

Ruby returned with a sheet of paper and handed it to me. "The printer's up front, and I actually sent this to print right after you called."

The printout was from a website page, and it was the biography for a Hollywood producer named Bernard Goldstein.

My excitement quickly crashed back to earth.

"Sorry to break it to you," I said gently to Ruby. "Bernard is a dead end. If this is the same stalker guy Voula had a restraining order on, we'll need a séance to ask him questions. He died a few years ago."

"Not according to his company's website. He's alive and well, with several big-budget movies in development."

I frowned at the sheet of paper before me, then pulled out my phone to access the notes I'd taken while my father was making calls the day before.

"My mistake, Ruby. The stalker's name was *Harold* Goldstein. Same last name, though. So, what's the connection?"

"I didn't know about the stalker until you told me. I think it's probably just a coincidence. Goldstein isn't that rare of a last name."

I studied the producer's picture. The printout was in color, but it was still a photo from a website, so the resolution was low, the image pixelated. Even so, it was clear how fit and attractive the man was. He looked about fifty, with just enough gray at his temples to give him a distinguished look, and his jaw was as square as a lantern, like that of a hunky man on a romance novel, or in a menswear catalog.

"He's too attractive," Ruby said.

"You're right. Voula Varga was not his type for dating. A powerful, alpha-looking man like this would have a trophy wife, blond, plus maybe a trophy girlfriend, too—also blond. I know the type. He wouldn't be with a curly-haired woman whose features got her cast in every witch role available."

"True enough, but what I meant was he's too attractive to be hanging around in Misty Falls without people noticing. If this man has set foot in our town, I'd have heard about it."

"How did you get his name?"

"Rumors about a movie deal." She leaned over and pointed to the section of the bio that listed projects in development. "This is the one."

I read out the movie title. "*House of Love and Lies.* Sounds dark. I thought Voula wasn't acting anymore. Did she have a role in this? Or was this about the house? The one she was renting is practically famous from that other movie."

"I'm not sure if the house was involved. All I've heard is that she was friends with this Bernard Goldstein gentleman, and he was letting her invest in the movie. She swore she was going to get ten times her investment back."

"She was borrowing money?"

"I'm not sure. You know how it is with rumors that go around. Everybody drops a little information and adds their own something."

"Yes. Small-town gossip is more complex than asymmetric encryption algorithms."

"Exactly!" Ruby used one elegant ring-covered hand to tuck her buoyant red-purple curls behind one ear. "If you want more information, you should go directly to her friends."

I sat up straight, feeling proud. "That's my plan. I'm hoping you have the contact information for some of the people in her knitting club. Even if you just know someone who might know someone, I'm happy to make a few calls."

"How about a website?" She held up one finger for me to wait for it, then reopened her nearby laptop. A moment later, she turned the screen to face me.

The photo on the screen caught me off guard. My shoulders jerked up and I leaned back reflexively. It took a few seconds for me to compose myself, then explain, "This group photo of the knitting club was taken inside... *the room*."

Ruby let out a torrent of apologies and ran to get me a glass of water.

"I'm fine," I assured her. "Just caught off guard. But the good news is that's definitely the right club, since the photo's inside her house."

"Your move," Ruby said. "The schedule says they have a meeting tonight, location to be determined."

"My father wants me to offer to host the club. You don't think that would look too suspicious, do you? They're all friends of hers, and then there's me, the chick who discovered the body. What if they decide I'm the killer?"

Ruby raised her eyebrows. "You think they'll have a vote and then stab you to death with all their knitting needles?"

I guffawed. "I'll get a friend to come, so the club can't hold a trial while I'm in the washroom." I batted my eyelashes. "What are you up to tonight?"

"I've got a date with a pilot." She reached across the table and patted my hand. "But I'll be thinking of you! I hope the killer's not in the knitting club, but something tells me it's a man." She eyed the printed bio for Bernard Goldstein. "Maybe he snuck in and out of town without anyone seeing him."

"I don't know, Ruby. If he was an old Hollywood friend getting her to invest in his project, you'd think he'd want her alive."

"My gut tells me he's involved, though. Look at the eyes. There's something disingenuous there."

"Bernard Goldstein," I said. "That's a very nice yellow tie you're wearing. It practically screams I'm-a-nice-guy-not-a-killer. Why the bright tie, Bernard? What have you got to hide?"

The photo didn't answer. I would have to ask Voula's friends.

CHAPTER 14

RUBY WAS IN no rush to kick me out, plus she seemed as interested in the case as my father had been, so I stayed for another pot of tea and made some calls to the members of the Misty Falls Crafty Knitters Club.

On the phone, I fudged the truth by saying I was a "new friend" of Voula's. The statement was justifiable, sort of. Our first and only meeting had resulted in me loaning her the masquerade mask, to cover her smeared makeup, and that was something a friend would do. Perhaps if she'd still been alive when I'd arrived at her house, it could have been the beginning of a friendship... once I got over my annoyance about her researching my ex-fiancé's name.

The first two phone calls went smoothly. If her knitting club friends thought I was responsible for her untimely demise, they hid it well. They seemed to be a tight-knit group (pun intended!), because the third person I phoned was expecting my call.

"What shall I bring to the wake?" the third woman asked.

"Uh..." *The wake?* I stammered for a moment, caught off guard.

"How about a deli tray?" the woman suggested.

"That would be perfect," I said. "Do you need my address?"

"Oh. Sure. Hang on, I'll get a pen." I heard some exaggerated shuffling of papers. This woman already had my address from one of the others, but we both played along out of politeness.

I made calls to a total of twelve women. All of them said they would be there, at my house, at seven o'clock.

I told Ruby the details, and then used her washroom so I could get right to errands and preparing for the wake.

The wake.

What kind of an Irish person was I, to have completely overlooked the obvious? Of course tonight's knitting club meeting wasn't just any old meeting—it was always meant to be a wake, of course. The only change was that now I was hosting.

An Irish wake is not so different from the death traditions of other cultures, especially now, in modern times. We don't typically lay out the body in the home of the deceased anymore, but there are traditions people keep up because they offer comfort. The true gift of ritual is that you have a blueprint, a guide for what to do next when you're in grief and can't think for yourself of what to do next.

I didn't know Voula Varga or her tastes, but I did know where to find the best whiskey in town. I loaded my car with supplies, and then drove by my father's, to borrow a clay pipe and some tobacco. It was unlikely the women would partake of that, or help themselves to a pinch of the snuff, but I would do my part and make my Irish ancestors proud.

* * *

THE CRAFTY KNITTERS would be arriving at seven o'clock. I got so worked up over being a good hostess that I nearly forgot *why* I was hosting.

Jessica stopped by at four o'clock with folding chairs from her apartment, and she asked, "Remind me again, why are you doing this?"

I'd already caught her up on recent events when I phoned about borrowing the chairs, but it was taking a while for everything to sink in—for her, as well as me. I'd gone from witness to investigator in a single day.

I explained, "To find out more about Voula's connection to this Hollywood producer guy. I've called his office in California, but I keep going straight to voicemail. They must be taking a long holiday."

"Couldn't you just ask her friends over the phone?"

"Sure, but this is about getting a feel for Voula and her interactions with people. The more you know about the victim, the closer you get to the killer. If you can walk in their shoes, the clues start to pop out."

Jessica tossed her red hair over her shoulder as she moved the standing lamp over to the corner to make more space for the folding chairs we were setting up.

"I don't want you walking in victim shoes," she said. "Promise you'll go straight to the police with whatever you find out."

"They'll get their information." I snapped two more chairs into their seats-down position. "Eventually."

I looked up to catch her rolling her pretty blue eyes.

"You'll do anything to annoy Tony Milano, won't you? Just leave him alone already."

I bristled at the judgment in her voice. Jessica was one of the few people who knew about my brief fling with Tony, so many years ago, and lately she'd been getting weird whenever his name came up. There was something she wanted to say about my friendship with him, but she wouldn't spit it out.

"You should have heard him this morning," I said defensively. "The way he was talking about women knowing their place, it was offensive. I should have thrown my drink on him, but you can't do that with coffee."

"Too hot?"

"Too wasteful. I buy the good stuff, you know."

"I've never thrown a drink on anyone," she said.

"Me neither." I checked the time on my phone. "We still have a few hours before people get here. Should we pour some drinks and toss them on each other, to let off a little steam?"

Jessica laughed and then sneezed. With a plugged-sounding nose, she said, "Let's wait until the guests arrive and put on a drink-tossing show for them before the food fight. Every good wake needs some entertainment."

We both laughed over this as we finished setting up the chairs. Jessica kept sneezing, though, and by five o'clock she was raiding my medicine cabinet for cold medication. She'd had a successful Polar Bear Dip the day before, earning her ten-year pin, but she'd also succumbed to a cold that must have been lying dormant.

She swore she'd be fine to stay for the wake and be my protection against the crafty knitters, but by five thirty, Jessica was asleep on my sofa, snuggled under a red chenille throw and a warm, gray cat. I checked the bathroom cabinet and discovered she'd taken the nighttime cold medicine, even though there was a brand-new bottle of the daytime version.

I knew exactly what had happened.

She knew darn well which version was which, but didn't want to crack the seal on the new bottle—not that cough syrup would go bad once opened, but some people are funny that way, and will only accept something if it's already opened. That's why you're supposed to open the bottle of white wine as well as the bottle of red for your dinner guests, so they pick the one they really want rather than politely accepting whichever one's already open.

I let Jessica snooze, and when she was still an immobile lump on my sofa at ten minutes to seven, I gently relocated her to the guest room. I got her tucked into the guest bed, and she thanked me by kissing the top of my hand. Strange, but cute. And germy. I immediately washed both hands with antibacterial soap.

My doorbell rang as I was drying my hands. Jeffrey hid, because he didn't like the chimes. I ran out to answer the door, pausing to turn around the mirror by the entryway table. I'd remembered to stop the clocks and turn the other mirrors, but this one had evaded me.

I could hear, through the door, some of the women talking. The sound was muffled, but a woman with a strident voice said, "If this Stormy Day woman is the thirteenth, she should be told. It's what Voula would have wanted."

The thirteenth? Of what? There were twelve women in the knitting club. Twelve wasn't the sort of number that set off any alarm bells in my head, but thirteen was. Were they witches? Was the knitting group actually a coven?

I pressed my ear to the door, hoping to hear more, but it was just a jumble of voices as more people arrived. Someone knocked on the door, their knuckles rapping loudly over my ear, and I jumped out of my socks.

Once I'd scraped myself off the ceiling, I put on a welcoming smile and opened the door to the Misty Falls Crafty Knitters.

Crafty Knitters… and *Possibly Witches.*

CHAPTER 15

MY TOP SUSPECTS for witches posing as crafters were Barbara and her sister, Denise. They both had straight black hair, which I knew was a stereotype for witches, but even stereotypes come from somewhere truthful.

These two had also been at Voula's table on New Year's Eve.

From the moment she stepped into my house, Barbara had taken charge of all the activities, moving chairs and rearranging the trays of food without asking me. She even scolded Jeffrey for trying to steal a slice of ham—not that he didn't deserve the scolding, but it didn't seem right. Worse, Jeffrey took Barbara way more seriously than he ever took me. He was so frightened by her hissing and her waggling finger that he slunk out of the room like he was packing a hobo bag and never coming back.

Like Voula, Barbara was an imposing figure of a woman, tall and angular, with her straight black hair cut on a crisp asymmetrical angle. Her sister, Denise, was the shorter, softer version. Both were in their sixties, but Denise did an unusual thing that made her look like a schoolgirl—she covered her mouth with her hand almost continuously, like she had something to say but wouldn't let it out.

Barbara, however, had no problem talking. She led the readings from the Bible, and I couldn't go to the kitchen for a glass of water without her at my heels, asking in her loud, strident voice what I was doing and how she could help.

Eventually, I used her eagerness to get her away from the group for a private discussion, leading her downstairs to the laundry room on an errand to get more napkins. I knew the napkins were on a top shelf, behind the extra laundry detergent, but I took my time, pretending to be searching around.

"Were the two of you close?" I asked Barbara.

"Who?" She seemed surprised by my question.

"You and Voula."

"Oh. No, not really." She looked around my dark basement with suspicion, like it might contain reptiles, which made me imagine beady eyeballs lurking in the shadows.

"I thought you and your sister were close to her. Didn't I see you at the Fox and Hound with Voula?"

"Yes, but she wasn't the sort of woman who let people get close. You had to *pay to play*, if you know what I mean."

"Pay to play? Oh, you mean all the psychic consultation mumbo jumbo."

"Mumbo jumbo? No." Barbara gave me a deathly serious look, her large brown eyes bulging and glossy under the light of the single bulb overhead in the laundry room.

This was it. She was about to tell me about the coven. I asked, "Was she really a witch?"

"No. There's no such thing as witches."

I nodded. *That's exactly what a witch would want you to think.*

"But Voula Varga was the real deal," she said, giving me a chill that ran up my spine like a snake made of ice cubes.

"Real? How?"

"She was a psychic. I wouldn't be surprised if her spirit was walking around this wake right now, listening to what people say about her. That's why everyone's so shy about sharing their stories." Barbara looked up at the low basement rafters. Suddenly, she jerked her arms, as though she'd seen or felt something.

"Are you feeling okay?"

"Just a chill." She rubbed her forearms, which were bare below the elbow, her elegant black dress having only three-quarter-length sleeves. "I haven't been in a house with a basement in years. It's cold down here, like a mausoleum."

"Sorry it's so chilly. You can go back up if you like, and I'll find those darn napkins eventually, I'm sure."

"Voula knew things," Barbara said, her voice much softer and quieter than it had been most of the night. "Voula knew my soon-to-be-ex-husband was holding out on me. I paid for sessions with her, and she did her chants, communicating with the spirits on the other plane. It took so long, and I was about to give up and write off her fees as a valuable lesson learned, when she told me about his secret bank account. I sent my lawyer in the right direction, and we nailed my ex. I was so grateful, I happily paid Voula double for the sessions."

"Did she ask you to pay double? Or to pay some sort of finder's fee percentage?" I remembered the con artist books at her house. The truly noteworthy thing about Voula's reading choices was the lack of literature on communicating with spirit planes.

Barbara shrugged her bony shoulders and used her left hand, bare of rings, but with an indentation where a wedding band had once been, to smooth her silky black hair. "She had a way of asking for money without asking. She made you feel like she was doing *you* the favor by taking it."

"So, she wasn't exactly a friend?"

"I don't suppose she had any friends at all. She wasn't the warm, fuzzy type. My ex-husband said she was a narcissist, possibly a psychopath. *He would know*."

An image flashed in my head: the gun, left behind at the crime scene.

Ruby suspected the killer was a man. If it hadn't been a lover, it could have been another male enemy.

Barbara's ex-husband, whose name I didn't even know, shifted onto my list of suspects. If he'd been hiding money during a divorce settlement, that confirmed he was the deceptive type. If he knew Voula was the one revealing his secrets, whether the information had come from a spirit plane or somewhere else, he might have been angry enough to kill her.

My mind reeled with the possibilities. Six months in town was long enough to set up alliances and gather a few enemies. I didn't believe Voula was getting information from spirits on another plane, but it was possible she had human spies, or other ways of getting information. She could have befriended someone who worked at a bank, or even within the police force.

I turned away from Barbara and started moving boxes around on the basement's storage shelves, buying time before I would "find" the napkins.

"Do you know if Voula worked with anyone?" I asked casually. "Like an assistant, or someone who set up appointments?"

"I don't think so. Why do you ask?"

I'd prepared myself for a question like this, so I had my answer ready.

"I'm not sure if you know about what happened to me in December, but long story short, I've decided to keep my eyes wide open from now on. This is a small town, and when something bad happens, I'm not going to blindly walk into another dangerous situation."

"Yet you invite twelve strangers into your home," she noted coolly. "One of us could be the killer."

The hairs on the back of my neck stood up, but I remained calm and didn't whirl around to face Barbara. There was a teasing tone to her voice, but no malice.

I answered with equal coolness, "If one of the Crafty Knitters is the killer and takes me out tonight, that leaves eleven witnesses."

"I suppose it does. What's this?"

Something cool brushed against my ear. My breath caught in my throat as I froze. The coolness was Barbara's bony hand, reaching… for the napkins, on the top shelf. In her heels, she was taller than me, and must have spotted the plastic-wrapped stack once her eyes had adjusted to the low light of the basement.

"Ta da," she said triumphantly. "Found the napkins."

"Must have been helpful spirits guiding you."

She made a wheezing attempt at a laugh.

I turned around and studied her face. Despite the small smile on her thin lips, her eyes were still wide, the whites showing around her irises. She was afraid. Not of me, but of something, or someone.

And why wouldn't she be? A murderer was on the loose in Misty Falls, and it could be her ex-husband, or someone else she knew. The killer could be someone sitting upstairs right now, helping themselves to smoked meats and cheese.

"Everything's going to be okay," I said soothingly. "The police will catch Voula's killer."

She turned away slowly, then stopped. With her face in profile to me, she nodded forward as one gleaming tear ran from her eye, down her cheek, and fell upon the bare concrete floor. The tear darkened a circle. I blinked, and the tear was lost in the pattern of the gray concrete.

"Then what?" she asked. "Nothing will ever be the same again."

I didn't know what to say, but then part of an Irish prayer I'd printed out to read at the wake came to me.

"*May you always hear, even in your hour of sorrow, the gentle singing of the lark.*" I paused. "That's an Irish proverb. I've got the rest of it printed out upstairs, but I can't remember the end."

"That was nice," Barbara said. She handed me the napkins without meeting my eyes, said she needed to use the washroom, then disappeared up the wood stairs.

I stood alone under the bare light bulb. The furnace kicked on, filling the basement with its rumble. I looked up at the other door, the closed one next to the one Barbara had just gone through. That door led to Logan's side of the duplex. I wondered if he was home, and if he could hear the party happening on my side. Someone turned up the music.

Logan wouldn't dare pop over, for fear of being cajoled into dancing.

I heard laughter, the clinking of glasses, and then one woman encouraging the others to take a pinch of the snuff, just for fun.

I got a feeling that, just like the other wakes I'd been to with my father, this one was going to last as long as the food and drinks held out, and many secrets would be spilled.

CHAPTER 16

I'D NEVER BEEN to an all-woman wake before the one I threw for the *Vibrant & Vivacious Voula Varga, Psychic Extraordinaire*.

By ten thirty, everyone but me was drunk. That wasn't the unusual part, though. All dozen of the ladies had brought their yarn and needles, and they were actually knitting. Someone started a drinking game: if you dropped a stitch, you had to take a shot of whiskey. Naturally, this led to more dropped stitches and more drinks.

Nobody seemed to notice that I was neither drinking nor knitting. I had my trusty ball of yarn, and I wound it partly onto one hand loosely, the way I'd seen others do, then wound it back onto the ball. Jeffrey had finally ventured out and sat on the coffee table, smack dab in the middle of the living room, watching all the wiggling strings he wasn't allowed to play with. For him, this knitting wake was either heaven or hell, or maybe both.

I kept my mouth closed and my ears open as people related their personal stories about Voula. Barbara told the same anecdote she'd shared with me in the basement, about Voula locating the money her ex-husband had squirreled away.

"She always saw right through people," said the youngest woman in attendance, a round-cheeked redhead. "She knew my boss didn't hate me, but was only behaving like a total freak because of a lawsuit by a former partner."

While the redhead called her boss colorful names, I realized I knew her from Jeffrey's veterinary clinic. She shared a few details about the lawsuit and I quietly smiled to myself—not because the case itself made me happy, but because this must have been the business Logan was attending to when I first met him, and now I knew things about his life he hadn't told me.

There's definitely satisfaction in knowing something that someone else thinks is a secret. Voula must have been the happiest woman in the world, with all the information she had. Over the evening, I heard story after story about her many insights.

How did Voula get her information, though? Some of the ladies in attendance believed it came from spirits, but I wasn't buying the psychic angle. It sounded more like the type of stuff private investigators dug up.

So, if she was basically just a private investigator, why did she operate as a psychic?

I stole away to the washroom for a few minutes and sent my father a text message with some of the details I'd learned, as well as that question.

He replied to my text with a tiny cartoon of three ants and a picnic basket.

Ants? Picnic basket? I flung my problem-solving skills down this new tangent. The picnic basket was a clue! My brilliant father knew something and was giving me a hint.

A moment later, he sent another message, this one with words: *Oops. Sorry. I meant this one.*

There was a new image, this one a head of lettuce.

I was so confused by this that I forgot what I'd even asked him in the first place. I called and asked him to clarify.

"Why, that's a head of lettuce, and lettuce is another word for money." He chuckled, clearly amused by himself.

"You think she got more money by claiming to be a psychic? Do private investigators not make that much money?"

"Why do you ask?"

Someone tapped on the washroom door and asked if it was occupied.

"Just one minute," I called out as I turned on the sink water. My voice low, I told my father, "I can't really chat now. I'll call you later. How late will you be up?"

"I'll be up until I'm asleep, at quarter after bedtime o'clock, which is two train stops before Snoretown."

I groaned. Of course he wouldn't just give me a time. That would be too easy. If you want information from Finnegan Day, be prepared to ask two or three times, and brace yourself for a text message with a head of lettuce or picnic ants or heaven knows.

The woman on the other side of my bathroom knocked again, with some degree of urgency, so I quickly said goodbye to my father, vacated the washroom, and returned to the party.

STITCHES WERE DROPPING, another bottle of whiskey was open, and still nobody would spill the beans about investing in Voula's friend's movie deal.

Finally, I just asked.

"Hey, did any of you ladies meet Voula's friend, Bernard Goldstein? I hope someone got in touch with him and let him know about her passing."

The twelve ladies exchanged furtive glances, and the ones who could still hold their needles straight kept on knitting while the others kept eating and drinking.

Only Barbara answered me, saying, "Who?" and frowning.

I repeated his name and swept my gaze around the circle, looking for reactions. It could have been my imagination, but I thought I saw lips get thinner, being pressed together. Barbara's sister had her hand over her mouth, but it had been there most of the night, so that wasn't new.

Barbara shrugged. "If someone's a good friend, I would imagine they'd notice she wasn't around. I don't think Voula had much in the way of family, the poor dear. She was a bit of a lost soul."

The redheaded veterinary assistant made a choking sound and began to shake. The woman next to her slapped her on the back while another woman asked if she could breathe. The redhead shook her head and held up her hands to signal she was okay.

"I'm sorry," she said, then began to laugh. "I'm so sorry, and you'll probably all think I'm a terrible person, but I've had four drinks, so whatever. I'm really grateful for the way Voula helped me, but… was it just me, or was she kind of a… *you know*. Kind of *not that nice*?"

The group fell silent.

Someone began to snicker.

Another woman, who'd seemed more interested in her knitting than anything else until that point, spoke up. "She was kind of horrible. I was going to drop out of the knitting club, actually, but I worried she'd put one of her voodoo curses on me."

"Me too," Barbara said in her strident, self-assured voice. "I was afraid to cross her."

With Barbara's admission, the energy of the whole room changed, like we'd all been held inside a bottle of champagne, and the cork popped off with a few magical words. *Voula Varga wasn't that nice.*

Everyone started sharing their true feelings. Voula had been a creepy, scary lady, and a bully, but nobody had dared to think about it too much, let alone talk about it, for fear of getting hit with bad mojo.

We passed the whiskey bottle around the circle, then raised our glasses.

Barbara stood and proclaimed, her voice as clear as a church bell on Christmas morning, "Ding dong, the witch is dead!"

THE LAST GUESTS left at two o'clock in the morning, at which point a confused-looking Jessica roused herself from the guest bedroom, made herself a plate from the leftover food, then quaffed another dose of cold medicine before returning to the guest bed.

As I lay awake in my own bed, mulling over the revelations of the evening, I considered taking a dose of the cold medicine myself, just to shut off my brain. What troubled me most was that I hadn't gotten anywhere with my investigation into Voula's connection to Bernard Goldstein.

The Misty Falls Crafty Knitters had been more than willing to talk about their distaste for the woman whose wake we were at, but nobody would spill the beans about Goldstein or the potential investment.

Something was going on, right under my nose, but I couldn't see it.

I rolled onto my side to check the time on my alarm clock for the millionth time. 3:17 a.m. There was a chance my father was still up—he gets insomnia sometimes, just like me—so I reached for my phone.

My bedroom was dark, and I didn't see His Regal Grayness sitting where I expected to find my phone. Naturally, he assumed that my clumsy gesture, in which I barely grazed the side of his body, was an attempt to grab him for something horrible, like a late-night car ride to the vet, or a bubble-bath party. He let out a mournful meow and made a daring leap for his life, in the direction of my dresser. Unfortunately, he was barely full-grown, and still had the dangerous optimism of a kitten. He overshot his landing by about three toes, and scratched his way down the front of the drawers, taking a few dresser-top items with him.

Once the breaking sounds stopped, I turned on the light to survey the damage. A ceramic good-luck cat I'd bought as a souvenir during my travels in China was in smithereens on the floor, along with the tiny cactus my father had given me as a housewarming present. The cactus would be fine once I swept up the sandy dirt and put it back into the pot, which was made of hammered copper.

I got a dustpan and started cleaning. Jeffrey circled around, looking equal parts curious and guilty.

"Don't feel too bad," I told him. "You're a naughty boy sometimes, but I know this was an accident. I groped you in the dark unexpectedly, and you ran off so fast, you weren't paying attention to where you were going."

I finished sweeping up, patted the dirt back around the thumb-sized miniature cactus, then bent down to kiss Jeffrey goodnight. He shied away and ran out of the bedroom.

I got back into bed and softly called to him, reassuring him that I knew it was just an accident. *Just an accident.* Sleepiness came, and I started to drift.

With my dreams came a nightmare: headlights glaring in my eyes from an oncoming vehicle.

I sat up in bed with a start, my heart pounding and my whole body drenched in sweat.

"The accident," I croaked to myself in the dark.

My subconscious had put it together, thanks to a clue from Jeffrey. He'd knocked my collectibles over because he'd been upset by something; on the day I found Voula's body, I was pushed off the road by a vehicle running wild. What were the chances that same vehicle had continued on a path of chaotic destruction? And what were the chances it was involved in the auto collision that had delayed the police in arriving at the murder scene?

There would be records of everyone in the accident, and eyewitnesses, too. I placed my hand on my chest, over my heart. I'd calmed down from the nightmare, but now my heart was racing because of something new: the identity of Voula's killer was just a phone call or two away.

It was 5:30 a.m.—early. I jumped out of bed and rushed to get dressed.

As luck would have it, Jessica was already up and making coffee, still sick but rested from twelve hours of sleep. I caught her up on my new theory.

She twisted her long red hair into a French braid while we talked.

"Sounds like I missed a wild party," she said.

"But I cracked the case."

"Did you? Your two suspects are Barbara's ex-husband, who was hiding money that Voula found, plus whoever was driving like a maniac on the first of January. Holy snickerdoodles! Stormy, what if it was him behind the wheel? That would pretty much clinch it, right?"

I wiggled in my chair excitedly. "Can you imagine? I'd be two for two on solving murders."

She kept braiding her hair, reaching the base of her neck for the easy part, fingers flying.

"Promise you'll be careful," she said.

"I'm not going to make a citizen's arrest. I'll pass the information on to the police, or… actually, I'll let my father do that."

"You'll let him take all the credit?"

"Um…"

My phone buzzed on the table with an incoming text, right on cue. It was my father, responding to my dozens of early-morning text messages explaining my theory about the vehicle accident and our possible suspects.

He'd replied—not with words, but with the cartoon image of a bear coming out of a cave, and a mug of coffee. I showed Jessica.

"His texting skills are improving," she said. "That actually makes sense."

"It does, right? Actually, it makes so much sense, I wonder if he sent the wrong images by accident."

Jessica tied her hair with an elastic, then snickered into her mug of coffee.

As for her question about letting my father take all the credit for solving the case, I wasn't sure. I'd never seen him as dispirited as the day he'd blown up about his painful hip rehabilitation, and I never wanted to see him looking that sad again.

I'd heard so many jokes about guys retiring and driving their wives nuts, but the jokes weren't so funny now that it was happening to Finnegan Day. What had he been thinking, taking the retirement offer? As soon as I asked myself the question, I already knew the answer. He'd retired so the department would have the budget for two new rookies. Now we had Peggy Wiggles and Kyle Dempsey. He'd done it for the town, without thinking of himself.

I would push all the credit over to him, to help him kick off his private investigation business—the one he still hadn't told me about.

First things first, though. We had to track down everyone involved in the accident, then check their alibis for the morning. The body had still been warm when I found it, so I didn't need a fancy crime scene investigation report to give me a window for time of death.

Who was the killer? I jumped to my feet as I drained the last of my coffee. I couldn't wait another second to find out.

CHAPTER 17

THE SUN WAS still an hour from rising as I drove to my father's in the dark. I saw very few vehicles, as it was still too early for most people to drive to work. The cars I did see were likely heading toward one of the town's factories.

Misty Falls is a former mining town that was just too beautiful to disappear after the mines closed down. We now have a strong tourism economy in the summer, plus some manufacturing year round. Back in the fifties, smart investors bought up land and employed the out-of-work miners as workers at one of three factories: chopsticks, potato chips, and furniture. These days, both the furniture and chopsticks are resold under various private labels. You'll never know if the chopsticks you're using to stab your sweet and sour chicken balls came from Misty Falls, but you can spot our potato chips by their brand name, Aunt Jo's Crispy Spuds.

It's a little-known fact that the potato chips were originally packaged as Uncle Joe's Crispy Spuds. That only lasted a few months, because a local man named Joseph Bacon, of no relationship to the factory owners or the actor Kevin Bacon, felt the artwork of the cartoon Uncle Joe on the packaging infringed on his life rights. The issue never went to court, because the cartoonist admitted to basing the image of the grinning, baldheaded, chip-eating man on Joseph Bacon, who ran the cafeteria counter at the town's only department store. Plus, anyone who had two eyes in their head could see the resemblance.

Rather than simply redrawing the cartoon with some hair, the marketing department at the factory ran some focus research testing—a newfangled practice at the time—and discovered that mothers who made the family's purchasing decisions preferred to buy potato chips from a cartoon *woman*, because they trusted a woman to provide a nourishing, vegetable-based snack for their children.

The marketing department offered every woman in town named Josephine or Joanna a fifty-dollar check in exchange for a personal release statement, just in case. Five hundred dollars later, Uncle Joe became Aunt Jo. It would have only been four hundred and fifty dollars, but an enterprising local couple changed the name of their just-born baby girl from Mary to Jody-Mary.

That's how my aunt Jody-Mary got her name, according to family legend.

These days, a new potato chip brand would probably launch with a fake old-fashioned label worthy of framing, plus a whole backstory about organic, fair-trade farmers who sing their baby potatoes to sleep. Personally, I'm a fan of Aunt Jo, with her curls freshly set from the hairdresser, and her good pearls worn proudly around her neck.

As I pulled up in front of my father's house, the DJ on the radio was talking about the unusual wind direction that was wafting the factory's potato chip smell into town. I rolled down my window to sniff the air, which did smell of deep-fried potatoes. I couldn't tell if the scent was real or my imagination, and puzzled over this, using my fingers to close one nostril and then the other.

My father came out of his house, using his cane to steady himself, and slowly climbed into the passenger side. He huffed and said, "It's an ill wind that blows nobody any good."

"You smell those potato chips too, Dad?"

"Only when I breathe."

I put the car into drive, but didn't step on the gas. "Where are we going, anyway?"

"I reckon the junkyard will be open to those who know which gates don't lock." He pointed in the direction of the town's only auto wrecker. "I checked the newspapers, both yesterday's and today's, but the only mention of the accident was brief and didn't include any names. Apparently there was some big murder in town that took up all the pages."

"You don't say. Any new details?"

He scoffed as he put on his seatbelt. "Only superstitious voodoo nonsense, but I did find one line about the accident, saying both vehicles were write-offs."

I started driving. The sky had turned navy blue, with a fringe of fuchsia between the snow-dusted mountain peaks.

I would have asked why we were driving to the auto wreckers instead of waiting until places were open for phone calls, but I suspected he was testing me. This was part of my interview, before he asked me to be his private investigating partner, assuming he was still moving ahead with that.

The answer came as we approached the chain-link fence surrounding the wrecker yard.

I turned to my father and said, with a sly smile, "You think I'll recognize the vehicle that nearly ran me down."

A grin spread across his face, making him look years younger. He was proud, and so was I.

"It's worth a shot," he said casually.

"A long shot." I'd been so surprised and shaken up by the incident that I hadn't been able to describe anything about the vehicle to the police, but there was a slim chance seeing it again might trigger my memory. Then again, it could be like the potato chip smell, where the mere suggestion played tricks on my head.

We pulled up to the gate for the enclosure. It was locked up tight, and the handwritten sign listed the opening time for that day as "Noon-ish." Beyond the gate was a sight that would have made my car shiver, if she only knew—a post-apocalyptic pile of cars and trucks in various states of destruction. My girl sported bullet holes, and the passenger-side mirror was still in the trunk, but that didn't seem so bad compared to the horror on the other side of the fence.

My father said, "Park here and we'll walk around the side. There's a hole in the fence Gene never fixed after the Cannonball Incident. He doesn't mind us police going in to look around on our own—prefers it over being woken up, actually."

"We're not police, Dad."

He already had his seatbelt off and was grunting his way out of the car. I switched off the engine and ran around to help him out.

"How's the hip today?" I gripped his elbow for steadiness as he held my forearm.

He answered me with a flash of his eyes.

"Did you do your exercises today?"

He nodded. "Don't you worry about your old man. I've signed us up for the Forest Folk Run in August. We'll go as a father-daughter team, with monster costumes and everything."

I laughed, thinking he was joking, but he just gave me a serious look. He wasn't kidding around.

As we walked along the fence, shuffling through the snow, I was quiet. August was still eight months away, and the run was only three miles. I'd never been a fan of jogging, but the Forest Folk Run was just goofy enough that training for it seemed almost fun.

"We're not going as zombies," Dad said.

"Of course not. We'll go as genuine Forest Folk, in Sasquatch fur, with the bones of our cannibalized victims strung on ropes we wear as necklaces."

My father chuckled in a that's-my-girl sort of way, then held open the break in the fence for me to go through first. We walked past snow-capped stacks of rusty, flattened metal. The stacks became more colorful, the paint still intact, as we got to the newer acquisitions.

He knew his way around the junkyard and pointed out the organization system, stopping to wave his cane this way and that, like a pointer. We reached the vehicles that had been involved in the collision, the crash date of January first written on them with a waxy grease pencil.

There were three wrecks from that day, two cars and a van. The van was a Dodge, blue, with a white stripe. The cars were both silver, different makes and models, and thoroughly average. We walked around the three vehicles, observing the damage and discussing how the crash must have happened. The side of one of the cars was shredded, courtesy of the Jaws of Life equipment used to extract the driver.

My father talked through his theory. "The van T-boned this car, which slid across the snowy road and rolled when it hit the ditch. The rolling crimped the doors on the other side and compressed the roof enough so the first responders couldn't extract through the front window." He rubbed his chin, which I noticed had been freshly shaved that morning—a sign he was feeling chipper.

"But the roof is barely dented."

"True enough." He kept rubbing his chin. "But the fire department gets rookies, too, and they like to train them up on the equipment. I've seen it happen a few times, especially when the injuries aren't too bad. It builds up their confidence."

I shivered and rubbed my forearms as I said a silent prayer for those who run into danger to help others.

"Anything look familiar?" he asked.

"The van." An image kept flashing through my head, of the blue and white van racing toward me on the dimly lit road. "I feel like I'm remembering this van coming at me… but how can I remember it now, when I didn't yesterday?"

He snapped his fingers and pointed at me. "Exactly."

"The problem with eyewitnesses," I said with a sigh. From my experience as an armchair detective, watching true crime documentaries on TV and talking about cases with my cop father, I knew too well that memories aren't photographs. They're more like watercolor paintings, and every time you visit a memory, you're going in with a wet brush and more paint, coloring and altering it with your changing perceptions, influencing it with your desires.

I wanted this blue and white van to be the one that ran me off the road, so my mind was fitting it into place, trying to help.

My lack of sleep the night before hit me hard. The sun crouched low on the horizon, bathing us with golden light, but sun alone couldn't energize me. I circled around to the back of the banged-up van and took a seat on the bumper.

"This was a waste of time," I said grumpily.

"Don't say that. Ninety-nine percent of all investigations is about chasing around hunches and eliminating theories." He came to stand across from me, his back to the sun and his shadow stretching tall across the rear doors of the van. "If you were working with Tony on this case, and someone thought they saw this van leaving the scene of the crime, what would you do?"

He looked me in the eyes as he hung his cane over his forearm and rubbed his hands together. He kept rubbing his hands, not to warm them, but as though he had something stuck to his palms.

"Gunshot residue!" I shouted. "The shooter would have that on their hands, transferring it to the steering wheel. If I were Tony, I'd have the whole driver's side of this van tested for gunshot residue, and the other two cars as well, just to be thorough."

"Very good. You call Tony and tell him you saw this van leaving the scene of the crime."

I blinked up at him, unable to read his expression in the shadows. The rising sun created a halo effect with his silver hair.

"That's it?" I asked. "Just call Tony and hand the whole thing over?" I got to my feet and began to survey the van with renewed interest, walking around to peer inside at the steering wheel. There was no way I'd be able to see evidence with my bare eyes, but it helped me to think, all the same.

When a gun is fired, particles from the propellant and primer in the bullet come out of the muzzle and the back of the gun, landing on the shooter's hands and clothing. Gunshot residue, or GSR, isn't a single telltale thing, like the ink packets that modern anti-shoplifting tags contain, but the general term for a combination of elements like antimony, lead, and barium.

Lucky for me, the typical components of gunshot residue were a normal dinnertime conversation topic in the Day residence. I also knew that the metal elements wouldn't degrade, and could be pulled onto the police department's test kit sticky tabs for testing as easily today as two days ago, the date of the shooting. That evidence wouldn't go anywhere, provided nobody got into the vehicle and transferred it onto themselves—which was a shame, because I really wanted to get inside the van and look around.

My father came up behind me and said something about rewarding ourselves with coffee, but his voice barely reached me, because I was deep in thought.

I knew who the owner of the van was. Even though the glove box sat open, the insurance and identification papers removed, the owner's presence was there—there in the sparkling prism hanging from the rear-view mirror, the wood-bead seat covers, and the plastic travel mug sporting the iconic logo of the Fox and Hound. This van belonged to Dharma Lake, the friendly, older waitress from the pub. She'd thrown a drink on Voula, in front of everyone, and now…

Dharma, what have you done?

I pointed out the items to my father and told him who the van belonged to. "Come to think of it," I said, "she mentioned owning a beat-up van the first night I met her. She was teasing me about my car, when she was trying to set me up."

"Set you up for what?" His forehead wrinkled with vertical creases.

"Not for murder, just for a date. Long story. Not relevant."

The air around me felt thick, but I didn't see any fog.

I unzipped the top third of my jacket and rubbed my bare knuckles on my sternum. He kept looking at me, his worry lines deepening.

"I feel funny," I said. "Like I can't get any oxygen, which is weird, because we're outside."

"She was a friend of yours? Dharma Lake? I know who you're talking about. Her uncle is Deiter Koenig, the man who could buy every house in Misty Falls and still have enough money to put the houses on stilts and convert the town to a canal system, like in Venice."

"Canals?"

He pointed his cane at the break in the fence and began walking away, riffing on this new idea of his. "Of course, the canals would need to be wired up, like those heated sidewalks in Sweden, or they'd freeze up in the winter."

I let him have a head start while I pulled my phone from my purse and took photos of the three vehicles. My chest still felt fluttery, but my breathing deepened when I focused on it.

Discovering the identify of the driver had been shocking, but my father's patter about electrified canals did lighten the mood. My whole life, he'd driven me crazy with his wild stories and circuitous answers, but I could see how stressful police work was, and how a playful attitude would help.

I circled the van, taking more photos. The vehicle looked artfully decrepit in my shots.

Dharma's uncle, Deiter Koenig, was the richest man in Misty Falls, but he certainly didn't spoil his niece, by the look of it. The van's paint job looked like an emergency fix, done with a brush and a can of Tremclad, to stop the rust from spreading like barnacles on an old boat. Three of the tires were bald, and the one with treads was skinny—obviously the spare tire, a temporary measure for a repair job that would never be done now that the vehicle was a write-off.

I put my phone away and ran to catch up with my father.

"I haven't called Tony yet," I said as I fell into step next to him. "We could pick up some donuts and drop by the station in person."

My father shot me a quick look, then grinned down at the snow in front of us. He didn't elaborate on whatever it was he found amusing. It might have simply been the donuts. We walked to the fence in silence and got back into the car.

"Well?" I asked. "What do we do next?"

"Depends on what you want out of life. Do you want a chunk of Koenig's fortune? If so, we could drive over there and tell him what we found out about his niece. He's not the type to spoil his family with lavish gifts, but he's a proud man. He'd pay up to keep the family name clear of things like murder convictions."

I stared at my father in disbelief. Was this another of his tall tales, or had retirement changed the former cop into a potential blackmailer?

I answered slowly and deliberately, "We split the million dollars fifty-fifty."

"Sixty-forty," he countered.

"Let's just up the ask to two million. More to go around."

"Good thinking. We start at two, but our bottom is one-point-five. Then we have room to come down on negotiations."

I put the car in reverse and backed down the narrow entry road toward the main road.

"Or... we could do the right thing and let Tony know about what we've found," I said.

My father tilted his head from side to side, pretending to grapple with a difficult decision.

"Not as exciting, and the end result is sending a sweet old lady to jail."

The tightness returned to my chest. He was joking around, but he made a great point about the outcome being unpleasant. Dharma Lake had seemed like a kind woman, whereas the stories I'd heard about Voula Varga made her seem like not such a kind woman. The B-word had been used a few times at the wake, and I don't mean *businesswoman*.

My father seemed to know exactly how I was feeling, because instead of joking around, he reached over and squeezed my shoulder.

"The right thing is always the right thing. That's the beauty of it, Stormy."

CHAPTER 18

WE PICKED UP a box of donuts and drove to the police station. The winter sun hung low on the horizon, and the day was as bright as it was going to get. I couldn't shake the feeling that sending the police after sweet Dharma was the wrong thing to do.

"Dad, would you mind if I wait in the car? Your old friends will probably be more comfortable if your daughter isn't hanging around."

"But everyone loves you."

"Says the World's Best Dad."

"What's wrong? You used to love visiting the station with me."

"Sure, but the last time I was here, I was in a housecoat, with my cat in tow. Let's allow the humiliation to age a little." Also, I didn't want to run into Tony, who I was mad at, or Kyle, who'd probably hit on me in front of my father.

"I won't be long." He opened the donut box and shook it until I took one for myself—lemon blueberry. He got out of the car, moving more easily this time, and went in on his own.

I kept the engine running and the heater on while I used my phone to check my various messages.

To my surprise, there was a message from my ex-fiancé. To my total lack of surprise, it was a rude message.

Christopher: *What's this about you wandering into a crime scene? Isn't this the second one? What the sam-heck is going on with you that this keeps happening?*

I rolled my eyes and shook my head. This was just like Christopher to break our months of silence this way, not by sending me something nice like a Happy New Year message, but by implying that everything bad that happened in my life was always my fault. And he'd said *sam-heck* instead of *hell*. Somehow that made it worse.

It took me twenty minutes to compose a long message explaining exactly where he could go, what he could do to himself, and the clothes he could wear while he did it. I didn't send the message, though. Out of the corner of my eye, I saw my father exiting the police station, and that gave me an idea.

I deleted the wordy message, then randomly selected a string of picture icons, including plants, animals, food. I hit send on the cryptic message and chuckled to myself.

Good luck figuring that one out, Christopher.

Finnegan Day got into the passenger seat. "Ooh, nice and warm. I do like this business of having a personal driver."

"That's all I am to you?"

"We'll discuss your official title during the annual review."

"Thanks. How'd it go in there? And don't tell me what everyone thought about the donuts. Cut to the chase for once."

"Those young guys." He shook his head. "They didn't even pretend they had leads on the case. I had to get out of there before they all kissed me in gratitude."

"Are you serious? They're going to look at Dharma's van?"

"Some of the crime scene guys are driving out already. Poor Gene will have to get out of bed before noon and let them in."

"Will they know right away about the residue?"

"With one of the test kits, yes. There are some other tests that get sent out to the lab, but a positive with the on-site kit will be enough to bring Dharma in for questioning. Tony stopped by the Fox and Hound yesterday and interviewed her about throwing the drink. He said she seemed nervous, in retrospect. Hindsight is twenty-twenty, as they say."

"It was definitely her van at the wreckers?"

He grimaced. "Yes, unfortunately." He rubbed his hands together. "Do you have any plans for the rest of the day? Can we run some errands?"

I started backing out of the parking spot. "Your driver is booked for the whole day. Your wish is my command."

He listed off some stores that wouldn't even be open yet, then said the name of a restaurant where we could get breakfast. My stomach growled, the sugary donut long gone.

I drove toward the restaurant, half listening as he talked about how much bacon he was going to order.

My heart felt heavy in my chest. As proud as I was of our work, I hoped the test on the van's steering wheel would come up negative.

"When will you find out the test results?" I asked. "Do we have to wait for tomorrow's newspaper and town gossip, or do you have an old buddy there who'll leak it to you?"

"Dimples—I mean Kyle—is going to keep in touch."

I shot my father a look. "You're going to get him in trouble."

"Oh, and you aren't going to get him in trouble? I heard you were"—he made air quotes with his fingers—"*helping* Kyle search the crime scene."

"What are you implying? What are people at the station saying?" I held my hand up between us. "Never mind. I don't want to know. Whatever other people choose to think about me is their business, not mine."

MY FATHER AND I had a quiet breakfast, then ran some errands that included getting a new area rug to put in the living room. Home decor shopping with my father was a learning experience. I had no idea my father knew the difference between teal and aquamarine, let alone that he had strong opinions about which color looked more "modern."

His new teal rug was too long to fit in my car without bending the roll, which the salesman advised against, so we would have to strap it to the roof of my car. The store offered us free delivery, but Finnegan Day, and his Hobo Pride in doing things himself on the cheap, wouldn't accept free delivery.

"Hobo Pride is not about being cheap," he said as he tossed me the coil of yellow rope through the interior of the car. "Being self-sufficient is an admirable trait. That's why people watch those TV shows about the zombies. The shows are mostly trash, blah-blah relationship talking, but sometimes they'll show something useful, like how to make a stew using just a squirrel and whatever you have on hand, in under thirty minutes." He continued looping the rope through the windows, front and back. "Or maybe I'm thinking of the cooking channel. Hmm. Have you ever had squab?"

"Squab? That sounds like something Christopher would order at one of his beloved fancy restaurants."

"Well, don't eat it," my father said. "Unless you like pigeon." He tied a knot in the rope, then pointed across the street behind me. "I need a new computer. A laptop."

"Why?" I turned to follow his gaze to Misty Microchips across the street. Was he serious? His old computer looked and sounded like it might catch on fire during startup, but his Hobo Pride meant he'd wait for the implosion before upgrading.

Could the private investigator application—the one he still hadn't mentioned—have something to do with this sudden interest in a laptop?

"Do you really want a new computer?" I asked. "Why now?"

"They're having a sale."

He started toward the computer store, looking both ways before crossing at the middle of the street. I ran after him, surprised yet again. First the interest in teal rugs and laptops, and now Finnegan Day was jaywalking.

Wonders never cease!

THE COMPUTER STORE was clean and bright. Some teenagers came in right after me and headed straight to the game section.

I hadn't seen the owners, Marvin and Marcy, since New Year's Eve.

Marcy gave us a friendly greeting, making me feel guilty about not returning the phone call from her—the one that I'd forgotten about until that very moment.

"So nice to see you," Marcy said warmly. Her gold-brown eyes had a bright gleam under the store's lights, and her sandy brown hair looked freshly styled, with copper highlights.

"You look healthy," I said. "Getting lots of fresh air walking Stanley?"

She laughed and started telling me how she felt like a whole new person, thanks to some new resolutions.

Out of the corner of my eye, I watched my father head straight for the most expensive laptops and dive right in without waiting for help. Within seconds, Marvin was at my father's side, patiently smiling and ready to ring up a laptop or two.

I wondered if selling one computer a day made their sales quota, or if they had to sell several just to pay the rent. I knew how razor-thin the margins on computers were. My gift store probably made as much profit on a set of napkin rings as the computer store did on a laptop sale. The real money was in the computer accessories—the little charging cords, foam cases, and sticker doodads that have a triple markup.

Over by the laptops, my father was gesturing wildly. Was he describing the recent explosion and demise of his old computer? If the *tough old bird*— as he called her—had expired, that would explain his need for a new one.

The teens in the games section were making just enough noise that I couldn't hear what my father was saying, but I did hear Marvin exclaim, "Really? That's cool! So cool!"

Not cool, I thought. If he was telling Marvin about his private investigator business before he told me, he could ride home strapped to the roof of the car, next to his new teal rug.

Marcy giggled. "He's been so wonderful lately. So attentive and affectionate."

"Who?" I asked, confused. I hadn't been paying much attention, but she was gazing with adoration at her husband, who'd I'd only witnessed being attentive to his wine, and affectionate toward, well, his wine. Those two secretly hated each other. She had to be talking about their dog.

She came out from behind the glass display counter and grabbed my forearm like we were high school girls talking in the hall about our crushes. "He wrote me a poem and read it to me."

"That's… wow. A poem." So, we were talking about Marvin after all, and not the couple's cute but needy Labradoodle.

The door jingled as the teens who'd been looking at the games walked out, chattering about who would spring for a round of frozen slushy drinks.

Now it was just the four of us in the computer store, and judging by the way Marvin was hustling past me toward the stock room, my father's business was nearly finished. It irked me that he'd selected an expensive laptop in less time than he'd taken that morning to decide on his pancake topping.

Marcy was still chattering about romance and date nights. I smiled as I nodded along. There was a pause, and she asked if I was feeling okay.

"Sorry, I'm a bit spaced out," I said. "I've got a lot on my mind."

"Has her ghost done anything for you?"

Now Marcy had my attention. "Ghost? What?"

She still had her hand on my forearm, and squeezed it now. "Everyone's talking about it.

Voula's ghost. She's been granting people's wishes from beyond the other side." Marcy grinned. "You should try making a wish and see what happens. Send her an email, and she might email back."

"Someone's been emailing people from Voula Varga's account?" I wondered if the police knew about this, and if it would stop once they had the matchmaking waitress in custody.

"Not just someone. It's her." She let go of my arm and stepped away to help Marvin ring up my father's new purchase.

As I watched her compliment my father on his excellent taste in laptops, then try to sell him the extended warranty—*good luck with that, Marcy*—I wondered if the woman was on some new medication with interesting side effects. Perhaps she was taking the dog's antidepressant pills.

Marvin switched places with Marcy behind the counter and came over to talk to me. "I hear you're having a fun shopping day with your father. Tell me the truth. Is he driving you crazy, or is this a good bonding experience?"

"Apparently, he likes teal."

"That explains why he wanted the laptop with the teal case."

I looked over at Marcy, who was pitching the extended warranty hard. Neither of them were paying any attention to us.

"What did he say to you?" I asked as I turned back toward Marvin. "Did he tell you why he wanted the laptop?"

Marvin waggled his eyebrows. "Wouldn't you like to know?" For a man in his forties, Marvin was acting strangely juvenile, almost stranger than his wife with her ghost stories. I switched to a new theory about the dog medication: Marcy was grinding up so-called "happy-dog pills" and hiding them in Marvin's food.

"How about you?" Marvin asked. "Are you in need of any upgrades?" He waggled his eyebrows again, and this time he let his brown eyes take a detour down the front of my body. Huskily, he said, "I do house calls, so if you'd like me to stop by your place sometime and do a private assessment of *your needs*, just call me and we'll make that happen."

"Uh, thanks." *And please stop being gross. Please stop right now, Marvin.*

"We can make lots of things happen," he said.

"No, thank you."

I moved away from Marvin, toward the ring of safety within my father's hearing range. If I'd been ten years younger, I might have continued naively talking to Marvin, excusing his behavior as just harmless joking. But I was thirty-three, and I'd had enough life experience to know that "I was just joking" is what a man says only after you've called him on his lascivious behavior. If Marcy wasn't such a nice woman, I might have done something dramatic, right then and there.

My father gathered up his new laptop and we walked out of the store. I shook my arms, trying to rid myself of the slime residue from Marvin.

We paused on the sidewalk while my father pulled out his phone to check for messages or missed calls.

"Bingo," he said, then handed me his phone.

There was a text message from Kyle Dempsey, whose contact info my father had programmed in as *Kyle Dimples-Dempsey*.

Kyle Dimples-Dempsey: *Good news. Nitrocellulose on the steering wheel of the van. Bad news. Suspect has fled town. Her husband seems as shocked as anyone. He called in a Missing Persons report this morning. My gut says he's telling the truth. He doesn't know where she is or what she's done.*

"That was fast," I said. "Do you think Dharma's rich uncle is helping her disappear?"

"We could pay him a visit and ask."

I laughed, because I thought he was joking, but his brown eyes didn't waver.

"How far are you going to take this armchair sleuthing thing?" I asked. "Nobody's paying you to look into this case, are they? Did Kyle ask you to help make him look good?"

"I should be offended. You're implying that Finnegan Day can be bribed into doing someone else's job for nothing more than a case of fancy-label beer." He nodded for me to follow him across the street, back to the car.

He opened the passenger side and slid in, but I didn't, because I couldn't even get my door open. The rope holding his new rug in place was threaded through three windows, forming a triangle shape.

As I stood there, wondering if he'd done this on purpose as some sort of life lesson, he called out, "For heaven's sakes, just jump in the window," like I was being ridiculous for wanting to go in through the door like a normal person.

Muttering a few choice words under my breath, I started climbing in, right leg first. I was halfway in when I heard a familiar voice laughing. I looked over to the sidewalk and saw Logan grinning at me.

"Stormy Day doesn't believe in doors," he said.

"Logan Sanderson states the obvious when he could be helping."

He jogged off the sidewalk and around the car to assist me. Before I could shoo him away, he had my arm around his shoulders and his hip bracing mine. I'd only meant to mock him, not get him under my arm, with his cheek practically touching mine and the warm, spicy scent of his skin tickling my nostrils.

He grabbed my leg behind the knee with one strong hand, and I was in his arms. It was not an unpleasant sensation at all. Too quickly, he aimed my left foot through the window and transferred me smoothly into my seat.

"Thanks," I said.

Logan leaned down to the window and reached in with his right hand. "Logan Sanderson," he said as he shook my father's hand.

I said, "Logan, meet my father, Finnegan Day. That's his new rug tied to my roof. He likes teal, apparently. He got a new laptop today, too, with a teal case. He just walked into the computer store and picked one out in less time than it took him to choose a pancake topping at breakfast."

Logan raised his eyebrows, his sky-blue eyes twinkling with amusement at my babbling. "Sounds like you two are having a nice father-daughter day."

"You're the lawyer and the tenant," my father said. "Good to finally meet you. Keep paying your rent on time and do as my daughter says, and our meetings can keep on being this pleasant."

"Yes, sir," Logan replied.

My cheeks flushed hot with embarrassment, and I felt about thirteen again, with my father trying to put the guys in my life off balance.

Logan wasn't wearing one of his lawyer suits that day, despite it being a weekday. He wore threadbare jeans and a chunky-knit sweater that looked like a hand-me-down—comfortable and clean, but not something you'd wear to impress a potential girlfriend's father. My cheeks burned even more as I realized that I wanted my father to be impressed by Logan.

"You're dressed casually," I said. "Day off from your law firm today?"

He'd glanced around.

"Working from home," he said quietly. "Just popped out to grab some lunch."

"I'll let you get back to it. Thanks for the help getting in the car."

He patted the roof, said goodbye to my father, then turned and left us.

I started the car and said, "Where to next? A lamp to go with your rug? A new desk for your laptop?"

"Next stop is the Koenig Mansion, of course."

CHAPTER 19

As we drove to the Koenig Mansion, my father talked to himself while he tapped out a response to Kyle. He was using words, not the cryptic symbols he preferred sending me. He was neither speedy nor accurate, but he could send words when sufficiently motivated.

After the exchange of a few messages, he said, "Dimples is hot on the chase of Dharma Lake. He's checking the local car rentals, the bus depot, travel agents, and the motels. He's a smart kid. Do you know how I know that?"

"Is it because he's come to you as a mentor?"

"Yes, and he called the hair salons. He found out that we're not looking for a woman with shoulder-length silver-white hair anymore. She's a brunette. Her hair's auburn now, and chin-length."

"Ouch." I sucked in air between my teeth. "It's hard to look innocent when you dye your hair and disappear. I didn't want to believe that sweet woman could be a killer, but actions speak volumes."

"That's right. Believe the actions, not the words."

We'd passed out of town limits and I slowed the car as I scanned for the turnoff to the Koenig Estate.

"Speaking of actions," I said, "Dharma tried to set me up with a guy the first time I met her. She and I weren't any more than acquaintances, but she wanted to help me, for free."

"Hmm."

"What does that sort of action tell you about her?"

"That she's nuts," he said.

I turned onto the access road for the Koenig Mansion. As we pulled up to the wrought iron gates, they opened for us, so I didn't even need to bring the car to a halt.

In a dramatically ominous tone, I announced, "They know we're coming."

"You think?"

He was testing me again, so I looked around as we passed through the open gates. I couldn't see any cameras or intercoms, so either they were tiny and hidden, or the gates were on a motion sensor.

"The gates must open automatically," I said. "They probably lock down at night, but auto-open during the day for visitors and deliveries."

"Sounds about right."

I sped up, as the mansion was still far ahead, up a hill. My heart rate also sped up, in anticipation of seeing the gorgeous home.

The Koenig Mansion was a miniature castle, with its Romanesque arches, recessed entryways, and cylindrical towers with conical caps.

I'd been to the mansion before, on school field trips. The owner permitted tours once a year, during the town's Cherry Blossom Festival. Ironically, there were no cherry trees on the property, and thus no blossoms, but the mansion was filled with cherry wood, much of it intricately carved.

When the building came into view, I said, "Amazing. It's just as big as I remember. It seems like so many other things shrink as I get older, but not this."

"Good job keeping your eyes open. Plenty of things are right in front of us, hiding in plain sight, because most people are so busy with their thoughts or their phones, they don't take the time to look."

He shifted in his seat and readied his cane, looking like he was ready to jump out of the car before I'd even pulled up to the mansion.

His cane was not the basic model you'd pick up at the drugstore or even a medical supply store. The handle was metal, maybe stainless steel, with intricate carvings. Around the perimeter was a Celtic design of interwoven knots, framing a nasty-looking creature that was either a bat or a flying squirrel.

A conversation we'd had a month earlier, when he'd been at the hospital following his hip surgery, came back to me. I kept my suspicions to myself as I followed the posted signs directing us to the Visitor Parking.

No other vehicles had been parked in that section, but I could see cars in another area, probably staff parking by the look of the modest economy models.

We still had the rug tied to the roof, so I couldn't open my door and get out the regular way. I started climbing out of my window, figuring it might be easier to get out that way than to climb in. And it was easier, until the toe of my boot caught on the rope, and I flailed off balance and landed on my butt. Hard. The packed snow was better than concrete, but not by much.

I stared up at the winter sky, the frozen ground cool under my back.

My father's face appeared above me.

Grinning, he asked, "Did it hurt when you fell from heaven?"

"Very funny." I groaned my way to my feet. "Hey, can I see your cane for a sec?"

He handed the fancy cane to me without question, then turned to admire the mansion. I examined the handle, then pushed down on the bat creature with my thumb. As I'd suspected, the center was a button. It depressed, but nothing else happened.

"Give it a twist," my father said. He was still facing away from me, admiring the peaked towers of the mansion. "That's the hiking model, for rugged use."

I tried twisting it, but nothing happened. Then I pushed the button while giving the handle a twist. The engraved steel handle popped up, revealing a few inches of what was unmistakably, undeniably, and unsurprisingly a sword.

"This is why you haven't complained about the cane," I said. "You love the excuse to carry a concealed weapon around. Is this even legal?"

"Admit that you wish you had one."

"It is pretty cool."

I glanced around to make sure nobody else was in the parking area. We seemed to be alone, but anyone could have been watching from one of the mansion's many windows. Most of them dark, the rooms unlit, but that just made the enormous house better for hiding in. I drew the sword all the way out of the cane anyway, then gave the air a few swishes.

My father had turned around and was smiling, his dark brown eyes crinkling with pride as he watched me. He nodded approvingly as I changed my grip on the handle.

"Take that, bad guy," I said. "Poke, poke."

"Interesting sound effects."

"Stab, stab," I said as I stabbed and slashed the air, then, "Schawoom, schawoom."

"It's not a lightsaber," he said.

I squeezed both of my small hands onto the handle and struck an exaggerated warrior pose. "Do I look like Conan the Barbarian?"

"Always, but even more so with the sword."

"Cool." I sheathed the blade back into the cane, locked the pieces in place, and handed it back to him.

We started toward the visitor's entrance. I caught a flash of movement in a window on the third floor. For an instant, I saw a face, framed by dark hair, and then it was gone. It had happened so quickly, I couldn't even say for sure it was a woman, but I had a feeling we'd found our fugitive.

My father asked me, softly, "Did you see her, too? Up there on the third floor?"

"Yes, but only a glimpse."

"Same here," he said, sounding excited.

"What next? We can't go in there and start accusing her of murdering people, or we'll be the next victims. Your cane sword is very cool in a James Bond way, but it's no match for a gun, assuming she has more than one gun, and why wouldn't she? All the better for shooting people who come around asking nosy questions for no good reason."

"Follow my lead," he said. We were nearly at the front door.

I glanced over my shoulder at the staff vehicles and tried to find their presence reassuring. Voula Varga had been shot inside a small house, with no neighbors for miles, and no army of on-site staff. Here at the mansion, there were plenty of witnesses, which meant we'd be safe.

At least, that's what I told myself as my father rang the doorbell.

CHAPTER 20

THE PERSON WHO opened the door had dark hair, and something silver in her hand.

"Freeze!" I yelled.

She froze.

We had ourselves a dark-haired woman, all right, but either Dharma had gotten a radical emergency facelift, or this wasn't her. And I didn't think a facelift could take off thirty years.

It made more sense that the brunette before us was a maid, given that she wore an honest-to-goodness maid uniform, with the white apron and everything. The gleaming item in her hand was the silver handle of a fancy feather duster.

"Freeze?" she asked.

"Freez...ing out here," I said. "Brr. Cold and snowy. Freeze is what we'll do if we stay out here too long. Isn't that right, Dad?"

My father reached over and ruffled my hair in a playful way. "Such a goofball, this one," he said. "How are you, Erica? I'm sorry to bother you at work."

She answered with a lightly accented, melodic voice, "I'm okay, Mr. Day, but now you have me worried. Is there something wrong? Is it my son? I'm not supposed to have my phone on while I'm working, so if the school called, I never know until my break. Stupid rules. Mr. Koenig is not here right now, but the head of housekeeping has eyes in the back of her head."

"Sorry to alarm you," my father said. "We're here to see you, Erica, but it has nothing to do with your son."

"You are not in your uniform." She waved for us to enter. "Come in, come in. No need to freeze."

"I'm not here on official police business," he said. He didn't mention that his lack of uniform was due to him having zero official police business these days. Apparently, Erica knew him, but not well enough to know he'd retired.

Inside, we brushed the snow off our boots on the designated area in the foyer, then followed the maid through the cherry-wood-lined hall, past the regal marble table lined up under a chandelier that was bigger than my car, and on to a sitting room. Following his lead, as he'd advised, I took a seat on a sofa with tufted burgundy upholstery.

The sitting room was not too grand to be cozy. The wood shelves along the perimeter contained books behind glass doors, and a good number of decorative objects, eclectic and probably valuable. Under a pinpoint of brightness supplied by recessed lighting sat what appeared to be a Fabergé egg.

Erica left us there, rushing off to fetch some refreshments.

I leaned over and said to my father, "I forgot how you know half the town. You must have met this maid, Erica, through one of your other cases."

"It was a domestic issue, resolved now."

This sitting room wasn't on the public tour, and for good reason. All the precious objects had to be worth a king's ransom.

My father kept his focus on the room's door, watchful for our suspect.

"Dharma could be anywhere in this huge mansion," I said.

"But that could have been Erica we saw in the third floor window."

"Or maybe another maid. Running down two sets of stairs to answer the door would have had her breathing heavily by the time she reached us, especially in a tall house like this. The ceiling height in here must be twelve feet. Must be nice to be rich."

My father chuckled. "I wouldn't wish this much wealth on my worst enemy."

"Speaking of rich, she said Mr. Koenig isn't here right now, but I'm guessing your plan all along was to talk to the staff, not the uncle?"

"The way you say the word *plan* implies I have one."

"You don't?"

"I have a *process*," he said cryptically. "Never have a *plan*. Plans go wrong."

I nodded, getting the feeling I should be taking notes. *A process is better than a plan, because plans go wrong.*

Erica returned with a tray of hot drinks. "Cocoa for your daughter, Mr. Day, because she was freezing."

I took the cup she offered. It was tiny, like from a child's play set. I chalked it up to a weird rich person thing, but when I took a sip of the cocoa, I understood why the serving size was so petite. It was thick, liquid chocolate, rich and creamy, sweet but not too sweet.

Erica asked if the cocoa was warming me up, and I nodded that it was, resisting the urge to jump up and hug her for the incredible treat.

My father reached to his back pocket and withdrew a slim notebook with a pen tucked into its elastic closure. It wasn't one of those fancy leather Moleskine books, but a plain notebook with a thick blue elastic, like the kind you get around broccoli stalks from the grocery store.

"Erica, I'm working on a cold case from a few years back. I know this is a long shot, because you were just a girl at the time, but I wonder if I might pick your brain anyway."

"Oh, Mr. Day, anything for you. What would you like to know?"

"Is it all right for you to talk to me now? Will someone else cover for you if the family needs something?"

"It's okay." She waved her hand in a floppy, relaxed gesture. "Nobody from the family has been here for days."

My father licked his thumb and flipped through the pages of his notepad, appearing to be looking at his notes on the cold case.

"No houseguests?" he asked. "I counted eight cars in the staff parking, out of twelve available spots."

"You're so cute," she said with a laugh. "Always counting things. We have everyone here today for taking down the Christmas decorations. Plus Mr. Koenig returns from Denmark next week, and the interior decorator is here because he wants his room painted the same color as the hotel he's in now. The decorator is so mad, too. She's going crazy. She says the light from the sun here is not like the light in Denmark and the same color is not going to look the same, but she will do it. You can't argue with rich people, you know? That's why they pay you better. So you don't say when they're being—"

She was interrupted by the appearance in the doorway of another dark-haired woman who could have been Erica's older sister. Her eyes were wide and her cheeks looked ashen. She waved for Erica to come talk to her in the hallway.

Erica excused herself, and my father and I waited all of two seconds to get up and tiptoe stealthily to the doorway to listen.

"The police called again," the second woman said. "They asked about Dharma, and they also asked about Mr. Koenig's gun collection."

"So? Why are you bothering me? She hasn't been here since dinner on Christmas Day. Just tell them the truth and they'll leave us alone."

"But the gun collection. Oh, Erica, I'm in so much trouble. I forgot to lock the room on Christmas Day. He wanted to show everyone his new rifles, but then I didn't lock it after he was done. I'm such an idiot. I'm going to get fired, and I'll have to go back to my old job, getting steam burns from the linen press." She made a sharp, gasping sound, then started sobbing.

"There, there." Clothes rustled, and I heard the sound of a back being patted. "I will make you some cocoa when I'm done in here. There's no harm in leaving a room unlocked, as long as…"

The two were quiet for a moment, then lowered their voices to a level where I couldn't make out their words. Shuffling footsteps echoed in the hall as they walked away. I turned to my father with raised eyebrows. He had one hand on his cane and used the other to mime a gun.

The women were well out of range, so we returned to our seats, ready to pretend we'd heard nothing.

My father said to me softly, "Now we know where the murder weapon came from. Dharma slipped into the room where her uncle keeps his collection, and helped herself to a gun. The photo you took wasn't very clear, but I thought the weapon looked antique."

"Antique? That's crazy. Even if it had been kept in a humidity-controlled case and been cleaned, it's an odd choice. Not to mention the fact it would be easily traced back to her if she just left it at the crime scene."

We both sat there in silence for a few minutes, pondering this.

"We're missing something," he said.

"Let's dig deep, then."

Erica returned, apologizing for the interruption.

"I understand someone has stolen a gun from the premises," I said.

Erica's eyes widened, and her hand flew to her mouth. My father looked nearly as surprised by my direct question, but recovered quickly.

"We heard you speaking in the hall," he said. "But to be fair, we have very good hearing. It runs in the Day family."

"We don't want to get in trouble," Erica said.

"I'm sure it's nothing, but since we're here anyway, perhaps I'll just mosey on over and take a look at the gun room, while you prepare a list of everyone who was here for Christmas dinner."

"Okay," Erica said.

Okay? I gave my father a look that said, for lack of a better description, EEEEEE!

Erica led us out of the sitting room.

My father gave me a look that also said EEEEEE!

Without looking back at us making faces, Erica said, "We just counted, and one of Mr. Koenig's handguns is missing. What's going on, Mr. Day? Is it the gypsy? The one who got killed?" She turned left, leading us down another cherry-wood-paneled hall.

"Ms. Varga's murder is currently an ongoing investigation," he said, neither lying nor being entirely truthful about the legitimacy of our involvement.

"Never cross a gypsy," she said as she led us to a set of stairs.

"Stairs," my father said through gritted teeth. He took a breath. "Actually, this is perfect. I skipped some of my exercises this morning, so now I can catch up."

"We'll take it slow," I said, but he was already five steps ahead of me, admiring the view of Erica's hips.

While we climbed the stairs, Erica kept talking about Voula Varga. "They say her ghost is everywhere. I have all the brooms upside-down by the door at my house. I do not want a visit by her."

"You never struck me as the superstitious type," my father said.

She looked over her shoulder, giving my father a smile that bordered on flirtatious, despite the fact he was twice her age. I looked away, admiring the stairwell's artwork, framed prints of modern art. Were they prints or originals? I wouldn't know, because my degree wasn't in the arts. It wasn't in criminology, either, so I was in way over my head.

THE ROOM WHERE Deiter Koenig kept his weapon collection had not been a part of the annual spring tours of the mansion, and that was a shame, as it would have been far more exciting than the mansion's organic vegetable garden.

And what a weapon room it was. Even my jaw dropped, and I've been to galleries and exclusive private collections around the world.

The room was twenty feet by twenty, with display cases along the walls, thick gold draperies on the windows, and a ten-by-ten display case in the center of the room. Inside the glass case, arranged on staggered plinths of varying heights, were knives, axes, arrowheads, and other ancient tools. Across the low case, on the far wall, were two stunning broadswords.

My father turned left and went to the wall case of pistols, discussing with Erica who would have had access to the room on Christmas Day. As the two talked, I turned right and walked over to the swords. The one on the left was simple in design, and the one on the right looked similar, but fancier, like the movie prop version of the same sword.

The neatly typed note card underneath the swords confirmed exactly what I'd guessed: on the left was the real thing, and the one on the right was a prettier fake that had been used in a movie.

My father continued his casual-sounding questions with Erica, homing in on the information he wanted, while I wandered around the room, admiring the weaponry.

If society were to suddenly collapse under a zombie apocalypse, I would head straight to the Koenig Mansion and its armory. The brain-craving living dead wouldn't stand a chance against this arsenal. And in this apocalyptic scenario, my father's recipe for thirty-minute squirrel stew might come in handy, too.

I wandered over to the arrowheads, turning my head so I could better hear my father's conversation with Erica.

"Most of the guests were from out of town," she said. "Everyone left again right after Christmas, and we didn't do a New Year's celebration here at the house because Mr. Koenig had already left for Denmark."

My father chuckled. "I like how you call this place a *house*."

She stepped in closer to him. "Can I confess something to you?"

My ears practically tingled with interest as I waited to hear Erica's confession.

"We did have a party, but just the staff. All of us were here, except for the two people who don't drink, because they took everyone's kids." She held up both hands in an expression of awe. "We had a wild, wild, wild party in the ballroom. Then everyone slept over and we didn't wake up until past noon the next day."

My father gave me a look, and I knew exactly what he was thinking. The mansion's staff all had solid alibis for the time of the murder. That ruled them out and left us with only Dharma. Things were not looking good for the woman, assuming the police could find her.

My father promised Erica he wouldn't tell anyone about the staff party, then pulled open the glass doors to a display case of pistols. "No locks on these doors. I doubt the perpetrator left any prints." He sniffed the door. "At least none that haven't been cleaned away by Mr. Koenig's hardworking and hard-partying staff."

"What can you tell me about the murder? I know you police aren't supposed to tell people things, but should I be scared? A woman who lived alone was killed. It's just me and my son at my house. I lock the doors and windows, but is that enough?"

"Keep your eyes open," he said. "Plus you can always call me." His voice had taken on a throaty quality.

As my father turned on the charm, I wished I could be anywhere else at that moment. Anywhere. Even trapped in a broken-down car while a horde of brain-craving zombies were closing in, admiring how my short hair revealed the tantalizing shape of my cranium.

"Really? I can call you?" Erica grinned so wide I could see her pearly molars.

I coughed abruptly and shot my father a look.

Erica stepped back and said, "Excuse me. I need paper to write down the names of the people who were here, like you asked." She wrung her hands for a moment, casting her gaze nervously around the room, then turned and left in a swirl of black and white.

"Dad, I don't think there are any clues on the backs of Erica's legs."

"No?"

"Hey, you can charm all the single yummy mommies you want on your own time, and not when we're at a crime scene, operating under the false premise of you still being employed by the Misty Falls Police Department."

"There's nothing wrong with multitasking."

"Speaking of which, you didn't ask her much about your cold case."

"It's not going to get any colder." He went to the door and popped his head out to make sure the hallway was clear. "She doesn't know her employer's niece is a suspect. I don't think Dharma is hiding here, or the maid would have been more nervous. Most people—the non-sociopath ones, anyway—find it incredibly difficult to lie, especially if you're nice to them."

"Good to know." I looked around at the many weapons. "Are we done? This room's amazing, but it's starting to give me the creeps."

Erica reappeared with pen and paper in hand. "Your friends just showed up," she said.

We went to the window, which faced the front entrance, and looked down. Tony and Kyle were walking toward the door from their police vehicle. They'd parked right in front, not in the visitor's parking, where they wouldn't have missed seeing my car.

My father turned to Erica. "Quick. Is there a sneaky back way out of here?"

CHAPTER 21

THERE WASN'T JUST one sneaky back way out of the Koenig Mansion, but a dozen. My father and I left through a delivery entrance, easily avoiding the official police.

Erica hadn't enough time to write out the list of dinner guests, but there seemed to be no point anyway, since the staff and out-of-towners were all accounted for on the morning of the murder. My father asked Erica to email him the list anyway.

I didn't breathe normally until we were driving away from the mansion.

"That was a bit close for comfort," I said. "You're sure Erica won't tell Tony we were there?"

"She said she wouldn't."

"Erica seemed nice. Is she about my age, or is she younger?"

He declined to answer that question.

We approached the gates, which opened automatically, as before.

"Talk us through the case," he said. "What do we know about Dharma Lake?"

"For starters, she believes in karma, which means doing good things for others, so it comes back to you. She probably has strong ideas about right and wrong. From what I heard at the pub, she thought Voula Varga's black magic was wrong. She wanted her to stop doing whatever she was doing."

"There's the motivation," he commented. "We need means, motivation, and opportunity."

"As for *means*, there's the gun missing from the armory back there. Now, whether it was Dharma, or her husband, or another accomplice who grabbed it from the room, it's easy to connect her and the gun. Then she made her own *opportunity* when she went to the house that morning. Maybe she showed up at the woman's door to apologize."

My father's head bobbed. "But when you go somewhere to apologize, you bring flowers or chocolate, not a gun. Maybe flowers *and* chocolate."

"You would know," I teased.

He had a point, though. A weapon was protection, or for threatening someone. If Dharma really believed Voula was practicing black magic, wouldn't a magic necklace be better protection?

After a moment, my father said, "Let's say Dharma showed up with the gun, acting like the sheriff of a Wild West town, trying to run the voodoo lady out of town. Things get heated. They argue, wrestle over the gun, and it goes off. Total accident. She'll serve some time for manslaughter, but she'll still have her good karma, because she thought she was doing the right thing."

"If the shooting was an accident, that would explain why her getaway driving wasn't exactly sneaky." I tapped on the steering wheel. "What if she didn't know the gun was loaded? That weapons collection back there was pretty intense. Is Mr. Koenig nutty enough to display loaded guns?"

"I checked a few of the other handguns. There were some nice pieces in there, and I couldn't resist. No ammunition in the ones I looked at, and I didn't see any bullets in the room. If I were him, leaving my cases unlocked to better show off my collection, I'd be damn careful to keep the bullets in a safe that only I had the combination to."

"How many places in town sell ammunition?"

He stared out the window for a minute, at the passing snowy terrain, then turned to me. "Just one place, and it's next to that sandwich shop that does the grilled panini with three kinds of cheese. I suppose we could swing by Wild Buck's, just to be thorough. I might be persuaded to buy you lunch."

I nodded. "We do need to eat."

MY FATHER KNEW the owner of Wild Buck's, the town's hunting and fishing shop. The man was neither wild, nor named Buck; he was Owen Johnson, a small man with a smooth scalp, a squeaky voice, and a warm handshake. When I was younger, I thought Owen Johnson was the cartoon Elmer Fudd, *hunting wabbits*, come to life.

Upon our arrival, Owen was restocking shelves with fishing lures. My father told him to keep working, and not to let us stop him.

I picked up one of the feathered lures to admire the design. "This could be a cute little earring," I said.

Owen Johnson smiled a crooked smile. I guessed it wasn't the first time he'd heard a woman say that exact thing.

He opened a cardboard box on the worn linoleum floor and started sorting through the packed items. He said, "Finnegan Day, you don't look dressed for ice fishing, so you must be here to ask me about that woman's suicide."

"Suicide?"

My father and I exchanged a confused look.

"Seems like an open-and-shut case to me," Owen said. "I'm no detective, but when a woman comes in and buys a box of bullets, then turns up dead the next day, a guy's gotta figure it was no accident."

A confusing mix of horror and curiosity came over me.

I knelt down so I could look into Owen's face while he stooped over the box of lures. "Mr. Johnson, are you sure it was Voula Varga who came in and bought bullets? She had long black hair, very curly, and was probably dressed in layers of dark, flowing clothes. Was it definitely her who bought the bullets and not another woman, say, with silver-white hair?"

"I know who it was," he said. "She was always driving around in that coffin-mobile with her name on the side. Sheesh. Can't miss a character like that. Then she wanted bullets for a twenty-thousand-dollar gun. I was like, hey, lady, why are you ripping off the good folks of Misty Falls with your little palm-reading act if you can afford a twenty-thousand-dollar gun? Sheesh. Some people."

"She told you she had a gun worth that much?"

"She said she was gettin' it the next day, and was in a mood to celebrate." He slowed down in his movements, but continued unpacking the fishing lures from the box to the shelf.

"It sounds like she was happy," I said. "Why do you think it was a suicide?"

"With some folks it's like that, toward the end. They come in all happy. And you think you're gonna see them around at the gun range for target practice, but then they won't take a flyer, and you think, *Owen, you should call someone*. You think about calling and saying someone might be thinkin' about murderin' themselves. But then you say, *Owen, that's not your business. Mind your own business.*"

My father put his hand on Owen's shoulder. "You couldn't have known. You did all right."

Owen unpacked the box with gusto, his whole bald head flushing pink with effort.

We thanked him for his help, and I purchased a half-dozen feathered lures as a token of gratitude for his time and honesty.

We got back into the car—me getting in the passenger door and sliding over to the driver's side rather than falling on my butt again.

We didn't have anywhere else to go, and we'd stopped at the cafe for panini sandwiches before the visit to Wild Buck's, so I started driving my father and his new rug and laptop to his house.

After a few minutes, I said, "Suicide? Is it possible?"

"Suicide by shooting the chest is less common than the head, but does happen. They don't usually shoot through clothing, though, which is just one of several reasons why the police are investigating it as a homicide. Hang on."

He pulled out his phone and explained he was reviewing notes from what Kyle had leaked to him.

After a few minutes, he said, "Okay, here we go. No suicide note, as you know. Coroner report confirms a single bullet wound to the chest, and the angle tilted down, suggesting a killer who was taller than her, unless she'd been on her knees. Probably not a suicide. If it had been a self-inflicted shot, those usually tilt upward slightly."

"There's no way we'll know for sure, is there?"

"No. We only know what's typical for a female."

"True, but Voula Varga wasn't the typical sort of female, was she? The woman drove a hearse."

"Some people are just nuts."

With my next thought, my stomach clenched around the panini sandwich from lunch, which suddenly felt like a stone.

"Dad, what if she meant for me to be the one to find her? I'm sorry to sound like I think everything is all about me, but this is two bodies in two months. Bad things come in threes. I'm not sure if I'll be leaving the house in February."

"Don't you start turning superstitious on me, wearing bracelets to fend off the evil eye, putting upside-down brooms behind the door, and all that nonsense. I've seen a lot of things in my years on the force, and I can guarantee you bad things don't come in threes. Bad things come all the time, one-two-three-four-five-six-infinity."

His words echoed in my head. *Bad things come all the time. Infinity.*

We drove in silence, leaving the town center. As we picked up speed, the wind played with the rug on the roof, making it flop against the metal like a prize marlin.

My father cleared his throat. "Good things come all the time, too. All the time."

"I know. Thanks for taking me with you today. I really learned a lot. You're good at this stuff. Really good."

He leaned over to check my speedometer. "You're speeding."

"Don't change the subject. You're good at investigating. So… what's the plan? You're going to help Kyle with this cold case, and then what?"

"We'll see."

"But what's next in your plan? Uh, I mean, your process?" *A process is better than a plan, because plans go wrong.*

With a smirk, he said, "Beer. Every time you say *cold case*, I think, *cold beer*. That's all I have planned for tonight."

We sat in easy silence until we reached his street, then parked over in front of his house. We still had to untie his rug, so I waited for him to shift out of the passenger side so I could get out. My hip was starting to ache from my previous smooth exit.

"How about you?" he asked. "Big plans for tonight?"

"Knitting. I've got a ball of yarn I should do something with."

"You could make a scarf."

"Yes, I think that's about my skill level."

He winked at me. "Don't sell yourself short."

CHAPTER 22
JANUARY 4

THE NEXT MORNING, I could barely get out of bed, thanks to a baseball-mitt-sized bruise on my buttock, acquired by falling out of my car window at the Koenig Mansion. *Some souvenir.*

"Look at the size of that thing," I said.

Jeffrey didn't seem particularly shocked by the shades of purple and ochre covering a good portion of the fleshy region I normally sat upon.

Groaning, I pulled on thick wool socks and the wild-patterned housecoat, because one's appearance should match how one feels, and I felt hideous.

The house felt empty without Jessica, who'd been my temporary housemate for two of the previous four mornings. I made my coffee and limped around, cursing my father's refusal to accept free delivery, and generally feeling sorry for myself.

My knitting attempt from the night before sat on the coffee table. Four rows. I had created four measly rows, and no two loops were the same size.

I was debating a second attempt at knitting, even getting a little excited about improving my technique, when my phone alerted me to a new text message from my father. He'd sent a single image, just an envelope with a red lipstick kiss over the flap.

I called his number, and when he answered, I said, "You got the email from Erica, with the dinner list?"

"A friendly email, yes." I could practically hear his eyebrows waggling. He continued, "Here's an interesting thing about Christmas dinner at the Koenig Mansion. Erica said they like to bring in an entertainer to keep things lively. You get three guesses who it was that night, and the first two don't count."

I limped over to my fridge and looked at the business card stuck there. "I'm guessing it was *the vibrant and vivacious Voula Varga, psychic extraordinaire.*"

"That's exactly who it was. Interesting, don't you think?"

"Please tell me someone took video of her interacting with Dharma. Maybe we can find out what set off their feud."

"No video, but here's the interesting part. Dharma was the one who suggested the psychic as a guest. Erica says the two met a few months back at some sort of hokey self-help workshop."

"They were friends? Wow." I tried to imagine what Jessica would have to do for me to throw a drink on her, much less threaten her with a gun.

"I have a new theory. It's a good one. Are you sitting down?"

I walked to the table and took a seat, wincing at the tenderness on my bruised side. "Sitting," I said through clenched teeth.

"Here's my theory: Voula contacted something terrible in the spirit world, and it possessed her and killed her, right after it spent some time in Dharma's body to steal the gun from her uncle." He chortled at his joke. "Just kidding," he said, as if I hadn't guessed.

"Dad, if Voula was at the Koenig Mansion, she could have stolen the gun. That makes more sense. She stole the gun and already had it when she bought the bullets. It's possible Owen Johnson misunderstood what she was saying. Then she shot herself, and did something to set up Dharma to take the fall."

"To what end, though? I'd be more inclined to believe the evil spirit thing. Let's see if Lizzy has any answers."

"Lizzy? Is that some new contact of yours?"

"Back in the olden days, when your father was young and dinosaurs roamed the planet, people called their horses Lizzy. That's why the first car was called a Tin Lizzy. My laptop's name is Lizzy, because… well, I guess I just like the name. Let's see now…" He tapped away at the keys. Unlike the keyboard for his old fire-hazard computer, I could barely hear this one's keystrokes.

"What are you doing?" I asked.

"Looking up demon possession."

"Do I need to stay on the phone for this?"

"If I start speaking in tongues, call an exorcist." He chuckled. "If you must know, I'm sending an email to my pharmacist contacts. If Voula had a demon possession problem, there's probably a pill for that."

"Gotcha." He was still looking into the suicide angle, and trying to find out if she was being treated for any illnesses.

For the next ten minutes, I stayed on the line while he talked through his email exchange with a contact. It sounded like the only prescriptions Voula had at the time of her death were the hormone pills and a new drug for lowering cholesterol. It wasn't exactly riveting, but it was interesting. My father also gushed over the speed and responsiveness of his new laptop.

When he'd finished with the emails, I asked, "What else is on the agenda for today? Do you need your personal driver?"

"Take the day off," he said distractedly. "I'm getting to know Lizzy."

"I've been replaced," I sniffed. "What about Dimples? I mean Officer Dempsey? Did you tell him about what Owen said about Voula buying those bullets herself? Are they any closer to tracking down Dharma?"

"Ask him yourself. I reckon he'll be there in about… eleven minutes."

I reached up and clutched my bathrobe closed. "What?"

"Listen, I can't give Lizzy the attention she needs and talk on the phone. I'll let you go."

He ended the call, and I tried to get to my feet, but I had a warm weight on my lap. Jeffrey blinked up at me sleepily. I hadn't even noticed him sneaking onto my lap in the first place, yet had a vague recollection that I'd been petting him for the last few minutes.

"Dimples is coming here," I said. "Here. Get yourself spruced up, will you?"

He gave me a grumpy look as I pushed him off my lap and rushed off to get showered and changed into real clothes. I hoped that a blast of hot water would help with the stiffness in my side and lower back, but my shower only spat out lukewarm water. My tenant must have used the entire hot water tank, which struck me as odd, because it hadn't happened before. On the plus side, my tepid shower was a fast one. I was dressed and had makeup on by the time someone knocked on my door.

I checked the front window first, spotting a police vehicle parked out front. I opened my door, expecting to find Kyle *and* Tony, but it was just Kyle.

He was in his uniform, which meant he was probably there on official business. He was smiling, and his blond hair shone gold in the morning sun. My mouth went so dry, I suddenly had to cough.

He held up the two travel mugs I'd sent out with Tony two days earlier. "I thought you might want these back."

I kept coughing and waved him in wordlessly.

He stepped inside, closed the door, and looked left to right, scanning my home's interior in a curious yet professional manner, as though assessing potential hiding places for attackers.

"Refill?" I croaked, pointing to the coffee pot. I coughed a final time to get my voice back to normal. "You can keep the travel mug. I have plenty. Or, if you have time, you could have a cup here, in a real mug."

"I don't want to catch flack from Tony, but I do have a few minutes, and that brew does smell good. I'll just take off my boots."

He hung his jacket on a hook, then bent over and unlaced his boots on the mat, so he didn't track in snow. *So polite.*

I grabbed a clean mug from the cupboard and brought him coffee at the table, where he was already taking a seat. "Does my father make you take off your boots?" I asked.

A smile spread out between his dimples. "I guess he told you we've been working together."

"He won't tell me much." I took a seat across from him, gasping inwardly when I landed on my bruise. "Thank you for letting him feel involved with your casework. He's one of those people who has to keep busy constantly, and can't relax like a normal person."

Kyle looked down at my hands, which were arranging the sugar bowl, creamer, napkins, and extra spoons into a neat row. He raised his eyebrows and then flicked his blue eyes up to meet mine.

"Fine," I said. "The apple doesn't fall far from the tree. My father and I both need to keep busy. Did he happen to mention to you what his retirement plans are? Like, officially?"

"He's your father. That's not really for me to say."

"You know something?"

Kyle blinked a few times, but kept his gaze locked on mine. His eyes weren't just blue. They were aquamarine blue. *Stormy! Look away from the aquamarine-blue eyes that sparkle like gems. He's a decade younger than you, lady.*

I squirmed in my chair, which aggravated my bruise and sent pain up my spine, making me sweat even more.

"Are you feeling okay?" Kyle asked, ignoring my probing questions about my father. "You look pale. I hope you're taking Vitamin D. It's basically mandatory in this corner of the world."

"I do take it, and calcium and magnesium, for my old lady bones, which are… super old."

He laughed over his coffee. "Yeah, you're really super old," he said.

I didn't want to talk about my age after all, so I switched the conversation to asking him how the homicide case was going.

He filled me in on his side.

They hadn't actually canvassed at Wild Buck's, and were puzzled by the information my father and I had found out. It complicated matters that the victim had purchased the bullets, but that was for the jury to deal with, he said. The department's sole focus was to apprehend their top suspect, and that meant finding her.

"I'll keep my eyes open," I promised. "By the way, that was good work you did, finding out she dyed her hair brown."

"Thanks." He looked troubled. "She's not exactly a criminal mastermind, but then again, people in a panic do strange things." He scanned the room again, swiveling his head left and right. "Mind if I look around?"

"Even better, I'll give you the Grand Tour."

I led him through my home, chattering about the renovations I had planned, and what I wished I'd known before I bought the place. He didn't say much, but he did look inside all the closets, and behind doors. My heart sank a little when I realized he was searching my residence, either for evidence or their suspect. He didn't care about my planned upgrades or color scheme.

When he let himself into the stairwell that led down to the laundry room and furnace, I started to feel offended. How could he think I was hiding something or someone? *He didn't trust me.* I calmly reminded myself he was just doing his job, and I bit my tongue.

When we were done with the tour, he stood by the kitchen table and finished his coffee. His suspicion of me had made his dimples slightly less adorable, and now I could stare right at them without feeling giddy. I could even glare at them.

"Thanks for searching the premises," I said icily. "I feel much safer now, Officer Dempsey. Do you have any recommendations? Bars on the windows? A girl can't be too careful."

"Just keep your eyes open," he said evenly as he laced his boots back up, then let himself out.

As soon as he was gone, Jeffrey emerged from wherever he'd been hiding. We were still getting to know each other's habits, and he definitely had mixed feelings about visitors.

I snorted. "Kyle's not much of a detective if he didn't find you right under his nose."

My joke didn't make me feel better, because now I believed it. Kyle was young and inexperienced. And Tony had become aggressive and impulsive lately. He'd actually kicked down the door at Voula's house rather than wait an entire thirty seconds for me to open it. Then he'd roughed up and handcuffed my tenant for the crime of standing in front of his own house.

Despite the best of intentions, I worried that the two weren't directing their energy in the best ways. Kyle had been creative in canvassing the hair salons, yet neither of them had checked the ammunition store.

Could those two even handle a complicated investigation? With every hour passing, the killer could be getting further away.

Someone had to do something.

CHAPTER 23

I TRIED TO shake off that morning's surprise inspection from Kyle, but it bothered me more with each passing minute.

Instead of trusting that me and my father were trying to help, he'd actually suspected I was hiding something.

I was in no mood to take the day off and knit, so me and my giant purple bruise limped our way to the car, then drove to my store, Glorious Gifts.

My employee, Brianna, was just opening for the day. She stood in front of the store, using a stiff-bristled broom to sweep the sidewalk clear, since there wasn't enough snow to justify using a shovel. Brianna was twenty-one, but so petite that she looked all of fourteen at first glance.

"Hey, boss." She stopped sweeping to give me a cheery smile and tuck her straight brown hair behind her ears so it wouldn't swing in the way while she was sweeping. Brenda had a round face, and rarely wore her hair pinned back, because she thought her ears stuck out, making her look like a monkey. I'd pointed out to her that monkeys were cute, and there were worse things to look like, but I didn't deny the comparison. She said she appreciated my honesty. As far as boss-employee relationships went, ours was as good as it gets.

"How's it been going?" I asked.

I hadn't seen her since the last day of December, and I probably should have wished her a Happy New Year, but it was the fifth of the month, and I wasn't sure if there was a statute of limitations. Plus, I felt guilty about not having been to my business, even though Brianna was more than capable of running it with minimal oversight.

"About the same," she said. "I haven't grown five inches, so I'm still using the ladder to get things off the top shelves."

I grinned. "Have you tried positive thinking? Just thinking yourself taller?"

"No, but I hear there's a ghost in town who grants wishes if you email her. Did you hear about—" Her face blanched and she stopped herself from telling me about the body I'd discovered.

"She wasn't my friend," I said. "I'd barely met her once, and the whole—" my throat pinched on my words "—the whole body thing wasn't too bad. I wouldn't want to see one every day, but I grew up hearing plenty of stories from my father."

"I'm still sorry about everything."

"You're sweet, Bri."

I noticed, out of the corner of my eye, someone walking toward us on the sidewalk. For privacy, I pulled open the door of the shop and nodded for Brianna to go in ahead of me.

The familiar scent of the store immediately made me feel both relaxed and invigorated. It wasn't a single specific potpourri or room freshener, but the mix of *everything*, every scented candle and box of natural objects like acorns or seashells, picked off the ground, soaked in essential oils, and sold with a high markup. Some company should market a candle called Gift Shop and have it burn through a thousand layers of everything from eucalyptus to cinnamon.

There were new items on the center table, so I eagerly went to look at them. I'd forgotten ordering the blown-glass pears and plums, and held them with wonder. Moments like these, when I walked into my store and enjoyed it the way a customer might, made me feel happy about my choice to buy the place— happier than when I looked at the financial reports.

Brianna finished switching on the lights and stood behind the counter, looking over the notepad we kept there for messages.

"Do you want these phone messages on your desk in the office?" she asked.

"Only the important ones. All the calls from salespeople can all go in the circular filing cabinet."

She nodded, tore the page out of the book, and tossed it into the circular filing cabinet, which was a round recycling bin.

I finished admiring the glass baubles and leaned my elbows on the counter like customers did.

"Bri, what did you mean about emailing Voula's ghost? Don't tell me you actually tried it." Her cheeks reddened, giving her secret away. "You did? What happened? Show me."

She pulled out her phone and showed me the email.

Brianna: *Dear Voula, I hope your spirit is at peace. I was wondering if you could tell me if my webcomic will ever take off? Sincerely, Brianna*

"I was joking," Brianna said. "Mostly."

There was a reply, with yesterday's date, and the timestamp was a little over three hours after Brianna's message.

Voula Varga, Psychic Extraordinaire: *Dear friend, I have consulted the mists that surround this beautiful world, and I have a message for you about your webcomic. Go outside and find a round, flat stone. Place it on your windowsill, and whenever you think of your most ambitious desire, turn the stone over, to bring your destiny closer. If you would like to meet with me, please see my phone number and rates below.*

Under that message was a list of rates and packages. I scanned back up and reread with interest.

Setting up an email auto-responder was easy enough, and most folks in the corporate world ran them while on vacation. You can even set one up on a time delay, so it seems more like a human response, if you want to trick people.

This message, however, seemed both generic and personalized at the same time. It contained the word *webcomic*, and that was awfully specific.

"Do you mind if I forward this to myself?" I asked Brianna. She said she didn't mind, so I sent a copy of the message to myself, and also to my father.

"I phoned the number," Brianna said. "Like a total loser, but whatever. The recording from the phone company said the mailbox was full, and when I tried again later, the number was disconnected."

"She's not checking her messages," I said solemnly. "She's really dead, I swear. If emails are going out, it's because someone hacked her account. Ghosts aren't real."

Brianna wrinkled her nose. "I know, but my friends all emailed her and they got different emails back. Why would someone bother to answer them? It would take a lot of time, wouldn't it?"

"Not necessarily. Some tech support companies have automated systems to cut down on wages. There are programs that scan customer emails for certain keywords and then respond to the most common problems."

She frowned like she didn't believe me, but in my corporate life I'd seen such things firsthand, even overseen deals licensing the technology. It wasn't magic, but it did make me curious.

And distracted.

I looked around my store, at the shelves full of wonderful things. *So many things.* If I stuck around, I would have to get started on annual inventory. My lower back was already aching, just above the bruise. I was taller than Brianna, but I still would need the ladder to reach the tallest shelves, and my aching backside probably wouldn't appreciate climbing up and down, reaching, or bending.

"You probably don't need me breathing over your shoulder today," I said.

She shrugged. "I don't mind, either way." She pressed her lips together, careful not to mention the big annual inventory job.

"I'm going to look into this email thing," I announced. "Just because."

She seemed surprised by this, but wished me luck on my way out the door.

You don't need to be an expert on all technology to run a computer shop, but experience told me I would get answers at Misty Microchips, which only two blocks off the main street and a short walk from my gift shop. I headed there, walking briskly.

It wasn't until I walked in the door that I remembered how creepy Marvin had been on my last visit. Thankfully, he didn't seem to be around.

Marcy was wiping down the glass display case that served as their checkout counter. She must not have heard me come in, because she jumped when she turned around and saw me there.

I quickly apologized for stress-testing her cardiovascular system, and while I was at it, I also apologized for not returning her phone call from a few days earlier.

"Stormy Day, don't worry about a little thing like that." She swatted the air with her cleaning cloth. "I don't even remember what I was calling about." She let out a high-pitched laugh.

"How's the sale going?"

"Sale?" She blinked, her gold-brown eyes unfocused.

"The big computer sale." I pointed to the window, and the sale banner my father had seen the day before.

"Oh." Her cheeks reddened and she shrugged. "Marvin has that sign in the window more often than not, but we're not really having a sale. Can't afford to."

I nodded in understanding. "Thin margins."

"As Ruby Sparkes would say, *thinner than margarine at a butter convention*." She shook her head and gave me a crooked smile that seemed forced. "What a character, that Ruby."

"She must be one of your best customers. She has a new tablet or some other tech every time I see her." I gave Marcy a double eye-raise and intoned in a funny voice, "Ruby sees all, and reports to the others."

Marcy gave me the dazed look again. "What others?"

Oops, I thought. *They're called the* Secret *Tearoom Ladies for a reason, Stormy.*

"Others? Uh, I don't know," I lied. "Sometimes my mouth says things at random." That part wasn't a lie.

Marcy gave the glass surface of the case another spritz and wipe while she worked her way around so that it was between us. Her mood was less friendly than the day before. I hoped her coolness didn't have to do with me, or with her noticing her gross husband's ill-advised flirtations.

She asked, "Is everything working out with your dad's new laptop?"

"Yes, fine. Her name is Lizzy."

I hadn't forgotten my reason for coming in, but didn't know how to bring up tracing a ghost over the internet.

"Your dad seems… energetic. You must have your hands full now that he's retired. And that cane! Wherever did he find such a thing? Marvin was on the internet all last night, looking up cane swords, and now he wants one. I told him it was a terrible idea to keep a concealed deadly weapon on himself, but…" Her cheeks reddened again, and she stared down at the floor, unmoving, like someone had hit her pause button.

"Marcy, are you okay?"

She looked up and forced another smile. "Just a bit tired. Friends kept calling last night to tell me about these emails. Did you hear? They're coming from that poor dead woman's email account."

I cheered internally that the subject had come around to exactly what I wanted.

"What do you know about auto-responder programs?" I asked. "My employee is spooked over the reply she got. I told her it was probably something automated, and maybe the program has been running for months, but nobody noticed when she was alive. My guess is it's a modified technical help desk script."

"Can you keep a secret?"

"Are you going to tell me you know who set up the script? Was it Marvin?"

Marcy patted her chest with one hand. "Me. I set it up. Please don't tell anyone, because I don't want to be associated with that woman." She grimaced, looking for an instant like she might throw up.

"You're the programmer?"

"Guilty as charged. I'm a big nerd. Programming is what I used to do for a living before we moved here. The setup was easy enough. I'm actually the one who suggested it. That woman was in here buying one of our refurbished laptops, and she wasn't that tech savvy, so she was worrying about having to answer a lot of emails. I said I could whip something up, and I didn't even charge her."

"Are you going to take the program down? Or are you trolling?"

"Trolling?" She had a blank look again.

"By trolling, I mean enjoying causing trouble. If you let it run, the whole town of Misty Falls will keep thinking there's a ghost floating around, granting wishes." I snorted at the idea. "You could tweak the responses to suggest people get new laptops because new computers are more lucky."

"Good one," Marcy said, but she didn't laugh.

Shadows passed over us; people were walking past the shop's front window. My gaze lingered on the exit. I'd gotten what I came for, almost too easily, and now I wanted to go.

"Marcy, I was just on my way to get coffee. Would you like to come with me? Maybe Jessica will take a break and sit with us."

"No, I have to stay here and mind the store." There was a tinge of bitterness to her voice. "I have to be the responsible one."

I walked to the door and called back cheerily, "If I see Ruby, I'll send her in so you can sell her something."

A big truck whooshed by just as I opened the door, so her response was drowned out, but she did give me a wave goodbye.

I stepped outside and breathed in the fresh air, which was cold and dry, and burned my nasal passages enough to make my eyes water. After a few blinks, I acclimatized. *Now where?*

Inventory?

Ugh.

Ever since my mouth had suggested coffee, the rest of me had decided it was a good idea, so I walked in the direction of the nearest cafe, which was where Jessica worked. Their coffee was nothing to blog about, but it was still coffee, and I could tell Jessica about yesterday's trip to the Koenig Mansion.

After a few blocks, a gust of wind dried out my nose again, sending tears to my eyes and down my cheeks. I couldn't see where I was going, and ran into a blurry thing that smelled like the Golden Wok and cursed mildly in a man's voice.

I stepped back and blinked my watering eyes clear. Logan came into focus.

"Yeah, I ran you down," I said. "That'll teach you to use all the hot water and leave me none for my shower. That's an awfully big tank for one man to drain. You must have been really dirty this morning."

"This morning?" He shifted a paper bag of food to one arm and scratched his beard. "I didn't do anything out of the ordinary. Maybe it's your taps."

"You used all the hot water, but you're blaming my taps?

He nodded. "It must be your taps, because my water's always fine. How about I come over and have a look at your shower? I'm working from home again today, just heading there now. How about I pop over to your side, you help me eat this Chinese food that I've ordered too much of, and I'll check your taps?"

I leaned forward to inspect the fragrant contents of his bag. He did have a lot of food, but his fidgeting made me think his offer was a hollow one. Logan was up to something. First, I'd heard the female voice in his bathroom on New Year's Eve, and now the hot water was running out. It did not take a private investigator's license for me to guess Logan had a new friend. A girlfriend.

"Sorry, but I'm busy at my store doing inventory," I lied. "It's going to take all day, and then some."

"Sounds fun." He shifted the bag again, sending the mouth-watering scent of the Golden Wok's sweet and sour chicken balls my way. The first time I'd eaten them, I thought they were terrible, but I'd found myself craving the deep-fried nuggets, and every subsequent tasting had been more delicious.

"What else is new?" Logan asked. "Have you seen your friend *Tony* around?" He pronounced Tony's name with an Italian accent. Tony didn't have an accent, so it just sounded like Logan was making fun of him.

"Not lately. I guess Tony's busy chasing after their suspect for the fortune-teller's murder. Did you hear about that? It was Dharma Lake. You've met her at least once, I think. She's the waitress at the Fox and Hound with the snowy white hair, only now she has brown hair. Keep an eye out for that one." I nodded solemnly. "Armed and dangerous."

"I'll keep my eyes open." He gave me a friendly wink, then walked around me on the sidewalk and continued on his way. "See you around, Stormy Day."

"Not if I see you first, Logan Sanderson!"

CHAPTER 24

Two hours after running into Logan, I pulled my car up my driveway alongside his truck. I quietly creaked my way out of the driver's seat and limped to my front door. The purple bruise from my fall only hurt when I sat on it, so the pain had to be from pulled muscles—muscles I'd never given a second thought to until now.

I unlocked my door, went inside, and closed the door gently, so the sound wouldn't travel to Logan's side.

Despite what I'd said on the sidewalk, I'd had no intention of doing inventory. I went to the cafe where Jessica worked, and sat at the staff table in the corner for almost two hours, mostly reading through the recent issues of the *Misty Falls Mirror*. I'd meant to only pop in for a few minutes to catch up with Jessica, but as the place filled up for lunch, I was well situated to overhear town gossip.

People talked at their tables, and even across tables. The murder had been juicy news, and now everyone had wild stories about the ghost of Voula Varga.

One woman said the ghost broke her washing machine, but it was a good deed in disguise, because her husband bought her a new, better one. Plenty of people had been emailing Voula's email address and getting the automated semi-customized responses from Marcy's program.

While at the restaurant, I emailed her using my phone. I tried it a few times and confirmed what other people were saying: the second message from my email account generated a different response, stating she was unable to further consult by email, and recommended an in-person session.

The town seemed so delighted by the mystery of the emails and recent ghostly occurrences—none of which seemed very ghostly to me—that they weren't even worried about the murderer, who was still at large. By the time I left the cafe, I'd learned nothing new about the case, but plenty about the townspeople; there was no shortage of creative imagination in Misty Falls.

As I got comfortable inside my house, I smiled over one story: a lady who swore her Siamese cat was routinely possessed by Voula's spirit from 11:00 p.m. to 11:16 p.m. every night.

I went to find Jeffrey to tell him all about it. He was on the floor of my bedroom, curled up in the empty cardboard tray his canned food came in. He preferred the plain box to the cute pet bed I'd gotten him for Christmas.

He didn't know what a Siamese cat was, but his tail flicked with enjoyment at being spoken to.

"This explains Kitty Playtime Hour," I said. "You're possessed by a ghost every night. It's so obvious now."

He stretched, scratched his nails on the cardboard, then stepped out, giving the box an accusing look for always making him sleepy.

I put away the clothes I'd tossed around that morning in my rush to get dressed for Kyle. He padded after me as I straightened up the house. I'd come home with the intention of getting into the tub, to soothe my sore muscles, but I hadn't taken a bath since a troubling incident the previous month. The idea of being naked and vulnerable bothered me almost as much as my sore body.

The only way past my fear was through it, though. I talked my way through the process. "Got my towels, my book, water, tea, fully charged phone. What else?"

Jeffrey gave the tub a suspicious look.

"Good idea. I'll zip down to the basement and look at the hot water heater, in case there's some sort of warning light flashing." I kept talking to Jeffrey, who followed me down the hall, where I opened the door to the basement.

"That was just a joke about the warning light," I said. "I know hot water heaters aren't cars. I'm checking for a leak, or a blown-out pilot light."

I patted Jeffrey on the head, then turned to go down the stairs just as the basement light flicked off.

Or had it? I hadn't been paying close attention when I'd opened the door.

"Hello?" I called down into the darkness. Some light seeped in through the basement's narrow windows, but only enough for me to make out the basic shapes of the appliances and shelves.

"Logan? You'd better not be hiding down here with your lizard farm."

No response, but I thought I could hear someone breathing.

"Hello? You should know I'm a master of martial arts, like, um, Krav Maga, and some of the other ones." I smiled, proud that I knew the *term* Krav Maga—not that I knew anything about *practicing* the technique of disarming your opponent in a fight by using anything within reach.

Still no answer. I reached for the light switch on the wall, but found nothing, of course, because there *was no* switch on the wall. The only control was the beaded-metal cord on the fixture. I usually left the light on all the time, because a few dollars on the electric bill was better than a broken leg from falling down the stairs.

As I stepped cautiously into the murky depths, basement scenes from horror movies played in my head. I sniffed deeply, detecting the invigorating scent of freshly washed and dried laundry.

Unless the killer was hiding in my basement, doing a load of laundry, it would seem Logan had washed some clothes that day and clicked off the light.

I was halfway down the steps when I stopped. What was I going to the basement for? I didn't have a laundry basket in my hands. Had I been going down for paper towels? I had to start taking some of those vitamins for memory.

It came to me: *I'm checking the hot water tank*. I went back up the steps and grabbed the flashlight I kept hanging on the wall. The batteries needed charging, but the light was strong enough to get me down the wood steps in one piece.

I got to the bottom and was reaching up for the light switch cord when I noticed a pair of slippers near the edge of the wall. I pointed the flashlight at the slippers, then moved the light up, up a pair of legs in jeans with rolled cuffs, then a dark blue sweater, and finally, a face.

Two eyes stared back at me.

It was a woman.

A woman was standing under my stairs, in my dark basement. She put up one hand to shield her eyes from the light of my flashlight.

Someone screamed. It had to be me, because her mouth didn't move. I screamed again. Then she screamed.

There were only two ways out of the basement, and the narrow window wasn't fast enough. I started for the stairs, but the woman was closer, so she beat me to staircase and bounded up noisily.

Jeffrey, who stood watch in my open doorway, arched his back and hissed like a tiny dragon when she got to the top.

The woman didn't turn back, nor did she enter my apartment. She opened the other door, the one leading to Logan's half of the duplex, and went through. The door slammed shut, and I heard the telltale click of the handle being twisted to lock it.

I'd only caught a glimpse of her, but it had been more than enough for me to identify the woman. Logan did have a houseguest, but it wasn't a girlfriend.

Unless he'd taken up dating much older women, he was harboring a fugitive.

Dharma Lake.

I'd found her.

Someone's karma was about to change.

CHAPTER 25

As I TURNED my living room upside down looking for my cell phone, I cursed myself for not having a landline. With a phone plugged into the wall, it could only wander the length of the cord.

Someone knocked on my front door. It was a polite knock, which only made it more terrifying.

"Stormy? It's me, Logan."

I latched the chain before I unlocked the door and opened it a crack.

"Just you?" I asked.

"I'm alone." Both of his hands came through the crack in the door.

I panicked, screamed, and tried to close the door on his hands. He quickly withdrew them, but he thrust his boot in at the bottom.

"Easy now," he said. "I was just showing you I was unarmed. Can we talk?"

I shifted so I could see him through the crack.

"Start talking. Why do you have a killer over there?"

He fixed his winter-sky eyes on mine.

"Dharma's not a killer. People are wrongly accused of things all the time. That's why we have lawyers."

"You're her defense attorney? Is that why she's at your place? Are you planning to hide her forever?"

"May I come in?"

ANGELA PEPPER

"I guess she can't stay at her house, because the cops are looking for her. And she can't exactly hide out in a hotel, not in a town this size, where everybody knows everybody."

"Exactly," he said. "You're pretty smart."

"Flattery will get you nowhere." I kicked the toe of his boot out of the door crack and slammed the door shut.

Yes, pretty smart, indeed. I'd been quietly putting on my own boot while I talked through the hotel issue.

He knocked again.

I yelled at the door, "I've got my phone and I'm calling the police right now. I'm punching in the number."

"No, you've lost your phone. I have to walk past your front window to reach your door, remember? I saw you tossing cushions off your couch. Something tells me you weren't redecorating."

I opened the door a crack. "Can I borrow your phone?"

"I've got something else for you." He slipped a sheet of paper through the opening. It was a check, made out to me.

It wasn't a rent check. The subject line at the bottom had a line written in messily: *Investigative Services Retainer.*

"Logan, you don't have to pay me for locating the fugitive in our shared laundry room. Honestly, it's a freebie. My pleasure."

I shut the door.

He knocked again. "Stormy, I need to employ you as an investigator. It's so I can talk to you and we can share privileged information. You see, there's this client-attorney thing, and—"

230

I pulled the chain free and yanked open the door. "I know." I waved my hand, inviting him in. "I think I'm familiar with attorney-client privilege. I've seen every episode of *The Good Wife*."

He stepped inside. "That's a great show. They take a few liberties, of course, but it's excellent. No spoilers, I haven't seen them all." He kicked off his boots, which hadn't been tied up, and rubbed his bare forearms. He'd run over in a hurry, with no jacket. I almost felt bad for making him wait on the step. Almost.

Logan took a seat at the kitchen table, and I rearranged the magnets on my fridge so I could affix the check where it was visible. It felt like the official thing to do.

He nodded at the check. "Does this mean you accept my offer of employment?"

"I do. I do accept your hand in… handing me a check for employment."

"Good. I have other paperwork for you to sign, but I came over in a hurry." He rubbed his forehead as a smile spread across his face. "That's quite the panic-inducing scream you have."

I grabbed two cans of beer, cracked both open, and set them on the table as I sat down. My bruise didn't even hurt, thanks to the adrenaline.

"What's your plan?" I asked. "A diminished capacity plea? She seemed plenty sharp to me, but a jury might buy it. I hope her hair dye washes out. White would look better on the witness stand."

"She's innocent."

"Did the psychic shoot herself?"

"Maybe she did." He stared into my eyes with intensity, like he was trying to convince me through mind control. I looked away and took a sip of my beer. He did the same.

"How did your client get gunshot residue on her hands?"

"It was on her steering wheel, not her hands. These are very different things."

"You're such a lawyer."

He frowned. "Thanks." He took another sip of his beer. "She doesn't remember anything about what happened that day."

I snorted. "How convenient."

"The old van didn't have airbags, and she hit her head in the accident. Concussion can cause memory loss."

"Very convenient."

"I have a consultant with medical training, and she's looking into it for me. Actually, you might have seen her around. She was in town for a few days after Christmas."

"Hmm," I responded as I took another drink. The beer didn't taste great, but sipping it did keep my mouth from running ahead of my brain. It must have been Logan's "consultant" friend who was over on New Year's Eve. I didn't want him to think I *cared* who he had visiting over there—as long as they weren't wanted by the police.

He sighed. "You probably think I'm crazy for taking on this case."

"On the contrary. Her uncle is the richest man in town by a factor of ten, so that makes you anything but crazy."

"Sure, but all the money in the world doesn't give her an alibi for the shooting, or remove the evidence from her steering wheel, or change the fact she was involved in fraudulent activities with the victim."

"You mean stealing the gun from her uncle?"

"You heard about the Koenig Mansion theft?" He shook his head. "I pay good money for information that's apparently common knowledge."

"Why did she steal the gun? Was it her?"

"Her memory's foggy on that, but at least she remembers the big altercation on New Year's Eve. Do you know the truth about that?"

"Just what I saw."

Logan looked pleased to have information I didn't. "The fight was pure dinner theater. All an act."

"You mean when Dharma chewed out Voula in front of the entire crowded pub and threw a drink on her, right after accusing her of being a witch and practicing dark magic and... oh. I get it."

"Part of the long con, I suspect. Who knows how far she might have taken it."

I ruffled my hand through my hair, pushing the short, wavy strands skyward while I put everything together. Dharma had a good reputation in town, so by accusing someone else of genuine witchcraft, it was as good as an endorsement.

"She lied to the whole town," I said.

"My client had mixed feelings about the fortune-telling, but she felt the ends justified the means. If buying magic rocks from a so-called psychic was the thing that helped people stick to their exercise plan, or save their marriages, Dharma figured the karma would balance out."

He tipped back the beer can, drained it, then set it down gently. "That's the worst beer I've ever had."

Of course it was. It was the beer I kept on hand just to serve my father when he stopped by.

"The worst?" I gave Logan a perplexed look. "You're in Misty Falls now, Mr. Sanderson. This is the town's official beer."

He examined the can. "But it's not even brewed in the state."

I shrugged and played innocent. My father would have been very proud.

Logan glanced over at the interior wall. "I must be crazy," he said. "If I can't figure out who else was at the house that day, she might go to prison."

"Any wild theories you want to run past me? You're paid up for the day. Did she have a boyfriend?"

"Voula mentioned a guy she called Bernie. I just wish I knew his full name."

"Bernard Goldstein." I grabbed the printout of the film executive's website bio. I explained what I'd learned from Ruby, and how it seemed the ladies in the knitting club were the potential investors.

"This is great." Logan's shoulders softened as he relaxed in his chair. "I'll call in an anonymous tip and get the local boys in blue to do the investigative work for me."

"But that's what you're paying me to do."

He laughed and glanced over at the check on the fridge, then back to me. "You're my landlady, not a real investigator. I'm only paying you for your discretion."

He kept laughing, which made my stomach feel like it was making a fist. He wasn't being rude, because to him I was just his landlady, a woman who needed help climbing in her car window because she'd stupidly tied a rug to the roof. Who would hire a bimbo like that to do serious work?

"Wait here a minute," I said. I'd remembered my cell phone was in the bathroom, right where I'd left it before my bath. I ran to grab it, came back, and started going through the crime scene photos again, showing him.

"Logan, I hope there was a third person, I really do, but these are from New Year's Day. You'll notice there are two cups in the sink, with lipstick prints, and no other glasses or mugs."

He flipped forward and back through the other shots I'd taken.

"That's a creepy doll," he said. "We should look for someone who matches that doll."

"You'd think, but there was a basket of dolls in the room, and they were all the same. She would customize them with the clothes of whoever they represented. The doll is a dead end, because it's wearing *her* clothes. If you look closely, you'll see there's a chunk of fabric cut from the hem of the victim's dress, and that was on the doll."

He shuddered. "I don't want to look at these photos, but can I get a copy?"

"Sure. You've more than paid for them." I took back the phone and tapped in the email address he gave me, then sent the images. "Anything else I can do for you as your paid consultant?"

He gave me a crooked grin. "How about a plausible explanation for what happened that day? You've been inside the house, and I haven't. Did you get any feelings? Any hunches?"

"My best theory?" Something had just occurred to me while reviewing the photos. "Well, the gun wasn't just any old gun. It was made by some factory that only produced a limited number before it burned down. It was the gun equivalent of a Fabergé egg owned by the Russian royal family. What if the gun was Dharma's investment in the film deal?"

"That's one way to come up with cash. Oh! The third person could have been an antiques dealer who decided to keep the gun and kill the witnesses."

"But he left the gun, and a witness."

"Right."

"Is her memory really that bad? I'd like to talk to her."

"She's too fragile." He shook his head. "She doesn't remember taking the gun from her uncle's house, but it's not unusual for a client to hide things from her lawyer." He pushed his chair back and stood. "I'll show her a few photos and see if that jogs her memory."

He started slipping on his boots.

"Thanks for being so understanding," he said. "You really are the best landlady I've ever had, and I never meant to draw you into this, but you said you were doing inventory, so I figured we had a few hours for her to wash some clothes. I thought some normal activity might relax her, but she's practically catatonic now."

"I'm so sorry I scared her. Please, tell her I'm sorry."

"I will. I'm not sure she can even hear me when I'm talking, though. It's not good."

"Hopefully she feels better soon."

He thanked me again, then left.

I watched as he walked by my front window.

Once he was out of sight, I closed the curtains, even though it was still light outside.

Logan said his client was practically catatonic. And that she had selective memory lapses.

This was the same woman who'd convinced an entire pub that she hated a woman who was actually her friend. Dinner theater, indeed.

Despite wanting to believe in her innocence, it was entirely possible I was living under the same roof as a killer.

Providing laundry facilities for a wanted fugitive.

Sharing a hot water tank with a murderer.

CHAPTER 26

I CALLED MY FATHER about half an hour after Logan left. I couldn't tell him about who was next door, or he'd call the police… which was what a good citizen should do.

I was the bad one, who took a check to stay quiet.

"How's the physiotherapy?" I asked.

"The stretches? Horrible. If I ever say they're great, that's how you'll know I'm not doing them. Why are you really phoning?"

"Do you want to have dinner with me?"

"Sure, come over right now. I'll take care of everything. Could you swing by the store on your way and pick up some steaks, russet potatoes, and sour cream?"

I enjoyed his version of taking care of everything.

"And coffee," he said. "Plus bread, eggs, and bacon. Are you writing this down?"

"Yes." I was writing his grocery list on my notepad, after the page I'd been using to doodle names for our investigation business.

When he finished the list, I tossed the notepad and some toiletries into an overnight bag, then got Jeffrey's kitty carrier ready. I found him on my bed, watching the door, and looking edgy. He'd been off balance since the screaming in the basement.

He gave a few protest meows, but was a champion all through the car ride to the grocery store, waiting for me to shop, then driving to my father's.

The sun was setting when Jeffrey and I arrived at my father's. As I unloaded the car, I couldn't shake the neck-tickling sensation of being watched.

I whipped around and caught the neighbor across the street peering at me around curtains. I gave her a friendly wave. She pretended to be tending her collection of tea roses on the windowsill.

My father opened the door just as I was lugging everything up the porch steps.

He frowned at the cat carrier. "No returns."

"We're staying overnight. Surprise! It'll be fun. We can make popcorn and watch movies in our pajamas."

He demanded more of an explanation, but I didn't feel right talking about it on the porch, with the eyes and ears of the neighborhood trained on us. I pushed my way in, asking if he had the grill ready.

HE DIDN'T ASK AGAIN why we were staying overnight until we'd finished cooking and eating dinner. The dishwasher was running, and he stood at the sink washing the salad bowl while I attended with the drying towel.

"The Boomerang Generation," he said. "That's what you are. You move away from home, then you come back like a boomerang. I heard all about it on the radio."

"I'm not moving in," I said. "This is just for a few days, because I don't feel safe at my house."

He rinsed the glass salad bowl, then handed it to me, steaming hot.

"Stands to reason you're scared," he said. "Before I retired, it was part of my job to assure people we didn't have a serial killer on the loose, but just because I *say* reassuring things, that doesn't mean you shouldn't be careful. I'm sure glad to be retired now, so I can be honest."

I put the bowl in the cupboard, then turned to make steady contact with his gold-flecked, dark brown eyes. "You keep saying you're retired now, but I saw the papers, Dad. I saw your application to get the license. When were you going to tell me you're becoming a private investigator?"

His dark eyes twinkled. "Never, because I'm not. The application's for you. That's why I left it where you could see it."

My hands went limp, and I dropped the dishtowel. He used his fancy cane for balance as he leaned forward to pick it up.

The application was for me?

For the previous four days, I'd been happily imagining an exciting new career as a private investigator—but that had been as my father's partner. Doing it alone? That was a whole different thing.

"Tea," he said, so we made tea.

THIRTY MINUTES LATER, we were sitting in the living room. He'd turned on the TV and was enjoying the view from his newly repositioned recliner. Jeffrey was making himself at home on the couch.

The show we'd caught the tail end of finished up, and he muted the volume on the set.

"What do you think?" he asked. "You could always apply for the police academy, and go that route, but I don't think police work is for you. You've always been so independent, and you need the intellectual challenge of investigative work. Stormy, are you listening to me? This is what you've been looking for. This is why you came back to Misty Falls."

"No," I said. "This isn't what I'm looking for."

"Promise you'll sleep on it."

At my side, Jeffrey woke up, walked across my lap like I was furniture, jumped to the arm of my father's recliner, then curled up in his lap.

My father reached for the remote control, careful to not disturb the cat, then flicked the volume back on.

I WOKE UP TO a mix of familiar and unfamiliar: Jeffrey's whiskers tickling my face, and me in a bed that was both too firm and too soft at the same time, in that quirky way of guest room beds.

My father and I had stayed up late, watching a funny movie about two mismatched cops. We didn't discuss the investigator's license again, but he did point out a few things during the movie, about how the cops were handling the investigation poorly. I pointed out that the bumbling officers were in pursuit of an alien artifact, then he pointed out that was no excuse for poor procedure.

I climbed out of bed and pulled on multiple layers of clothes.

"Dad's new timer shuts down the heat at night," I said to Jeffrey.

Curled in a tight ball on the pillow, where my head had warmed it, he shot me a no-kidding look. I was glad he seemed comfortable at my father's, but did he need to act *that* happy about my father's lap?

Was it really better than mine? I suspected the little tramp had spent the night traipsing between both of our rooms.

I brushed my teeth in the downstairs bathroom, then went up the stairs, the scent of bacon and coffee quickening my pace.

He wouldn't let me help with breakfast, so I took a seat at the table in the kitchen and checked my phone for messages.

There was one from Logan: *Since I've paid for that retainer, I wonder if you might do one small thing for me? Very small.*

His message irritated me. Maybe it was just the lack of sleep and absence of coffee in my system, but he'd said I wasn't a real investigator. I planned to return the check, but now he wanted me to run errands? I had a bad feeling. Whenever someone says something is a very small favor, it's usually the exact opposite.

I replied: *How small?*

He responded within minutes: *I hear you hosted the knitting club last week. Would you be willing to host again and ask a few questions?*

The idea did not thrill me, but I still responded to say yes. Maybe the twelve ladies could help me with my knitting.

My father set a plate holding two perfectly round, perfectly golden pancakes in front of me.

"What's the message about?" he asked.

"I can't tell you."

He sat in his regular spot, across from me. "Can't, or won't?"

"I can and I will, but there are conditions."

"Like?"

"I'm working as a consultant to Logan Sanderson," I said. "The lawyer. You met him when he helped me climb into the car the other day, when your stupid Hobo Pride wouldn't let you accept free delivery of your rug."

"How's that coffee going down, *Stormy*?"

"Don't say my name like that," I snapped. "You know I hate it."

"Drink your coffee, then we'll talk."

I glowered at his insinuation that my irritation was unreasonable. I sipped some of the coffee, then grabbed a dollar bill from my wallet and slid it across the table toward him.

"I'm hiring you."

He frowned at the bill. "We're getting paid two dollars?"

I told him how much Logan's check was for, and he brightened up.

"But you don't have your license," he said. "Or do you?" He gave me a sidelong look that made me wish I had gotten my investigator's license already, just to surprise him. But I couldn't have gotten it on my own. In addition to sleeping on the idea, I'd also done some research the night before.

"Dad, the state of Oregon requires me to have fifteen hundred hours of investigative experience before I can apply for a license. But you knew that, didn't you? I need to apprentice with somebody."

He glanced up at the ceiling, his brown eyes almost as innocent as the green eyes of the cat sitting on the chair next to mine, eyeballing our bacon.

"This was your plan all along," I said. "Instead of just asking me to be your partner, you wanted me to think it was my idea."

He held his hands up in a gesture of surrender. "My idea, your idea, it's still a good one."

"Why couldn't you just ask me? Sometimes you drive me so nuts, the way I have to drag stuff out of you. And you wonder why I'm grumpy sometimes."

He got up and tidied the kitchen counter for a moment, grabbed the coffee carafe, then came back to the table with a somber expression. I finished drinking my cup and held it out for a refill.

"I couldn't ask," he said. "Investigating can be dangerous. I nearly got you killed once already."

"Twice if we count the tub thing, but that wasn't your fault. You couldn't have known."

"But it was because of my choices. Bad choices. And other people paid the consequences."

He stood with the coffee pot in hand, not moving, the pain of his regret on his face.

"Dad…"

"The reason I haven't asked you yet is because I made a promise to someone a long time ago. She didn't want her girls doing anything dangerous."

"Oh."

He started pouring my coffee. The room was so still that I could hear the liquid splashing in my cup. The air around us felt thick, like time was frozen.

Not every significant moment of choice feels like one. I'd walked away from an engagement and a whole life without having one of these moments. Leaving Christopher and the business had just felt *inevitable*—the natural outcome of all the players and forces involved, without any choice.

This moment, however, felt like standing in the forest at a fork in the path. My mother wouldn't have wanted me to be an investigator.

As for me, I didn't know what I wanted.

245

"Forget about your promise," I said. "She's not here anymore. I get to do whatever I want. We both do."

CHAPTER 27

WE WERE QUIETLY finishing breakfast when I got another message from Logan: *Who did you get this printout from? It's a fake. The website address printed on the footer gives me a blank page. I've searched the film company's name and found nothing.*

I replied: *Bernard Goldstein doesn't exist?*

Logan: *There are dozens of Bernard Goldsteins on the internet, but none of them are this guy. I did an image search and found his face on a stock photo site. Our voodoo lady was pulling a Ponzi scheme. I need to know where this printout came from.*

Me: *Don't worry about that. The website was real. I saw it myself when I made the printout on the day of the wake.*

Logan: *That means the site was taken down after her death.*

Me: *She did have a partner. OMG.*

Logan: *Did you really just say OMG?*

Me: *I'm hip, I'm cool, I say OMG. Especially when we get a big lead.*

Logan: *How did you come by this information about Bernard, anyway?*

Me: *It came to me through the grapevine. I'm not at liberty to discuss.*

As I waited for him to reply, I really hoped he wouldn't press me for the name of my contact. I couldn't tell him the information had come through Ruby and her Secret Tearoom Ladies.

Two minutes later, Logan still hadn't replied to my last message. I sent him a smiley face to lighten my previous dismissal, but still there was no response.

"Why are you scowling?" asked my father.

I relaxed my face. "Scowling?"

"You have a terrible poker face when you're texting. Terrible. I saw at least five emotions on your face just now, and you weren't paying *any* attention to your surroundings. You were sucked into that little screen. I could have leaned over and read the whole exchange, if I wanted to. Was that the lawyer?"

I narrowed my eyes at him playfully. "That's information for my partner. Are you taking the dollar?"

He flung his hand in the air dramatically, swept it down to snatch up the dollar bill, then tucked the money into his shirt pocket.

"Partners," he said.

"Well, partner, prepare to have your mind blown," I said proudly. "I found Dharma Lake. She's at my house, staying with Logan. He's defending her, or at least he will be, once she turns herself in."

"I knew that."

"You did not."

He grinned as he reached for the last piece of bacon. "You should put a better password on your phone than your cat's name."

I groaned. He did have a point.

I pulled up the option to change my phone's password, and tried to think of a new one. I'd only put a password on recently, after taking the crime scene photos at Voula's creepy house. I didn't want a friend grabbing my phone to check the time and accidentally getting an eyeful.

What would be a good password?

Security experts always tell you *not* to use birthdays or your pet's name, but they never give you ideas about what you *should* use. Given how suggestible the mind is, this leads to you staring at the password input screen unable to think of any word *except* your pet's name.

My father said, "Don't use your birthday, or 1234, and don't use the word *password*."

I glanced around for something basic yet memorable, then tapped it in.

"Your password is *bacon*," he said.

I stared at him in disbelief. "Are you a mind reader?" He couldn't have seen the screen, because I was careful to hold it facing away from his prying eyes. However, if my father did have supernatural powers, it would explain a lot.

"Yes, I am a mind reader. But it's a learned skill." He pointed his finger at my eyes. "I was watching your eyes. Your attention settled on the bacon plate, you raised your eyebrows, then tapped in a five-letter code. I might have guessed plate, which also fits, but *plate* wouldn't have made you lick your lips the way *bacon* did."

"Okay, that's pretty cool. I need to learn how to do that."

"You will."

I set the phone on the counter. "I'll leave the password as *bacon*. Other people won't guess, and it's okay if you have my password." I narrowed my eyes at him. "Should I be upset with you for looking at my phone last night while I was sleeping?"

"It was when you went to the washroom."

"Hmm."

He started clearing away the dishes and said, casually, "We'll go over the crime scene today. Not the photos. The actual crime scene."

"Has it been released? Do you have someone in mind who'll get us access?" My mouth got an unpleasant metallic taste at the idea of revisiting the creepy house.

"I haven't shown you how to pick a lock yet. This will be a good teaching moment."

"No." I crossed my arms. "Absolutely not. We're not breaking into anywhere. Can you imagine the ruckus if we got caught?"

He smiled, because he could imagine the ruckus, and that made it more fun.

"Let's just keep a low profile for a few more days, until the next knitting club meeting. Logan wants me to host again, and pump them for information. That reminds me, I should call Barbara and have her put out the word."

My father told me to go ahead. He got his new laptop out and checked his email while I called Barbara.

We set up the next knitting club meeting, to be held at my house again, and then she gave me an earful about her ex-husband being so difficult.

"That sounds really upsetting," I said after hearing some details. "Exes have a way of passive-aggressively getting under your skin."

"He says he's *concerned* about me," she sniffed. "He says the one thing in common with all my disasters is *me*. Like everything's my fault."

"Sounds familiar. Hey, what's his address? I'll go over and give him something to be concerned about."

To my surprise, she immediately gave me her ex-husband's full name and business address.

Hank Kettner had an insurance company, located in the business strip connected to the grocery store. I tried to tell her I'd only been joking about threatening him, but she'd already hung up, probably to blow her nose and then eat a box of cake mix by the sound of it.

I looked up at my father. "Anything good?"

"That fake film company's website is definitely gone, and they must have used tags to prevent the search engines from caching a copy of the pages, because there's nothing on the internet."

"You know about cached files?"

He sat up straight in his chair. "It's pretty simple, really, just a file called robots.txt that you upload to the root directory with a *noindex*, *nofollow* code." He closed the laptop lid. "Don't be too impressed by your father's hacker skills. The domain name is registered privately, and I don't know how to get past that."

"We could check with Marcy at Misty Microchips. And she might know something about the website, too. Marcy knew Voula Varga. Not well, I think, because they didn't talk to each other at the pub, but Marcy set up a custom email auto-responder for Voula's business."

My father's right eye twitched. "They didn't talk at the pub, yet they knew each other?"

"You think Marcy's somehow involved in the investment scheme? Hmm. She does complain about money issues."

"That meek little woman didn't strike me as the scheming type, but sometimes people surprise you."

"We can pay a visit to Misty Microchips today." I grinned. "My laptop's seen better days."

He leaned back and rubbed his hand lovingly over Lizzy, his teal laptop. "You're jealous. You can't handle me having a newer computer than you."

"Let's go see Marcy, and let's go by Barbara's husband's place. Hank Kettner. He's got an insurance place by the grocery store. We can ask him some bogus questions about insurance for investigators, then try to get a reaction on how he felt about our victim. Before we found Dharma's van at the junkyard, he was actually on my list as a suspect. Voula found some assets that Hank has, so he might have been angry enough to kill her."

"Hiding assets? Sounds like the scheming type."

Scheming? Sure. Hank Kettner could have been Voula Varga's partner in an investment scheme, but then something went sour, and she revealed his secret assets to his ex-wife for the low price of a few hours of fortune-telling mumbo jumbo. He shot her for revenge, or maybe because he had even more secrets. She could have been blackmailing him.

I explained my new theory while we finished clearing up the breakfast dishes. I called my employee to let her know the inventory job was delayed yet again, then we made sure Jeffrey was set with all his kitty supplies—the litter box was still in the back mudroom, where it had been when he'd lived there—and walked out to the car.

The day was bright, thanks to the gleaming white snow. The mountains rose around us in their majestic embrace. It was a beautiful day to chase down leads on our first day as the official paid research consultants to a lawyer.

Or a beautiful day to get ourselves arrested for harassing people.

Either way, it was a beautiful day.

Our first stop was Misty Microchips. We arrived just as Marvin was rolling up the exterior metal screen that covered the window and door overnight. Property crime wasn't a huge threat in town, but the security screens were still necessary for a few shops with the most high-value, easily resold goods.

Marvin had the couple's dog with him. Stanley was on a leash, and gave me a tail wag, but kept back a cautious distance. He was wearing a rainbow-striped dog collar, affixed to a rainbow-striped leash. Both items looked handmade, possibly crocheted.

I called to Stanley, "Here, boy! Don't be scared. We've met before, lots of times, when you came into my store. I gave you a dog biscuit. Remember?"

He gave me a bigger tail wag, so I extended my hand in a balled fist and let him have a sniff before I gave him some shoulder pats.

Stanley's fur was pleasantly soft and curly, the result of being the offspring of a Labrador Retriever and a Standard Poodle. This type of dog, called by the adorable name of Labradoodle, wasn't an official breed, but they were becoming more popular, or so it seemed to me. Stanley leaned in to my pets and offered me his chin for scratching. His fur matched the sandy brown hair of his parents.

"Stanley likes you," Marvin said. I looked up to find him making intense eye contact with me. "He thinks you're a pretty lady."

"Thanks." I tried to keep my disgust at Marvin's flirtations off my face. "Is Marcy coming in today?"

"She's gone to pick up some coffee. The ol' ball and chain loves her lattes. That's four dollars, two or three times a day, but I guess things could be worse."

"That's right," I agreed. "It could be two or three bottles of wine a day."

He winced, looking guilty for an instant, then turned to my father. "How's the new laptop working out, Mr. Day? I hope everything's running smoothly, and you're stopping in to show me how that cane sword of yours works. Is there a button?"

My father smiled. "I'll show you, but not out here on the sidewalk. Sorta defeats the point of concealing a sword if you're flashing it all over the place."

"Let's go inside, then." Marvin tugged Stanley's rainbow-patterned leash, but the dog gave me a pitiful look and didn't move.

Marvin said, "What's the matter, boy? Not enough walking? Why don't you ask beautiful Stormy if she'll take you on a date?" Marvin offered the leash to me. "You could go meet up with Marcy. Hurry and she might even buy you a latte."

I exchanged a look with my father. He gave me the smallest nod, so I agreed to take the Labradoodle for a walk, so my father could go inside to chat about swords and laptops.

"Stanley doesn't like other dogs," Marvin said. "He's not aggressive or anything, but he's easily scared if he doesn't know them."

I took the dog's leash, and a minute later, I was strolling down the sidewalk with Stanley the Socially Awkward Labradoodle.

We'd gone all of a block when we encountered a man walking his dog, also a Labradoodle. The dogs greeted each other with wagging tails and then friendly sniffs. *So much for Marvin's dire warnings*, I thought. But then again, Stanley probably knew this dog from regular walks in the area.

We turned the corner, and were alone again. I reached down and ran my fingers through his delightfully fluffy fur while we walked.

"Stanley, you sexy beast," I said. "I'm totally cheating on my Jeffrey with you. He'd be so jealous. That would serve him right for cheating on me last night, on someone else's lap. Yes, it was cheating! I know my father was sort of his original owner, but it's complicated."

Stanley turned his fluffy head to give me a knowing grin. When he returned his attention to the sidewalk ahead of us, his body language changed, his body getting stiffer and slower with tension.

There was a dark-haired woman with a smaller dog, a Corgi, walking toward us. I stopped and tugged the leash, thinking we could cross to the other side and avoid the strange dog, but Stanley tugged me forward, toward the Corgi. He wasn't scared, he was excited. Not being a dog owner, I hadn't read the signals right.

Stanley and the brown and white Corgi gave each other a good sniff, tails wagging. The dog's owner, a willowy girl with raven-black hair, gave me a suspicious look.

With a voice lacking any sweetness, she asked, "Hey, aren't you that creepy guy's wife?"

"Do you mean Marvin? No. I'm just walking this dog for a friend."

"Whatever. He's gross." She pulled her dog's leash and hauled it away down the street without further explanation.

"She's not wrong," I said to Stanley, who just smiled, pink tongue flopping out.

We continued on our way, stopping to mark a few pristine patches of white snow, then arrived at the coffee shop. Marcy was sitting at a round table outside, smoking a cigarette.

She saw Stanley first. "That dog looks just like…" She looked up and saw my face. "Stormy and Stanley. You two make a cute couple."

Stanley greeted his owner with snowy paws, then tried to climb onto her lap.

"Oof! You're not a lapdog," she said.

I could see there was a lineup inside the cafe, so I took a seat across from Marcy. The metal chair was so cold, it made my sore muscles feel even stiffer, but at least I wasn't as bad as the day before.

"What's going on here?" Marcy asked. "Is this a regular thing, you taking my Stanley-boo-boo on expeditions?" She ruffled the dog's ears. "Stanley, are you cheating on me?"

"I'm the cheater."

She grabbed another cigarette and lit it from the stubby one in her mouth. "Is that so?" she said on the smoky exhale.

"Cheating on my cat, Jeffrey. He's a Russian Blue, not quite a year old. Super energetic."

"My husband is allergic to cats," she said on another smoky exhale. "Did you know that?"

"He hadn't mentioned it."

She offered me the package of cigarettes, out of politeness, and I declined.

"Since when do you smoke?" I asked.

"New Year's resolution," she said. "With all those people quitting, some of us had to start back up to restore the balance."

I laughed at her joke, even though it didn't seem very funny. Marcy had looked healthy and happy just a few days earlier, and now she looked like she'd been washed in a puddle and crammed into a gym bag.

She asked me what I was up to that fine morning, with her dog, and I explained how we were in the market for another laptop, since my father was so happy with his.

"Is that all?" Marcy extinguished her cigarette in a makeshift ashtray, the lid of her takeout coffee. The chemical smell of singed plastic hit my nostrils.

"And I wanted to access your computer expertise for a few minutes, if you don't mind."

"Don't worry, I'm going to shut down that email responder. I've been meaning to get to it. At first it was funny, but now I don't feel right contributing to the mass hysteria." She twirled one finger next to her ear. "This town gets a bit cuckoo over things."

"Shutting it down is probably for the best. But, actually, I was wondering a couple of things. First of all, did you ever do graphic design? Like for websites?"

"No, programming only. I don't have the eye for design. Marvin says even my crafts are hideous. He doesn't like this beautiful leash I made for Stanley." She held up a length of the rainbow rope. "Crochet," she said. "I prefer it over knitting. I'm working on a blanket right now. Marvin hates it. Of course."

"I'm sure it's beautiful," I lied.

"What's the other thing you wanted to know?"

"Oh, just if there was a way to find out who registered a domain name. I tried the basic *whois* searches, but it's a private registration."

She leaned in over the round cafe table and whispered, "There's no such thing as private on the internet. What's the domain name?"

I pulled a notepad from my purse, along with a pen, and jotted down the website address for the disappearing film studio. I could have told her the name, since it wasn't that long, but I had a plan, courtesy of my father's lesson that morning.

"This is just some silly thing involving my ex-fiancé," I said. "He told me about this hot investment thing, but I think he's playing a prank on me."

I handed her the piece of paper. I kept my hands moving in my purse, pretending to be paying attention to that, but my eyes were on Marcy's face as she looked at the paper.

She tilted up her chin and frowned, but no more than any person would when reading a shakily handwritten note.

"You want the company that registered this?" she asked.

"The company, or the person. If it's a guy named Christopher, I won't be surprised."

"Give me a day or two." She tucked the paper into her coat pocket in a gesture so casual that I assumed she'd already forgotten about it. "What's Jessica been up to?"

"Not much. She's got a cold."

"From the Polar Bear Dip." Marcy shook her head. "Silly girl. She just had to get her ten-year pin."

I laughed, and we talked about Jessica for a bit. The line had disappeared inside the shop, so I got a small coffee to drink with Marcy while she had one more cigarette.

It's illegal to smoke on the sidewalk in Misty Falls, thanks to the Oregon Indoor Clean Air Act. Contrary to the *Indoor* part of the name, the act extends to outdoor public spaces. A few people walking by gave Marcy a pointed look, but nobody said anything, because most of the locals adhered to the philosophy of Live and Let Live.

Well, except for the ones who shot people.

CHAPTER 28

BACK AT MISTY MICROCHIPS, I did buy a new laptop, the same model as my father's. Since his was in a teal case, I got mine in red to match the case for my phone. Marvin and Marcy gave me a small discount for paying with my bank card instead of my credit card.

As we walked out of the store, my father patted me on the back. "I'm proud of you for not using credit."

"I wanted the discount."

"Yes, but a lot of people your age wouldn't have the choice, because they don't save up for big purchases."

I used one hand to wave away the undeserved compliment. "I'm just lucky to have had a few jobs that paid well, plus it's easy to save when you're a workaholic."

"Whatever you say." He chuckled at my modesty.

We got into the car, and I started the engine. It came to life with an expensive purr. My father was right about me being responsible with money. The car had been a splurge, but at least I'd bought it outright, no lease, after one test drive. That was my party side, though. My conservative side would probably have me driving the same vehicle until well into the future, when everyone else had flying cars and jetpacks.

As I looked past my father to check the lane before pulling out, he caught my eye and gave me a hopeful look. "Crime scene next?"

"I don't know, Dad. We start with a few unlawful entries, and before you know it, we're pulling stockings over our faces and holding up the Misty Falls Credit Union." I put on the turn signal and drove in the direction of our next lead, knitting club member Barbara's ex-husband.

On the drive, I told him about Marcy's non-reaction to the website. He agreed with my assessment that she hadn't been involved, and we both crossed our fingers that she would find something useful with the domain name.

FINNEGAN DAY HELD his finger to his lips and pressed his ear against the crack in the door. "Someone's worked up about something," he whispered.

We were at Kettner Insurance, the workplace of the eponymous owner Mr. Hank Kettner. I'd never been there before, because I purchased my home, business, and car insurance from a business in a convenient location that didn't look nearly as luxurious as this place.

I pressed my ear to the crack at the other side of the door and ran my fingers over the wood surface. It was a beautiful, dark wood, and not hollow core, or we would have been able to hear what the people inside were arguing about. All I could pick up on was the tone: angry.

My father wasn't doing much better, by the look on his face.

Still trying to listen, I asked in a whisper, "Is a lot of detective work just like this? My heart is racing.

This is so much fun, and we're not even doing anything."

Suddenly, the door began to vibrate. We both stepped back, eyes wide. The vibration was accompanied by a whirring, mechanical sound. The door swung open. A fifty-something, attractive man in an expensive suit came through in a wheelchair.

We stood back to let him by, and then walked into the insurance office. The Kettner Insurance reception area was spare and elegant, with fragrant fresh flowers. A red-faced woman stood behind the reception counter, looking like she was either going to cry or smash the flower vase on the gleaming marble floor.

My father beat me to asking her if she was okay.

As her answer, she brought her palms together in front of herself and said, "I express my anger in appropriate ways." She took a breath and let it out. "Starting now. How may I help you?"

"We don't have an appointment, but who would I need to kiss up to for a few minutes with Mr. Kettner?" My father leaned on the counter in a casual pose. "I bet you're in charge of things around here," he cooed.

"The schedule's pretty tight," she said.

"Speaking of *pretty*, what color would you call your eyes? Would you say they're a teal sort of blue?"

She tittered and started tapping away on a keyboard. "Let me check the schedule again."

While they talked, I perused the framed photos on the wall. The images gave me a sinking feeling. I checked the inscription under one of them, then tapped my father on the shoulder to get his attention.

He and the receptionist were talking about office politics, and how important it was for support staff to be respected. I managed to pull him away, and excused us for a minute.

"You should be taking notes, not stopping me," he said.

"That was Mr. Kettner we saw leaving, in the wheelchair. He couldn't have shot Voula, because it happened on the second floor, and the only access was stairs."

"He could be faking. A wheelchair is a great alibi. You could kill a dozen people, as long as it's always up a flight of stairs."

I rolled my eyes. "Some of those photos are a decade old, and he's in the wheelchair in all of them."

"And isn't it *rather convenient* that dated photos of our suspect in a wheelchair have been left out here for us to see?" He grinned. "I think we need to dig deep on this possible lead. I'll take the receptionist out for lunch, somewhere that serves martinis."

I shook my head, but I was smiling.

"Dad, I have a better idea. Let's drive to the victim's house and look around. Maybe we'll see something outside."

"Or maybe we'll find a window that's been left unlocked."

He turned and thanked the receptionist, then apologized that something had come up and we didn't need an appointment after all.

As we drove up to the victim's house, my father said, "You're right. That house does have a face, and not a nice one."

"At least it's been released. I don't see any crime scene tape."

We pulled up and parked where the victim's hearse had been on my previous visit. A chill ran through me at the memory of that day, then suddenly things got weird. My head was full of stars and my mouth went dry. I mumbled a warning that I was going to throw up, mere seconds before I pushed the car door open and did so on the snow. My butt was still in my seat, thanks to the seatbelt, and my position couldn't have been more awkward if I'd tried.

My father leaned over and patted me on the back. "You'll be okay, sport," he said. "Everybody barfs. I wish I had something more profound to say, but it is what it is. Stormy, everybody barfs."

I'd stopped heaving, so I got out of the car, stepping over the dirty snow.

"Don't tell anyone," I said.

He leaned over the driver's side and peered up at me from inside the car. "Who would I tell?"

"Tony. Or Kyle. Or your other buddies. Just don't tell them I barfed, okay?"

"Not a word," he promised.

I looked up at the leering face of the house and shivered. My stomach lurched, but had nothing to fling around anymore, so it settled down. I found a clean patch of snow and scooped some up to freshen my mouth. The snow worked well enough, and I felt much better already.

My father had gotten out of the car and was examining something on the underside of the handrail on the stairs leading up to the house's porch.

I watched over his shoulder as he tried a few different combinations on the lockbox—a miniature safe that real estate and rental agents commonly use to leave keys for each other.

The lockbox opened. "Hot buttered rum," he exclaimed. "We're in business."

A minute later, I was following him into the house. I didn't ask about the legality of entering this way, and when he gave me the half-dozen codes the local real estate agents commonly use for their lockboxes, I stored them inside a note on my phone, just in case of emergency.

The house was cold inside, the heat on barely enough to keep pipes from freezing.

"What's different from last time?" he asked.

We walked through the lower floor and I described what had been in the rooms before. All the furniture had since been removed. As we went from room to room, I led the way to speed things up. The house hadn't felt homey with the sparse furniture, but now it felt downright menacing.

"I heard from Kyle that they located some distant cousins," my father said.

We stood in the room where the red velvet sofas had been.

"Good," I said. "They took the red sofas?"

"The cousins told the property management company to go ahead and sell off the furnishings to pay for the cleanup bill. From the photos you took, I'd say the rental outfit's still going to lose out. I can't blame them for moving quickly to get it rented. The longer the house sits empty, the more people are going to talk about it being haunted."

I zipped my winter coat all the way up. "There's something truly spooky about the interior of a house being this temperate."

"Absolutely." He rubbed his chin and scanned the room again. "That's odd. This house feels smaller on the inside than it looks from the outside."

"Must be the lack of furniture. I had a friend in the city who did staging. She said the right furniture will make a room look bigger. Of course, they cheated, with special beds that were shorter than normal, so they looked like doubles or queens, but weren't. I tried lying down on one at an open house, just to see for myself, and my toes hung off the end."

"Hustlers and scammers." He shook his head. "Part of me thinks this woman got a taste of what she'd been dishing out. What do you call that again?"

"Karma."

"Right. Karma." He headed toward the staircase and used his cane to steady himself on his way up.

I gave my stomach a moment to settle, then followed him.

The bedroom was empty, devoid of anything resembling a clue, and the bathroom was clean and bare as well. We went into the big room at the end of the hall last. This room spanned the width of the house, and the two windows on its long wall were the ones that formed the *eyes* of the house.

There was something off about the room, but I couldn't put my feeling into words. Perhaps it was the bloodstain on the floor.

We stood on either side of the dark shape, looking down in respectful silence.

My father said, "There's an old saying. It might be from monks, or that Confucius guy. Something about going on a journey of revenge and digging two graves, because one is for yourself."

I crossed my arms and shivered as I looked around the room again. It was empty, except for one tapestry-style rug hanging on one wall. Why had the people who removed the furnishings left the rug? Did it come with the house? Did a ghost tell them to leave it? I shuddered again, then walked back to the doorway to get a better look at the windows.

"Do you notice something odd about this room?" I asked.

He came over to stand with me and see what I was seeing. "An amazing view of the whole town, but I wouldn't call that *odd*."

"What makes the windows look like eyes is that they're symmetrical from the exterior. But from here, that one's in the middle and that one's right at the edge of the room, not symmetrical at all."

He let out a low whistle, then we raced each other to the rug. He beat me, even with the cane, and lifted up the rug to reveal a square-shaped hole in the middle of the wall. We both stuck our heads through the hole, which was the size of the other windows. The home's true exterior wall was set out about five feet, and the gap between was unfinished wood, suitable for storage, but not much else.

"Why would someone do a stupid renovation like this?" he asked.

"It must have been for that movie. Remember when they shot it on location here? They renovated the house to make it match a certain look, the cover of the book the movie was based on, I think."

"This is a lot of wasted space, but I'm guessing the property management company left it this way, because it wasn't worth doing a full renovation for a bit more space."

"Or maybe the old house needed to keep these original walls for stability."

I started to put my leg through the box, but my father stopped me. "Evidence," he said.

"Evidence?" From where I stood, I looked at the door to the room and imagined myself walking in that day. I saw myself kneeling over the body, running out, then coming back.

All that time, when I'd assumed I was alone, and that I was safe because I'd checked all the closets and logical hiding places, someone could have been standing right here.

The killer had been here.

Watching me.

I stepped aside while my father used a compact flashlight to illuminate the space between the home's original wall and the movie-set wall.

"You walk around with a flashlight?" I asked. He wasn't focused on talking, though, so I answered my own question. "Of course you do. Every good sleuth carries a flashlight. You probably have a magnifying glass, too." I adjusted my hold on the rug to let more of the room's light through. "I'm in way over my head, Dad. I should have searched the house better."

He leaned his upper body through the square opening, grunted as he reached for something, then stood up and handed me a button.

"Stormy, you can thank your lucky stars you didn't encounter the owner of this button. If he or she was still on the scene when you arrived, and you'd looked behind this rug, it would have been a double homicide. There was a loaded gun inside the room, and don't take this the wrong way, but you're not exactly physically intimidating." He looked me up and down as he tapped his cane rhythmically on the wood floor. "We need to get you a weapon, and training. What's your ideal weapon for defense?"

"Shooting fireballs from the palms of my hands."

He didn't have a response for that, so he went back to examining the space with his flashlight. I examined the button he'd handed me. It was too small to provide fingerprints. We could turn it over to the police, along with our tip about the hole in the wall, but if they wanted to close the case with Dharma as the killer, new evidence might not do any good.

We talked this over as we examined and photographed the gap, then looked through the rest of the house. We didn't have any plastic bags for preserving the evidence, but I found a receipt for gas in my pocket and folded it into a makeshift envelope.

The button could have gotten into the space by falling out of a storage box, or from anyone who'd accessed the space over the years, including the movers and the crime scene cleanup crew who'd done the best they could with the stain on the floor.

However, there were two things that made us think the button belonged to a killer.

First, it was a genuine mother-of-pearl button—the kind you'd find on an expensive tailored shirt. The gap was a perfect hide-and-seek spot for kids who might have lived in the house over the years, but kids didn't typically wear shirts with mother-of-pearl buttons.

Second, the button hadn't just fallen off a garment. The threads were still intact, and bunched up at the back of the button was the smallest shred of fabric. The button had caught on the jagged wood or one of the exposed nails inside the space, and ripped from the garment. If that had happened to me, I would have noticed, and grabbed the button so it could be sewed back on. A killer, however, might have been too distracted.

We finished looking through the house, locked it up again, then returned the key to the real estate agent's lockbox.

"How long do you think this lockbox has been here?" I asked. "Getting access to the house was almost too easy. Voula would have dealt with the rental agent when she leased the place, right?"

"Good point. I'll call my friend and find out how long this lockbox has been here." He stopped on the porch steps and stared straight ahead, the lines on his face smoothing out.

"What is it? Something click together for you?"

He shook his head. "We live in a beautiful town. Look how it's nestled in the valley like that. Kinda takes your breath away."

I followed his gaze to the center of town, with its handful of tall buildings. Purple-blue mountains stood like stone guardians in the distance. Over the residential areas, trees camouflaged rooftops, and puffs of smoke from wood-burning fireplaces swirled from chimneys, seasoning the air.

"You're right, Dad. Our little piece of heaven."

"Also, I know how to get the killer's name," he said, then he started down the steps and toward the car, whistling happily.

CHAPTER 29

WE WERE PROBABLY on a wild goose chase, but my father wouldn't admit it.

I'd had enough of investigating for the day, and didn't feel well at all. It might have been the throwing up, or the realization I'd nearly gotten myself killed five days earlier.

The idea of a hot bath and a quiet night at home had never been so appealing, but there was no resting yet.

My father led the way toward Sew It Goes, which was just a few doors down from Blue Enchantment, my new favorite place for clothes. In fact, he had to nudge my elbow and remind me of our important mission so I didn't run into Blue Enchantment and buy the whole outfit off the sharply dressed mannequin in the window.

"I don't remember you being much into clothes," he commented as we walked down the street. "That was your sister who used to spend her full allowance on dresses and purses, then hit me up for money to go to the movies. I'd tell her no, of course, so she'd learn her lesson about saving."

I laughed. "She didn't learn, though. I'll tell you a secret. Do you know why I was so good at saving my allowance? Because I'd wait until she was broke, then pay her to do all my chores."

"At rock-bottom rates."

"You knew? She must have told you."

He gave me a smile as we reached the door of Sew It Goes. "Finnegan Day sees everything. I saw the button, didn't I?"

I groaned. "Do you really think you can get us a name from one little button and some threads? We should probably take it straight to the police, so they can enjoy a good laugh."

"Sure, Stormy. You explain to them how we came to be in possession of the button."

"Right."

I glanced around, guiltily expecting Tony Milano to suddenly appear, as though conjured by my thoughts. People were shopping and going about their business on the town's main retail street, but I didn't see Tony. I breathed in deeply through my nostrils. Someone nearby had to be wearing the same cologne as his, because my senses told me he was around.

The glint of winter sun on a glass door closing alerted me to the fact my father had already gone inside Sew It Goes. I looked up and down the sidewalk one more time for Tony, then entered the store.

For the second time that day, I heard a man and a woman arguing. The tiny store wasn't really made for shopping, so there was nobody else inside, except for us and the woman who worked there. She stood behind a long counter fitted with rulers for measuring fabric, jabbing her finger at my father and berating him.

"Finn Day, you make a lot of promises, but you don't follow through," she said angrily. "You're the reason Pam snapped. She wasn't nuts before she met you. People around this town worship and adore you too much to say it to your face, but some of us know it was all your fault!"

She hadn't heard me come in, so I stayed near the entryway and looked around the store. In addition to garment repair and tailoring, Sew It Goes produced a line of custom-made suit shirts. According to the shop's signage, the shirts took four weeks from the time the measurements were gathered. More importantly, their top-of-the-line shirt came with their signature mother-of-pearl buttons.

Maybe this wasn't a wild goose chase after all.

The woman at the counter was still berating my father. He shuffled his cane from one hand to the other, like he was resisting the urge to pull out the hidden sword.

"Easy now, Denise," he said. "Let's not say things we regret. Words can hurt."

"I wish they did," she huffed. "I've got a few more words for you. Liar. Scumbag. Bas—"

Something tinkled to the ground next to me. She stopped talking and stared at me as I scrambled to pick up the clothes hanger I'd just knocked to the floor by accident.

"That's your daughter," Denise said. The fire had left her voice, extinguished by my presence.

"Let me introduce you two," my father said.

"No need." I set the hanger with the sample shirt back on the display stand and walked up to join them at the counter. "We met at the wake for Voula Varga. Dad, I'm not sure if I told you, but I've joined a knitting club, and Denise and her sister Barbara are in it."

"Sounds vaguely familiar," he said, playing along.

Denise nodded, but didn't speak. She held her hand over her mouth the way she had when I'd met her at my house. Her straight black hair was impeccable, cut in a crisp bob that made even more sense now that I knew she was a professional tailor. Her softly rounded cheeks were flushed from yelling at my father, but she looked rested and healthy.

"Denise, you're coming to the next knitting club, right? It's at my house."

"I think so," she said softly, from behind her hand.

I reached into my purse and withdrew the folded-paper envelope containing the button. I tried to hand it to my father, but he used a chin-lift gesture to let me know I'd have better luck than him. He looked embarrassed, perhaps because he'd forgotten that the owner of the store had been good friends with his ex, Pam, and might have a few hard feelings.

Now I understood why Denise had been so uncomfortable around me at the wake. She'd been restraining herself from telling me exactly what she thought of my father. Of course, Denise was angry at the wrong person, but I wasn't about to tell her that. Not when I needed her help.

"Denise, I wonder if you could tell me about this button." I flipped open the makeshift envelope and rolled the gleaming button onto the counter.

"That's nacre," she said as she picked it up. "Nacre is the name for what we call mother-of-pearl. It's so beautiful, considering it's a defense mechanism. It would be funny to imagine the reverse, with mollusks going around wearing humans' discarded Band-Aids as decoration."

"Ew," I said. Denise certainly had a unique way of seeing the world. "Do you sell these buttons? They're the ones you use on your custom men's shirts, right?"

She squinted at the button between her fingers.

"Careful," I said. "Don't pull that bit of torn fabric off the back." She gave me a quizzical look. "Sentimental reasons," I explained.

"Just a minute." She turned and walked deeper into the store, past two industrial sewing tables.

My father said, softly so that Denise wouldn't overhear, "We need a list of customers who bought custom shirts in that color."

"Hold your horses," I hissed. "Let me get there. We have to ask people nicely for things. We don't have warrants, remember?"

"Just because I forgot ol' Denise was friends with Pam doesn't mean I'm losing my marbles."

"Denise is *not* fond of you. Maybe you should go wait in the car."

He looked like he was going to argue with me, then he admitted it was a good idea, and left.

Denise returned with an armload of fabric and set it on the counter between us. She glanced at the space where my father had been, then at me. It was the first time she'd ever made direct eye contact with me, and I was surprised to find her eyes were different colors, one green and one blue.

"This is the same fabric, and here are the same buttons," she said. The folded ream of fabric on the counter was sandy beige with a bit of a sheen— brushed cotton, if I knew my fabrics. "When do you need your shirt by?"

"My shirt?" So, this investigation was going to cost me a custom-made shirt, which wasn't cheap. I could see how quickly incidentals might add up, buying things here and there to curry favor. "Oh, the standard four weeks is fine."

"And is it for you or for a gentleman friend? I'll need to get some measurements, either way."

"Do women get those shirts for themselves?"

Denise looked at me like I was being strange, and I suppose I was. "We sell about ten for men to every one we make for women. Personally, I prefer the women's shirts, with all the fitted darts and everything being a smaller scale. We should probably charge more, because of the extra labor, but I don't mind the challenge. I wouldn't want life to get too simple." She pulled open a drawer and retrieved a well-worn cloth measuring tape. "Well?"

"Right." I started taking off my jacket. She nodded for me to follow her around behind the counter and into the back, out of sight from the front window.

She took my measurements, her touch feather-light on my arms, and her voice lullaby-soft. Denise was certainly a woman of contrasts, with her sharp black hair and her soft body and gestures. If I hadn't seen her yelling at my father, I'd never have believed it.

Would Denise have had any issues with Voula?

I could think of one possible problem: if Voula really was a psychic, as the knitting club ladies believed, why hadn't she warned Denise about something her friend Pam was about to do? *That's pretty far-fetched*, I told myself, but once the theory came to me, it wouldn't shake loose, so I had to ask about her alibi.

"How are your New Year's resolutions coming along?" I asked.

"Great," she said brightly. "Hold this."

I held the end of the measuring tape in place at the top of my arm. "You were at the Fox and Hound for the big New Year's Eve party, weren't you? I think I saw you there, with Voula."

"Yes." She measured the length of my right arm, and then repeated the process on my left arm. I was impressed. Most tailors would assume both of a person's arms were the same length.

Then she measured my right arm a second time.

"I don't think it grew," I said.

She sniffed and wiped a tear from her eye.

"Denise, are you okay? Would you like me to come back at a better time?"

"I'm just thinking about poor Voula. She kept asking if either I or Barbara would go to the Polar Bear Dip with her the next morning, but we said no, because we were driving to the city to see Barbara's daughter and her family that day." She pulled a cloth handkerchief from her pocket and dabbed her tears. "We should have invited her to come with us. She'd still be alive if we'd made more of an effort to include her. I tried to be nice, but she was just so…"

"Weird?"

"Bitter," she finished. "Like having all those amazing roles in major movies wasn't enough for her. She had an amazing career."

"You don't think she was a bit typecast? She only played those small parts, for gypsy fortune-tellers and witches."

Denise blinked her tears away and looked straight at me with her unusual eyes.

"I was one of those girls who went to Hollywood with dreams of being discovered," Denise said. "They said I was born a few decades too late. On black and white film, my eyes are the same shade of gray, but in living color, these are just too distracting for an actress in a supporting role. Nowadays, there are contact lenses, and I hear they can fix colors with the computers, but I was born a few decades too early for that."

"I'm sorry it didn't work out for you in Hollywood."

She tucked away her handkerchief and smiled. "Meeting Voula made me happy. Her bitterness made me glad my prayers weren't answered."

She went back to the measurements, and I mulled over what she'd said. Voula must have given up on going to the Polar Bear Dip when she invited me to come to her house on New Year's Day. And assuming Denise was telling the truth, both she and her sister had an alibi for the time of the murder.

My thoughts returned to the button, and the job I was supposed to be doing. If I went back to the car empty-handed, my father would probably insist on trying by himself, and it could go even worse than his first attempt.

"Denise, you must keep a database of all the customers you do custom shirts for, right?"

She let out a light laugh, sounding relieved after her moment of sadness. "Database? Yes, you could call it that. Here, watch me enter your measurements into my *database*."

She grabbed a paper ledger book, flipped it open, and handwrote my name and measurements onto a new line. Denise had only paper records, by the look of it, which explained the lack of computers on the premises.

"Your computer is so fancy it looks like a book," I joked.

"Marvin at the computer store is trying to get me into this century, but I have enough problems with the hand-me-down computer I keep at home for watching movies."

The ambient sound inside the store changed, from that of a cave to a tunnel, and a gust of cool air made me reach for my jacket.

"Please excuse me," Denise said. "A customer's just coming in to pick up their order." She went to a nearby shelf, pulled off a stack of garments in a baby-blue color, and walked toward the counter.

"Do you mind if I use your washroom?" I asked.

"Not at all. It's to your left."

I thanked her, waited until she was busy talking to her customer, then took the ledger book with me into the washroom.

My pulse was racing as I shut the door behind me and opened the book. I didn't like lying to Denise, but I didn't want to disappoint my father. If she suspected I wanted the list of customers for him to use, nobody would be getting it without a warrant.

Denise's system for special orders seemed logical enough, but her handwriting was tense and compact, impossible to skim quickly. I used the camera on my phone to snap images of the pages, starting with today's order and my name, then working my way back. The ledger had been started in October, so it only had a few months' worth of transactions, but this information was better than nothing.

While I hurried to finish taking the photos before the store owner got suspicious, my eye was caught by one name in particular.

I flushed the toilet and ran the sink water for cover, then left Sew It Goes without incident. I jog-walked down the street quickly, eager to tell my father he was right, and we *did* have a name.

CHAPTER 30

MY FATHER WASN'T waiting in the car for me, which made sense, given that I'd locked it and he didn't have the keys. Most people in town didn't lock their cars, but it was a big-city habit I hadn't shaken yet.

I looked around, trying to put myself in his shoes. If I was Finnegan Day, where would I go?

Lunch! We hadn't eaten since breakfast. I scanned the nearby businesses, then settled on the bagel place. My stomach told me that was where he'd gone. Or maybe my stomach just wanted to go have a bagel. We do see what we want to see, after all.

I crossed the street, checked my reflection in Ruby's mirror, gave her a wave in case she was watching from the other side, then proceeded to the bagel place.

My father was inside, sharing a table with two police officers in uniform, Tony Milano and Kyle Dempsey.

I turned on my heel and walked right out again. I slipped my hand into my pocket and felt to make sure I had the button. I'd gotten it back on my way out of Sew It Goes, and Denise had thoughtfully transferred the button and fabric swatch into a tiny self-sealing plastic baggie.

"Guilty conscience?" came a male voice behind me.

I sped up.

Sounding closer, he said, "Stormy Day, what's the hurry?"

I stopped and turned to face my pursuer. It was Kyle, looking almost serious that day.

"Don't let me interrupt your lunch," I said.

"Too late. Would you check my teeth for poppy seeds?"

He was already grinning in anticipation, so I checked his teeth and gave him the all clear, then started walking away again.

He followed, falling in step at my side. "Nice day for a walk. Where are we going?"

I didn't answer, hoping he'd give up. I'd last seen Kyle the day he'd returned my travel mugs, then searched my home for a murder suspect. There was definitely some irony to the fact that I'd been annoyed at him for suspecting me, yet now I was *actually* hiding crime scene evidence, as well as the location of their fugitive.

Oops. I did have a guilty conscience, which was why I'd run out of the bagel shop.

I had to act fun and casual, not guilty. I wouldn't want Dimples to frisk me for purloined evidence, after all.

Or did I?

No!

No, I did not want to be frisked. *Not right here in the center of town, anyway.*

He asked again where I was headed, making it clear he wasn't leaving my side.

I slowed my pace and pointed ahead. "Just going up to Central Park."

"But that's an off-leash dog park," he said.

"Exactly. All the better to kidnap small dogs and hold them for ransom." I playfully held my hand over my mouth. "Oh, rats. I forgot you're a cop."

"I'd better come along and keep an eye on you."

"Officer, I don't really capture the dogs for ransom. That was just a joke. I just keep them in my house and dress them in doll clothes for high tea. I *never* give the doggies back."

Kyle narrowed his aquamarine-blue eyes at me. "Stormy Day, you are definitely up to no good."

"Tony Baloney calls you Dimples behind your back."

"You keep trying to evade me. Whatever you're hiding, it must be juicy."

We arrived at the fenced-in park, where an assortment of dogs frolicked in the snow like it was a white sandy beach, and today was everybody's birthday.

Kyle and I turned to the right, taking the path that led around the perimeter.

The official name of the park is something boring, like Pine Park or Cedar Grove, but everyone in Misty Falls calls it Central Park, after the much, much, much larger and grander park in New York. At my gift shop, we sell collectibles that celebrate local landmarks, including mugs and refrigerator magnets that read, *Get your bark on at Central Bark, Misty Falls, Oregon.* The word *Park* is intentionally spelled *Bark*, I think.

We kept walking, and Kyle didn't say why he'd run out of the bagel place after me, and I didn't ask.

"What about that one?" I asked, pointing to a large dog with black, brown, and white markings.

"The Bernese Mountain Dog? Not a great candidate for your dognapping spree, on account of the size."

I nodded in agreement. "None of my little doll clothes would fit. Plus he'd slurp all the tea in one lick. I'm looking for more of a toy size."

"You've put a lot of thought into this. That's the problem with most criminal masterminds these days. Too much criminal, not enough mastermind."

"Really? Bored with the job already? Does that mean you apprehended that sweet little old lady and locked her away for good?"

"No, we haven't found her yet, but we will." He gave me a dimpled grin. "The streets will be safe once more, I promise."

"You should have checked my laundry room when you were ransacking my house. I keep all my fugitives down there."

He chuckled. "I bet you do."

"Next to my spare rolls of paper towel."

We neared a woman with a small, brown-velvet-eared Beagle, plus an even smaller, juvenile Beagle that made me squeal. With the owner's permission, we both knelt down to pet the pooches, who wore matching sweater vests.

Kyle's voice changed when he talked to the dogs. He kept saying, "Puppy, puppy, puppy," in the excited way a little kid would.

The dog's owner eyed Kyle, then me, and back and forth over and over, trying to figure out our relationship. Her visible confusion made me painfully aware of the age difference between me and Kyle. She thought I was a cradle-robber!

"Puppy, puppy!" Kyle said.

Then, just when I thought it couldn't get any worse, the dog owner gave me a sly wink, as if to congratulate me. My cheeks flushed hot with embarrassment, and I avoided looking at Kyle's beautiful aquamarine eyes as we continued our walk.

"How's your father's hip?" he asked.

"Not slowing him down too much."

"How about you?"

"My old lady hips are just fine, thank you. I took a solid fall the other day, just to test everything."

He reached across my back and squeezed my shoulder in a gesture halfway between romantic and buddy-buddy.

"You've still got a few good years left," he said. "When are we going to get that drink together?"

"Um…"

He jumped ahead and blocked my path. "Stormy, look me in the eyes. Just for a minute. I want to see something."

I scanned Central Park for a distraction, but found nothing I could use as an excuse. Finally, I looked up into Kyle's blue eyes. I opened my eyes extra-wide, like you do at the beginning of a staring contest to intimidate your opponent.

After a moment of silent staring, he said, "Just as I suspected," then he turned and continued walking.

I skipped to catch up with him. "What was that about?"

"I can't look into your eyes without wanting to kiss you." He gave me a sidelong look. "That's all."

"Your interest has been noted."

"And?"

I nodded toward a miniature dachshund. "Steal that dog for me. I must have it."

He laughed, and let me change the topic back to my dognapping story, to my relief.

Kyle was handsome, and so sweet, but whenever I looked at him… *puppy, puppy, puppy!*

He was such a young pup.

KYLE WALKED ME BACK to the bagel place, where we found my father and Tony standing outside, chatting.

I noted the expressions on their faces when they saw me and Kyle walking up together. My father seemed amused, a crooked smile on his lips, and Tony just looked annoyed. He donned a pair of mirrored sunglasses, which only drew my attention to his flared nostrils and pressed-thin lips.

My father handed me a paper bag. "Smoked meat, extra Dijon." He gave me an eyebrow raise. "Was your errand successful?"

I answered guiltily, "We just went for a walk in Central Park. Saw some dogs. There was a cute puppy. Tiny. Just a baby, really. Way too young for me."

He raised his eyebrows higher. "I meant your other errand."

Right. The list of names from Sew It Goes.

"All done."

We said goodbye to the two police officers, then headed back toward the car.

Once we were alone on the sidewalk, I told him about the conversation I'd had with Denise while she was measuring me up for a custom-tailored blouse.

We got into the car, where I showed him the photos I'd taken of the customer receipt book.

"Lots of names in here," he said.

"But there's only one who ordered a shirt in the same tan color as mine. John Lake. That's Dharma's husband. We've been assuming he knows nothing about the shooting because he's the one who reported his wife missing a few days ago, but what if he's playing everyone?"

"He wasn't at the Christmas dinner at the mansion, though. Or was he?" He reached for his phone. "Erica would know."

I looked up the address for Dharma's husband while my father called the maid from the Koenig Mansion. He flirted for a few minutes, then asked about Mr. Lake.

"Interesting," he said, then went on to ask Erica about her home security measures. This went on for a while.

He ended the call and turned to me. "Mr. Lake wasn't feeling well that night, but Erica says he always comes down with something right before mansion events. It's been so long since she's seen him, she's forgotten what he looks like." He put on his seatbelt. "Let's go pay Mr. Lake a visit."

"Not so fast. We should check in with our employer and tell him what we've found so far. I don't even know if John Lake knows his wife is staying at my house. We don't want to blow her cover."

My father groaned with impatience, but waved his hand for me to go ahead. Rather than drop in unexpected, I called first.

A woman answered, "Logan Sanderson's office. How may I help you?"

"I need to speak with Logan, please. This is Stormy Day."

"Mr. Sanderson is not available, Ms. Day. I'll let him know you called. What shall I put on the subject line?"

"Hot water."

"And? Is this regarding a specific case?"

"Nope," I lied.

She repeated back my number and ended the call.

I explained to my father that Logan had his cell phone forwarded to either his office or an answering service. Then I verbally debated our next move, and whether we should visit the house, or wait to hear from Logan, or turn ourselves and the button in to the police, or any number of possible choices.

"It's a setup," my father said excitedly.

"Were you even listening to me?"

"John Lake set up his wife for murder, so he could get rid of her. I don't know the man, but let's say he married Dharma thinking he'd get his hands on her uncle's fortune, but recently he's given up on trying to ingratiate himself with the in-laws and he just wants out."

"Wouldn't divorce be easier?"

My father gave me a one-shoulder shrug. "Sometimes you ask a woman to leave, and she won't go. Let's go pay him a visit and take his temperature, so to speak."

I checked the address and started the car. "I've got a bad feeling about this."

"Eat your smoked meat sandwich." He picked up the paper bag and shook it at me.

"I don't eat in the car," I said as I pulled out onto the street. "Don't look at me like that. It messes up the interior, and it's a dirty habit, plus it's bad for digestion."

He opened the bag and rolled half of it back to expose the sloppy smoked meat trying to escape its poppy-seed bagel, then set the thing on the dashboard in front of me.

"Don't be fussy, Stormy. Detectives eat in their car. Eat, sleep, conduct meetings, you name it. I knew this tough old bird who gave birth to her son in her car, on stakeout. She cut the cord with her pocket knife, tucked the little guy into her shirt, he latched right on, and she went back to surveillance."

I rolled my eyes at his tall tale, but the sandwich did smell good. I reluctantly grabbed it and munched away while we drove to the Lake residence.

WE STOOD ON the porch of the Lakes' house. It was a small blue rancher, much like the other houses along the street. We'd prepared a cover story, but I had to fight the urge to giggle nervously while waiting for Mr. Lake to open the door.

Sometimes when I'm overwhelmed, I start to giggle like a maniac. The more I try to control myself, the funnier it gets.

As soon as John Lake opened the door, my urge to giggle dissipated.

He looked to be about my father's age, but with a sickly pale face and sweat glistening on his brow. He nodded along while my father gave him the spiel about how we were considering buying a house up the street and wanted to know what the neighborhood was like.

He mumbled one-word answers to our questions about schools and safety. When we got to the part where I was supposed to ask if I could use his washroom, my father gave me the signal, and I said,

"Thanks for the information. Maybe we'll see you around. Goodbye!"

He grunted an acknowledgment, shuffled back into his home, and closed the door.

My father gave me a stern look.

"What? It's not him," I said.

"I know you're thinking that old fart couldn't be the one, but trust me on this one. Guilt can look a lot like grief, and people who lie about one thing can lie about another."

"That poor man. He's probably devastated, with his wife missing and suspected of murder."

"Stormy, I never told you this job was easy."

"No, you didn't." I knocked on the door. "Let's try again."

I put on my sweetest smile, waiting for John Lake to return.

He didn't, so I knocked again, louder this time.

We waited another minute, and I started to get annoyed, because I hadn't used the washroom at Sew It Goes, and I'd had a lot of coffee that morning, and I really did need the facilities.

My father walked to the edge of the step and leaned over to look in the man's front room window. "I think he's passed out on the floor," he reported back. "Did you smell alcohol on his breath?"

"No, but he had a medical alert bracelet." I joined my father in peering through the window. We couldn't see much—just legs on the floor, extending from behind an interior wall. "Did he seem confused to you? He was pale and sweaty. Diabetic?"

"I saw a tremble in his hands. He's either passed out, or gone into a hypoglycemic coma. A married man like him probably counts on his wife to let him know when his blood sugar's getting low. She's not around, so he doesn't know how to look after himself."

I had my phone in my hands. "Ambulance?"

He shook his head. "We'll break the door down." He hobbled over to the edge of the step to get a good run at it, with his cane and everything.

"Let's try the handle first." I easily opened the unlocked door before Finnegan Day, the one-man battering ram, could throw himself through it.

JOHN LAKE WAS diabetic after all, and had slipped into shock. It was a good thing we'd been there. The paramedics gave him a glucagon injection and revived him. He said he was feeling better, but they insisted on bringing him down to the hospital anyway.

The paramedics kept congratulating us for being there, and thinking fast, but I only felt worse with every bit of praise.

It was my fault Mr. Lake was in such bad shape. Not my fault, exactly, but because of me. If I hadn't gone to the junkyard and tipped the police off about the van, they wouldn't have made her a suspect. The couple would be having lunch together right now, if not for my meddling.

My stomach pushed acid up, giving me pain in my chest. I surreptitiously raided the Lakes' medicine cabinet for some antacid. My heartburn was either from stress, or gobbling down a smoked meat sandwich while driving. Either way, it was a message from my body that this investigation stuff had consequences.

As they loaded Mr. Lake into the ambulance, the older paramedic joked around with my father, who knew most of the local first responders. The two

ANGELA PEPPER

were on such good terms that the paramedic didn't even question why we'd been there, or why we were volunteering to stay behind in the house to make sure all the appliances were safely turned off.

I watched the ambulance drive away, and silently promised Mr. Lake I would do what I could to get his wife home. Unless he was missing a mother-of-pearl button from a tan shirt.

Left alone in the home, my father and I got to work quickly. Well, I used the washroom, and then we got to work.

"You're not allowed to impersonate a police officer," I told him. "It's part of the rules for investigators. If people don't know you're retired now, and you don't tell them you are, that might get us in trouble."

My father led the way to the master bedroom and opened the closet. "Someone's been thinking about her research. Does that mean you've decided?"

"I don't know. At the moment, I'm kind of focused on finding a tan shirt with mother-of-pearl buttons."

"Like this?" He pulled the shirt from the closet.

Despite the gravity of the situation, seeing the shirt we'd been looking for made me happy. I jumped up and down, clapping my hands like I'd just won the first round on a game show called *Find the Killer's Shirt and Win Huge Prizes*.

We both inspected the shirt and let out a shared groan of disappointment at the result. This custom-tailored tan shirt still had all of its buttons, and the fabric underneath was in pristine condition. If a button had been ripped off this shirt, a genie had magically repaired the tear.

We searched through the closet thoroughly, then checked the clothes hamper, plus the washer and dryer. From the look of it, Mr. Lake hadn't done laundry since his wife's disappearance. We found several custom-made shirts from Sew It Goes, but none with missing buttons, let alone missing buttons ripped from tan fabric.

Since we were in the house already, we took a look around. We found several days' worth of unwashed dishes, but nothing suspicious, and nothing that would lead us to believe Mr. Lake was anything other than a man who was terribly lost without his wife.

And what a wife she was.

From the framed photos on the walls, to the inspirational signs and decorative angels placed throughout the home, Dharma was clearly someone who believed in kindness, goodness, and karma.

My heart sank low at the idea of her being carted off to jail, her husband devastated and alone. My father might have been feeling the same way, because he didn't have much to say, not even one of his wisecracks.

We turned off all the lights and left the house.

Back in the car, we both checked our phones. In all the excitement, I'd forgotten about the message I'd left for Logan with his secretary.

He'd sent me a text message: *Urgent. Please meet me at the house to discuss the hot water tank.*

I showed my father the message, and we drove to my house in silence.

Something bad was going down. I could taste it.

CHAPTER 31

Parking in my driveway and then walking to my tenant's side instead of my own felt familiar yet unsettling, like brushing your teeth with your non-dominant hand.

Logan opened his door and waved both of us in without a word. His place was dark for the daytime, all the curtains presumably pulled shut for privacy.

"You've met my father, Finnegan Day. He's working with me on the case," I said. "He's retired now, but as you know, he's worked in law enforcement since before I was born. Definitely an asset to the team."

My father shook Logan's hand. "Sorry to be seeing you again under these circumstances."

Logan nodded. "It's always darkest before the dawn."

"Don't I know it."

A woman sniffed.

We all turned toward the woman sitting on Logan's sofa with a box of tissues next to her. Dharma Lake appeared small and frail, a shadow of the energetic woman I'd seen at the Fox and Hound. The auburn dye in her hair didn't suit her at all, and made her look even more haggard.

"Thank you for saving John's life," she said. "He called from the hospital as soon as he got there."

My father and I exchanged a look. Her husband knew where she was, and he was still in a sorry state.

We joined her in Logan's living room, which was arranged in the mirror image of mine. The familiarity only added to the strangeness of the situation.

Logan dragged over a chair from his kitchen table so he could sit across from me and Dharma.

"Your husband knows you're here?" I asked Dharma.

"He's known for a few days. I've been using the special phone your boyfriend got for me. He's such a clever—"

"Logan's not my boyfriend," I said quickly.

She looked even more lost, like she was about to slip into a catatonic state.

I reached out and placed my hand on hers. "Sorry, please keep going. I hope your husband's feeling better now. He seems like a very nice man."

She forced a smile. "You've got passion, dear. You give me hope for the future."

Logan interrupted to ask me, "What were you two doing at the Lakes' residence, anyway?"

I scratched the top of my head and gave Logan a look that said we probably shouldn't say everything in front of his client.

Dharma picked up on my body language and excused herself to use the washroom.

With her out of the room, my father and I explained the events of our day, from asking Marcy to trace the domain name, our brief visit to Kettner Insurance, then the search of Voula's house and subsequent discovery of the hidden space as well as the button, the research into the custom shirts, and finally, the call we paid to the Lake residence.

"That's very thorough," Logan said. "I wish all your hard work wasn't wasted."

"We've got more leads," I said.

"But I called you here to tell you it's over."

"Over?"

Dharma returned to the room, taking small steps. "It's all over," she said. "I'm sorry I've put everyone through all this fuss for nothing."

"Not for nothing," I said. "Just give us a few more days. We're looking into this ghost of a movie producer, and we have other leads."

Dharma shook her head. Her voice weak and trembling, like her spirit had been broken, she said, "There's no need for anyone to waste their time or money. I'm turning myself in."

She sat next to me, then squeezed my hand, like I was the one who needed comfort. "Everything will work out," she said.

My father said, "We'll have you out on bail in no time, I'm sure."

She withdrew her hand from mine and looked down at the floor, avoiding my eyes.

"No bail," she said.

"I'm sure your uncle would help," I said.

"There's no need," she replied, her voice barely louder than a whisper. "I need to pay for what I did."

My mouth went dry, and my words came out hoarse. "What did you do?"

She flicked her gaze up to mine. "Isn't it obvious? I shot her. I shot her to death."

CHAPTER 32

LOGAN DROVE DHARMA to the police station to turn herself in, while my father and I drove back to his house. We were both in shock, and possibly denial.

"But she didn't do it," he said, yet again.

"She says she did."

"I've seen people confess to crimes they didn't commit. The public wants to believe every confession must be true, but it isn't. Being accused is such a nightmare for the suspect, a nightmare they desperately want to wake up from. Some of them see confessing as the only exit from the nightmare."

"Would they convict her based on her confession? She'll come to her senses before the trial, won't she?"

"I don't know. Did you see how weak she was? She might not make it to trial."

"Don't say that."

He reached over and fiddled with the volume for the radio. The DJ was talking about donuts, and even though I didn't usually have any feelings about that particular radio announcer, his voice was suddenly the most irritating thing on the planet and I wanted to punch him in the mouth.

We drove in silence while I tried to settle my anger.

Before turning herself in, Dharma had told us everything she could remember.

She remembered driving her van to Voula's house that morning, and how they'd had tea, then her memory got fuzzy. She did remember the feeling of the kick of the pistol in her hands, and how the shots were louder than she'd expected, even with thick earplugs in her ears. Then she was staring at Voula's body on the floor, blood pooled around her. She picked up the little doll from the floor, and then… nothing else. Her memory was a blank until after the vehicle accident, when she had some flashes of memory with an older female police officer draping a blanket over her shoulders.

I slammed on the brakes, checked over my shoulder, and made a U-turn.

"Dad, Dharma said *shots*. She said the *shots* hurt her ears, but Voula was only shot once."

"You're right. Just one wound, and the shooter didn't miss. There were no other bullet holes found in the room, but then again, the crack CSI team didn't locate the hidden room, so we can't say they're infallible."

"Dharma probably did fire the pistol, which was how the gunshot residue got onto her steering wheel, but what if it was at something else?"

"Or *someone* else. She grabbed the gun from the killer and ran him off!"

"The killer would have left on foot, because I only saw the van on the road. And the only other person I saw was a girl walking her dog. Does that seem suspicious to you? There's not another house around for miles."

"Lots of folks walk their dogs through there." He pointed through the windshield, at the hill the house sat atop. "There's a trail from town that leads right through there. It cuts across the property, which actually extends down the back of the hill in a wide swath, well into part of the forest. The kids ride their dirt bikes around there in the summer, and I remember we had a problem a few years back when the rental company put up fences and the kids kept taking them down."

He filled me in on the property and surrounding area, and we went over our game plan to search the house for other bullet holes to support our new theory. He explained how the holes were smaller than a layperson would expect, easily hidden in a ceiling of rough plaster if you didn't look inch by inch.

We pulled onto the road leading to the scary-faced house for the second time that day. The drive along the access road took us three minutes at moderate speed. I'd gotten run off the road at the midpoint, which meant... I got to use the algebra formula for two trains leaving two cities at different speeds, racing toward each other. Somewhere, a math teacher was smiling. We concluded that our mystery person could have gotten away in a vehicle unseen by me, if they'd had a one-and-a-half-minute lead on Dharma.

We parked in front of the house, got out, and paused to look down at the town again. Dusk had descended already, well before suppertime, as it does in a mountain valley in winter. Street lamps blinked on and shone like pearl garlands decorating the town.

My father said, "Before the sun goes down completely, we should check around the exterior. Who knows, we might get lucky and find a body under the snow."

"You call that *lucky*? I don't consider finding a body under the snow to be all that fortunate."

His jaw moved, but Finnegan Day was actually at a loss for words. I'd gotten him with that one.

We trekked around the house, to the back area, which wasn't so much a yard, but a giant snowy field that sloped down toward the forest edge.

"They planned to subdivide this land," my father explained. "They cleared the trees, but then the developer built that house in the prime location and decided he didn't want any neighbors after all. The land's changed hands a few times over the years, but I'm guessing we won't have houses back here for a while. Nobody wants to look out of their windows at a murder house. Kinda ruins your appetite."

"Is that how you feel about the house next door to yours?"

He didn't answer, so I let the topic drop.

We kept walking. I scanned the snowy field for human-sized lumps, but found none. I did, however, see something interesting at the edge of the forest—the horizontal line of a fallen tree, with a red Coca-Cola can resting on the sideways trunk.

"Dad!" I ran toward the can and leaned down to inspect it. "Bullet hole! Right through the letter O."

He was slower than me, using his cane to keep himself steady, and huffing from the exercise. By the time he reached the area, I'd used my boots and bare hands to clear away the snow underneath the horizontal log. I'd found a dozen soda cans, all empty, but only three with bullet holes.

"We found our second victim," he said as he stuck his pinkie finger into an indentation in the nearest standing tree.

"Arboricide," I said with a chuckle. "Get it? We're looking for an arborist with lousy aim."

He struggled to not roll his eyes at my pun.

"These cans haven't been outside for long," he said. "Careful not to touch that one on the log. They might be able to pull some prints. Maybe."

He looked over his shoulder at the house, which seemed to be watching us, even though the eye-shaped windows were on the other side.

"Really? You think we'll get fingerprints?"

"The little button was too small to pull prints, but this is different. We're going to have to call it in."

"Sounds like a plan. You can make the call." I used my phone to take photos of the can and the target practice area, using the flash.

We started the walk back up the slope, slower than the speed we'd come down.

"I should send the photos of the cans to Logan," I said. "He can show his client and hopefully give her an alternate explanation for her memory of shooting the gun."

In a harsh tone, he said, "Don't get your hopes up."

I stopped walking and waited for him to catch up. Even in the dark, I could see the look on his face was pure misery.

"Are you feeling okay? How's the hip?"

He scowled. "I don't want to talk about it."

"You're doing great, though. Your walking is much better."

"How would you know?" he snapped. "You're always three paces ahead of me, dragging me all over hell's half-acre, without so much as a glance over your shoulder."

I bit my tongue, waited for him to catch up with me, and then walked beside him, consciously slowing my pace.

"Tell me to slow down if I'm walking too fast," I said gently. "I'm not a mind reader. You haven't taught me that yet, remember?"

"I could fill Gene's junkyard with all the things I haven't taught you."

I mouthed the word *okay*, but didn't say it. Everyone has their limits, and it had been a long day for both of us. The sun had slipped behind the mountains, and the sky was dark and cold.

I pulled out my phone again. The light from the screen obliterated my night vision, but I used it anyway, relying on my father to keep us heading in the right direction.

I'd finished exchanging a few messages with Logan by the time we got back to the house.

"Logan's still at the police station with Dharma, where she's giving her statement," I reported.

"You sent the photos?"

"Yes, and he told them all about the cans with the bullet holes. He said it was an anonymous tip, so they won't know it was us." The sound of a vehicle somewhere in the distance gave me a jolt of adrenaline. "Unless they come here right now and find us on the scene. I guess we'd better skedaddle."

"To the Batmobile," he said with a gritty forced cheerfulness.

We got into the car, and I started driving right away without letting it warm up.

In the dark, I could feel the bad mood radiating from him. I knew I should just let him be with his thoughts, but I couldn't help myself.

"Hey, how did lunch with Tony go?" I asked casually. "Did you two talk about the case?"

"I wish."

"Yeah?"

"Diaper stories," he said.

"Tony was telling you diaper stories? I really missed out."

"You haven't missed out on anything. Don't compare yourself to some impossible standard. Not everyone's cut out for marriage and raising kids."

I stared straight ahead. I'd meant that I'd missed out on the lunch conversation with Tony, not that I'd missed my chance at starting a family.

Had he given up? I hadn't felt hopeless until now, hearing my own father imply it wasn't going to happen for me. Instead of saying I wasn't at all worried about the bleakness of being single and thirty-three and one cat closer to spinsterhood, I busied myself with the car's many heater settings.

On the main road, we passed what I thought was the crime scene investigation van, but it was unmarked, so there was no way to know for sure.

My father warmed up along with the car interior, and started explaining what he knew about fingerprints. If the aluminum can had been outside since New Year's Day, it had been exposed to the sun and other elements for about four days. For fingerprinting, this meant finding the clear ridge detail necessary for a positive identification was unlikely, but not impossible.

It would be simple enough to match the bullet lodged in the tree to the one that had ended Voula Varga's life, though, so that was something.

I told him I was crossing my fingers they'd find Dharma's fingerprints on the cola can, or maybe even fingerprints from another party.

For the second time that evening, my father told me not to get my hopes up.

I attributed his bad mood to pain from his hip, because it wasn't like him to be so negative. He sounded resigned to the idea of Dharma going off to jail, even though it probably meant a death sentence for her husband.

That wasn't acceptable to me, though.

My father didn't raise me or my sister to be quitters.

I would hold on to my optimism, because I remembered what he'd said so many times, whenever I'd been down.

Never lose hope in your quest for the truth, because even a little hope can light the way.

CHAPTER 33

AT THE END of a very long day, I dropped my father off at his house and picked up Jeffrey in exchange.

In the car ride back to my place, Jeffrey sang me the songs of his people. I asked him if he took requests, and if he knew "Free Bird."

He did not.

All was forgiven when we got home and Jeffrey got his favorite dinner.

I kept the curtains open a crack and watched the window for Logan returning from the police station, but he still wasn't back by the time I went to bed.

January 6th

In the morning, I called my father three times before he finally picked up.

"You could have left a voicemail," he grumbled.

"Sorry. Were you in the shower?"

"No."

"Well, I don't know about you, but my back is killing me." I rubbed my sore hip while I slowly stretched from side to side. "I fell on my butt and got a bruise, but you had major surgery. I feel like I'm broken, Dad, so I can't imagine how rough your pain must be."

"It's a little better today," he said, his tone softer.

"Do you feel up to some investigating? We can look over the customer names from Sew It Goes. I have a new idea. We can cross-reference customers with photos from the Polar Bear Dip that day. It was on the opposite side of town, so whoever was at the dip would have a good alibi."

"Don't bother. I talked to Tony last night and told him everything. He'll get the other customers from Denise, if they decide to pursue the button thing."

"You called Tony?" I took a deep breath and resisted the urge to yell at him. "Dad, you shouldn't have done that. We took the job working for Logan, which means we're working for Dharma Lake, not the people who locked her up."

"They wouldn't have even been looking for her if you hadn't identified the van, though."

"Thanks for pointing that out," I said flatly. "Because I haven't been torturing the *hell* out of myself over that little fact, nonstop."

"Listen, I understand you're frustrated, but Tony called me, and he was just confirming everything Logan had told them. Your friend didn't name us, but Tony's the kind of guy who can put two and two together. He's a good cop, and he's handling the investigation."

"So, this is it? We're done?"

There was a long pause, and then he said, "I'm going to make some calls to some old investigator friends and see if I can find you someone else to apprentice with."

"You're firing me?"

"Stormy, calm down."

The irritation in his voice, combined with those three irritating words—*Stormy, calm down*—set me off. What happened next wasn't pretty, it involved some swearing, and it ended with me saying something to the effect of, "You can't fire me as your partner, because I quit!"

January 8th

Doing a full inventory at my gift store took three days, which was two days longer than I'd promised myself it would take.

The previous owner's system for assigning codes to items that didn't have barcodes was slightly worse than no system at all. By the end of the third and final day, I was throwing non-coded mystery objects into cardboard boxes that were heading to my house, or the garbage dump, or back to the circle of hell from which they'd come.

My employee, Brianna, knew exactly what I was up to.

"Boss, you don't really need that many heart-shaped candles at your house, do you?"

We were standing in the stock room, which had been pulled apart and mostly put back together again, along with the rest of the store.

"Candles are nice," I said defensively. "I like to set a mood when I take a bath. A heart-shaped mood."

She rubbed the back of her hand across her sweaty forehead, smearing dust across her skin. "Tell me the truth. You're only taking this stuff home because you don't want to code and count the final odds and ends."

"What's the point? We could put it all into the computer inventory, but nobody's going to buy this crap."

I tossed another unlabeled and uncoded object—a carved wooden tiki god with red eyes, a long nose, and giant teeth—into the cardboard box, then taped it shut.

"Bri, some of these bizarro tchotchkes have been in the stock room since before you were born. *Before I was born.* Where does it come from? Honestly, I suspect some of the garden gnomes come to life after closing time and make random crap out of garbage from the alley."

Brianna quirked one eyebrow at me. "We could have a sidewalk sale. Some of these old things are cool in a retro way."

"If by *sidewalk sale* you mean leave them on the sidewalk and hope they disappear, I'm in."

"Cheer up, boss. Remember how I said we had three more shelves left? I lied. It was only one, and we did it. As of this moment, we're finished doing inventory."

"We're done?" I pulled a tissue from my pocket and pretended to be weeping from joy.

Just then, the door chime beeped to let us know someone had come in the front door.

I grumbled under my breath about silly people not being able to read the signs posted on doors, but then switched to a cheerful greeting when I saw the visitor was Marcy from Misty Microchips, with Stanley in tow on his rainbow leash.

"Sorry to bust in on you," Marcy said.

"You saw the sign on the door: *Storewide Inventory In Progress. Unauthorized Entry to the Premises Indicates Your Consent to Count Inventory on a Volunteer Basis.*"

Marcy laughed. "I did read your sign. Did you have a lawyer write that up?"

"I did. Logan Sanderson stopped by on the first day, so I put him to work."

While we were talking, Stanley had been walking around the store, smelling everything with great interest. He'd been in before with Marcy, but now everything was in different places.

Marcy picked up a red glass apple and buffed it on her lavender tailored blouse, just like it was a real apple she was about to take a bite of.

"Logan Sanderson," she said. "That's the new lawyer, right? The one who rents an apartment from you?"

"He rents half my duplex. We're just friends."

She picked up a yellow-green pear and buffed it next.

"Isn't he involved in that whole thing with that waitress, Dharma or whatever her name is?"

I studied Marcy's face for some clue as to why she was pretending to be ignorant of the hottest bit of gossip going around Misty Falls for the last three days.

"If you mean representing her criminal defense, then yes, I believe he is."

"Right. So, have you heard anything? Between knowing that lawyer, plus your dad's connections, you must have the whole inside scoop on the case."

I sighed. The truth was, I could have gotten the inventory finished in two days, but I'd taken my time because it was a good excuse to shut out everyone and their nosy questions.

As for my inside scoop, I'd heard a few things the rest of the town wasn't privy to. I knew the bullet pulled from the tree matched the murder weapon. I knew the shot-through cans would be helpful in Dharma's defense, but that, sadly, the lab technicians hadn't been able to pull even a print from any of the cans, let alone a clear match. I knew Dharma's bail had been set at an astronomical amount that she had no hope of paying without help from her uncle, and I also knew her uncle was a jerk, because he *hadn't* put up the bond. Dharma Lake was sitting in a jail cell in the city, and her husband was still in Misty Falls, being monitored by a neighbor, but not doing well without his wife.

Those last two things were exactly why I didn't take any pleasure in participating in local gossip.

"I've got nothing juicy," I said to Marcy. "The whole thing makes me feel like crying, so can we talk about something else?"

She blinked rapidly and backed away from the glass fruit. "Like what? Do you mean that website you wanted me to track down the owner of?"

"Sure," I said. Not that it would do any good now. The cops were sure they had their killer, thanks to Dharma's confession. They weren't even following through on the button, because a quick glance at the full records for Sew It Goes revealed that half the town over forty owned a tan shirt with mother-of-pearl buttons. Even Marcy was a customer, by the look of the snazzy buttons on the lavender blouse she'd been using to buff glass fruit.

"I forgot all about your website thing, but I'll get right on it," Marcy said. "Are you busy tomorrow night? We should get the gang together for some Golden Wok."

"Sure, that sounds…" I smacked my forehead. "I can't, actually. I'm hosting a knitting club at my house." I snapped my fingers as a new idea hit me. "Marcy, you strike me as the crafty type."

Her eyes widened. "What do you mean?"

"Crafts and stuff. I loved the beautiful masquerade masks you made for yourself and Marvin for the

New Year's Eve party. And you crocheted Stanley's leash and collar. You need to come to the knitting club? My place, at seven."

"Oh, I don't know…"

"I'll twist Jessica's arm and get her to come. It'll be fun, I swear. What are you working on now?"

"A blanket."

"Bring it! That is, unless knitters and crocheters have some sort of longstanding feud. I wouldn't want a violent confrontation."

She didn't laugh at my joke.

"You'll have fun," I said.

"Okay. I guess I could give it a shot." She tugged on Stanley's leash. "Come on, Stanley-boo-boo. We'd better get home and make our dinner."

"Marcy, before you go, can I ask you something?"

"Sure. Anything."

"Did you go to the Polar Bear Dip? Jessica didn't get any pictures of herself jumping in, and I was hoping someone got a photo I could make a print from, to celebrate her tenth year."

"No, I didn't go. I spent the entire day at home, in my house, with my husband. We didn't go out, and then we ordered pizza for dinner."

"That sounds cozy. Which pizza place? I'm still learning all the good places."

"Romeo's Ribs and Pizza. They make the best deep-dish crust. Anything else is just a waste of good tomato sauce, as Marvin would say."

"Sounds good," I said with a laugh. "I'll keep Romeo's in mind. See you tomorrow night. Here, let me give you my address."

I pressed the button on the receipt printer to roll out a scrap of paper, jotted down my address, and handed it to her.

"Hey, I have an even better idea," I said. "Come over a little earlier, like six, and bring Marvin. I'll get delivery from Golden Wok and open a bottle of whatever wine goes best with sweet and sour chicken balls."

"Marvin wouldn't want to impose."

"I insist. The four of us will have fun, just like we always do."

She paused for what felt like an eternity, then said, "Sure," before leaving with Stanley.

January 9th

I checked and re-checked everything, under the watchful eye of Jeffrey.

"All systems are go," I said to him.

He sat by the front door on the rubber boot tray, watching me freak out. He was using a pair of my boots to "hide" behind, and held absolutely still, except for the very tip of his twitching tail.

"Jeffrey, you do realize I can see your fluffy gray body around the edges of my boots, don't you?"

The tail twitched again, while his eyes held steady and hypnotic. Why would he flick his tail and give himself away? It had to be part of his hunting skills, to draw the attention to his harmless, fluffy gray tail, and away from his sharp teeth.

The doorbell rang. I was so wound up over my plan that I dropped the spoon I was holding.

Jeffrey interpreted the ear-piercing doorbell as a sign of something horrific impending, which it was. He skittered across the wood floor, spinning out wildly on his way down the hallway to a safety zone.

I wiped my palms on my jeans and opened the door.

It wasn't just my dinner guests, or the takeout food, but everyone, all at once. Jessica held back and attempted to pay the delivery driver for the food, but I'd already paid when I'd placed the order. We thanked the driver, and Jessica helped me bring the food inside.

In the kitchen, she leaned over and whispered to me, "Let me know how much I owe you for my share."

I told her she could get the next one, or just help me plate everything so we weren't serving ourselves from cardboard boxes.

While Jessica got the food set out, I gave Marvin and Marcy a tour of the house.

Marvin rapped his knuckles on a doorframe and said, in a deliberately deep and manly voice, "Solid investment you have here, Stormy."

"You don't think it's too big for a single girl living on her own?"

He walked into my bedroom, took a good, long look, and then pushed down on the corner of my mattress. "I'd say everything is just right, and you won't be single for long."

I joined him inside the room and took a seat on the mattress, then gave it a bounce. "I'm not exactly single," I said in a flirty voice. "There's a new man in my life."

Marvin couldn't conceal his excitement over me being friendly toward him. His voice rose and caught in his throat. "Oh, really?"

I shot a guilty look over to Marcy, who stood in my doorway with a murderous look on her face. I jumped up from the bed and rubbed my palms on my jeans. It wasn't hard to act nervous, because I was.

"My new man is Jeffrey-boo-boo. He's hiding under the bed because the doorbell scared him. You know what he's like." I rubbed my hands together and crossed my arms. "I mean, you know what cats are like."

From down the hall, Jessica called out, "Dinner's ready!"

Marcy gave Marvin a scathing look. "Darling, remember to go easy on the wine tonight."

"Yes, dear," he said.

The three of us returned to the open space at the front of the house and took our seats at the table. I smiled at Jessica, who was playing her part as perfectly as someone who didn't know she was playing a part. I had myself to thank for that, because I hadn't told her a single word of the plan.

Jessica sat to my right, with her back to the kitchen, and opened the bottle of white wine. She had her long red hair down in loose ringlets. She had some chafed, dry skin around her nose, but was over the cold she'd gotten after the Polar Bear Dip.

Marcy, seated to the right of Jessica and across from me, looked nearly as pale as Jessica, but in a sickly way. She reached for her glass of wine like she hoped an answer, or maybe a nicotine patch, was at the bottom.

Marvin, who'd waited until I was sitting before choosing his spot next to me, couldn't take his eyes off the space eight inches above my dinner plate. My blouse was unbuttoned, exposing a bit more cleavage than I would typically have on display for a dinner party with friends.

"Cheers," I said, and we clinked our wine glasses.

"Delicious," Jessica said. "Not too sweet, either."

"Extraordinary," Marvin said in agreement.

I'd chosen an off-dry Riesling that would complement the spicy noodle dishes, because, contrary to what Marcy wanted, I hoped people would *drink like fishes*, as the saying goes. I'd even gone so far as to hide the real white wine glasses, so our only option was the enormous globes I usually reserved for red.

I took another sip of the flavorless Riesling, noting to myself that my glass wasn't as tasty as theirs. Stress can make you lose your sense of taste, so you need more of everything to compensate. It's one of the reasons why people drink too many martinis at business lunches. Having an expense account doesn't hurt, either.

Marvin finished his first glass just as the doorbell rang.

"Someone's early for the knitting club," Jessica said. "It's a good thing we have enough to share!"

I kept my eyes down as I rose from my chair and went to the door. It should *not* have been someone early for the club meeting, because I'd canceled it a few hours earlier, citing stomach flu. I'd spoken to everyone personally, so whoever stood on the other side of my door either wanted to either sell me something or ruin everything.

Close. It was my father.

"Dad. How did you get here?"

"Rode my trusty cane like it was a broomstick. How do you think I got here? I took a taxi." He stepped inside and kicked off his slip-on boots. "Smells good. Golden Wok?"

With a loud, clear voice, I said, "I'm so glad you decided to join us, Dad. This is very unexpected, but perhaps Jessica can find you a plate."

He grabbed one of the folding chairs I had leaning against the wall for the meeting that wasn't happening, unfolded it with a snap, and joined us, parking himself between my chair and Jessica's.

He reached across the table and shook Marvin's hand, then Marcy's. He either didn't see, or was ignoring, my dirty look.

We'd barely spoken over the last four days, ever since he'd fired me as his apprentice. I'd used the time to count inventory during the day, and then go over my notes for the case in the evening. I'd spent much of my time looking at photos, zooming in and out, or running slideshows with images coming up in random order.

In addition to my crime scene pictures, I'd logged into some social media and downloaded pictures taken by local residents on and around New Year's Day. I'd found very few photos of Voula Varga, which made her seem—to me, anyway—like she'd been a ghost long before she passed away.

The night before Marcy dropped in looking for gossip, I'd been looking at pictures from the Polar Bear Dip. When I saw Marcy's mother-of-pearl buttons, something had tickled the back of my brain.

And then… to my utter delight… she had lied. Marcy said she and Marvin had stayed home all day, but that wasn't true. One of them had been at the Polar Bear Dip, because I'd seen their dog, Stanley, in photos from the chilly event. He wasn't the only brown Labradoodle in town, but he was the only one with a distinctive rainbow collar and leash. I couldn't see the person holding his leash, but if it had been Marvin, that meant Marcy lied to me so she'd have an alibi.

We passed the dishes of takeout food around the table, and I studied Marcy when she wasn't looking. Was it her who shot Voula? Could it have been over Marvin? No, Marvin wasn't the sort of catch you'd kill someone over. It had to be about money.

In a few minutes, when the opportunity came up, I'd back Marcy into a corner and turn on the heat.

Jessica and Marcy kept on talking about their holiday weight gains, and attempts at new fitness routines. My father and Marvin discussed computer viruses.

Now? Was it time?

I looked into my father's eyes. In his expression, I felt his support. He understood what I was about to do, and he had my back.

I took another breath, and then I went for it.

CHAPTER 34

I WAVED MY HAND to get Marcy's attention, then asked, "Did you ever get the report for that domain name I asked you about last week?"

She slowly pulled her purse from the back of her chair. My heart pounded while she rummaged in the bag. Marcy's shoulder bag was big enough to easily conceal a handgun, and I hadn't exactly frisked her on the way in.

She pulled out something rainbow-hued. It was the blanket she'd been crocheting.

"Cute!" Jessica exclaimed.

"You don't think it's too loose?" Marcy asked. "I made the loops so big, it's not much of a blanket. The holes let the heat out."

"But it's so cute," Jessica said. "And you don't need to use it as a blanket. It would look so cheerful draped over a piece of bland furniture."

"I guess so," Marcy said glumly.

Jessica got up, took the loopy rainbow blanket from Marcy's hands, and draped it loosely over the comfy chair by my sofa. Jessica was right; the chair did look more cheerful now.

Marcy set her bag aside and went back to eating her Golden Wok.

I crumpled inside from disappointment. Now everybody was talking about crochet projects and their favorite colors.

ANGELA PEPPER

I eyed Marcy's bag. Did she have the information about the domain name or not? I wanted it so bad, I could barely restrain myself from grabbing the bag. Perhaps I could distract her with an errand? Not to the basement, but maybe I could ask for her help with my hair or makeup. Or I could try flirting with Marvin again. (Gross.)

"Earth to Stormy," Marcy said. "What's going— oh, you wanted that domain name information, didn't you? Hang on, I've got it right here."

She reached into her voluminous bag, then handed me a sheet of paper. It was an official-looking printout of the registrant of the fake movie production company. I'd been expecting Marcy to say her contact couldn't get the private information after all, but here it was.

It was the registration record, all right, but not the real one.

I excused myself for a minute, while the table continued their conversation about crocheted blankets and other things that didn't seem nearly as important to me. I walked into the washroom, closed and locked the door, opened the below-sink cupboard, and pulled out a sheet of paper I'd hidden between the towels.

Marcy wasn't the only one who knew hackers who could get information. I'd made a few calls and gotten my own report. This one hadn't been edited, though.

After a brief pep talk in the mirror—*Stormy, you can do this! You've closed multimillion-dollar deals in the boardroom with sharks and sociopaths. You may not be an investigator, but you've got skills. Plus there's more wine in the fridge to wipe everyone's memories if you blow this thing. Not that you'll blow*

324

it. You probably won't. Go get 'em, champ!—I walked back out to the dining table and placed both of the sheets of paper next to Marvin.

"Marvin," I said sweetly. "Why do you suppose your wife is telling lies about her involvement with this company? It's a fake business set up to convince some foolish investors to put their life savings up for a movie that will never get made."

Everyone at the table fell silent. I heard the wood-on-wood sound of someone dropping their chopsticks.

"The movie's called *House of Love and Lies*," I said. "Isn't that the funniest thing? I do enjoy a bit of irony. Marvin, why do you suppose your *loving* wife would be *lying*? She gave me this printout for a domain name registration. Nothing too scandalous, right, but here's the real one." I pointed to the email address on the real registration. "That's the customer service email for the computer store, isn't it?"

Marvin's eyes flicked back and forth between the two papers. Nobody made a peep. I could feel the heat coming from Marcy's end of the table, but I didn't dare look over at her face. It wasn't time yet.

I looked at my father, sitting to my right and across from Marvin. He said, with gentle authority, "Son, if you know something, now's the time to speak up. Don't cover for your wife. She's the one who's going down for this. Don't let her drag you into the nightmare. Speak up for yourself."

Marvin slowly looked up from the papers and turned to his wife. "Marcy, how could you? I told you that woman was dangerous. I told you to stay away, but you got greedy. I was never enough for you."

Now.

Now the entire focus of the table turned to Marcy, all at once.

Marcy's jaw worked up and down for several seconds before she squeaked out words. "I didn't… I would never… just shut up, Marvin! Shut up!"

Marvin glared at his wife. "When I woke up on New Year's Day, you weren't in bed. You were at Voula's house, weren't you?" He covered his mouth with his hand. "Oh my God, you killed her. Marcy, how could you?"

"Shut up!" she yelled. "Marvin, shut up!"

Marvin did shut up. We all waited. The two white sheets of paper screamed their damning evidence in the silence.

Marvin looked weirdly relaxed. He had no more expression on his face than he'd had on New Year's Eve, in the masquerade mask.

Marcy, however, looked like she was holding her breath underwater.

Jessica was white as the sheets of paper on the table, visibly recoiling from Marcy while leaning toward my father.

And Finnegan Day was… helping himself to a second round of noodles. I heard the greasy suction sound of the food's surface tension breaking as he scooped three clumps of the glistening food onto his plate.

I kicked him under the table.

He took a bite anyway. Around the food in his mouth, he said, "Calm down, everyone. We all know Marcy here wouldn't hurt a fly." He gave Marvin a pointed look. "You, however, may not be so fortunate when she gets you home tonight." He chuckled at his joke.

Jessica came out of her daze and jerkily reached for the wine bottle. She sloppily refilled the glasses, then drank hers, still leaning close to my father and keeping her eyes on Marcy.

I looked down at my plate, hoping the noodles would spell out something to guide me. If I squinted, one of the noodles looked like the letter *g*. That didn't help.

Apply the pressure, Stormy. Nothing happens in business without passion and pressure!

I poked at my food, tilted my head to the side, and let the next question come without force.

"Marcy, I'm sure there's a logical explanation for why you tried to cover up your connection to Voula's investment scheme. I'm thinking you started off trying to help her, then backed away when you realized she was trying to rip off the good people of Misty Falls."

"Yes," Marcy said, lunging at my explanation. "That's exactly what happened. I never did anything illegal." She lifted her wine glass with a trembling hand and splashed most of the Riesling into her mouth.

My father reached for the broccoli. "Anyone mind if I snag these greens?"

The group murmured that he could go ahead.

I turned and gave Marvin the sweetest smile I could muster. "Tonight's been so interesting," I said huskily as I gazed into his eyes. "We're all learning so much about each other."

He swallowed hard enough for me to hear the gulp. He finished his glass of wine, then said, directly to my father, "Mr. Day, don't worry about this nonsense with my wife. I was overreacting before. She didn't know Voula that well. Nobody did."

"You'll handle the situation," my father said. "That's what we men have to do, when the women get themselves in trouble."

"Women," Marvin said with a shrug. "Can't live with 'em, can't shoot 'em."

My father laughed, but Jessica gasped, "Marvin, what a terrible thing to say! It's no joking matter."

Marvin looked pleased that he'd annoyed Jessica. "What? It's just an expression."

"I'm not an idiot," someone said.

It was Marcy speaking. Her voice sounded disembodied, mechanical. She stared into the middle of the table, at nothing.

The lifeless voice came again: "Marvin, I know about your secret bank account, and your *indiscretions*."

Marvin's face reddened. "Uh-oh. I'm in trouble," he said, while chuckling, to my father.

A breaded chicken ball flew through the air, whizzing through the space between me and Marvin. Marcy had thrown it, and had another chicken ball in her hand, ready to toss.

Marvin's careful mask slipped into anger, and his brown eyes grew very dark. Through clenched teeth, he practically growled, "I think it's time for us to go now, Marcy."

"I don't want to go." She lobbed the chicken ball at him. This one struck his chest, and he jerked his body, as though shot.

He pushed his chair back, but didn't stand.

Marcy turned to Jessica. "He thinks he's smarter than me. He thinks he's smarter than all women, but he isn't."

Jessica looked like she was about to throw up, but she managed to reply, "I thought things had been going better for you two lately."

"I guess I am stupid," Marcy said sadly. "I thought we had a chance, but now I can see he's trying to set me up for what I did." She lifted her chin and addressed my father. "Mr. Day, the GPS tracking on our car will put it at the edge of town, near Voula Varga's house, on New Year's Day. I've found long, black, curly strands of that woman's hair in my vehicle, on Marvin's clothes, and even in our bed. Do you think the police would be interested in that information?"

Marvin stood. "We're done here."

"Not so fast," I said. "I've got a beautiful lemon mousse chilling in the fridge for dessert, and I think we'd all like to hear what you were doing the morning Voula Varga was shot. Was it self-defense, Marvin?"

"What?" He looked at me like I was nuts, and maybe I was.

"Were you stalking her?" I asked. "Did you sneak into her house to watch her get dressed, then shoot her when she caught you being a pervert? Marvin, that's what you are, right? A dirty little pervert? Even right now, you keep looking down my shirt, when your wife is sitting four feet away."

His eyes as dark as night, he spat at me, "She said she was in love with me, but she was just using me. It meant nothing to her."

Marcy began sobbing noisily.

"Ha ha!" Marvin boomed. "I was just joking. Everyone, look how quick my wife is at jumping to conclusions. This is why we've been having some relationship issues. Private issues." He started moving toward the door. "Marcy, get your boots on. We're going."

My father got to his feet and moved between Marvin and the door. "You're not going anywhere. You've had a lot of wine and shouldn't be driving. Let's get some coffee in you first."

Marvin growled, "Out of my way, old man," and pushed my father to the floor.

"Logan!" I yelled. "Logan, help! Now!"

Logan Sanderson came bounding into the room from where he'd been hiding, on the other side of the basement door. He ran toward Marvin, then stopped abruptly, his hands in the air.

"Easy now," Logan said, breathing heavily. "Nobody else needs to get hurt today."

From where he was groaning on the floor in my kitchen, my father said, "Careful. It's as sharp as it looks."

I joined Marcy and Jessica at the far edge of the room, with the table between us and Marvin, who was now wielding the sword that had been concealed inside my father's cane. The sword wasn't long, but it was sharp, and dangerous.

Marvin lunged at Logan, sword flashing. Logan staggered back, bumping into our huddle.

"Uh-oh," Logan said.

That wasn't something I wanted to hear. *Uh-oh* was not part of the plan. My father was right about plans. They do go wrong.

Logan clutched his stomach. The fabric of his shirt had been sliced, and red blood wicked at the edges. His eyes were wide and fearful as he said to me, "We didn't plan for this."

Marcy, who'd been stunned into silence since the revelation, sprang into action like a small but aggressive dog who thinks she's bigger than she is.

She marched toward her husband. "Marvin, put the sword down!"

"No."

"Put it down!" she barked, walking around him in a wide circle, until she, Marvin, and my father were in a straight line along the exterior wall. "NOW! Marvin! DROP IT!"

Her husband cowered, leaning down with the sword limp in his hand, but then he looked around at the rest of us. He straightened up and held the sword high, pointing at his wife.

"Marcy, you're drunk," he said evenly. "Listen to me. These people are trying to trick us into turning on each other. Marcy, I love you."

"You... you love me?" Her angry-dog posture softened.

"Of course I do. Get over here and open the door for me while I hold these crazy people off. We're leaving this place, leaving this whole backwoods town. We should never have come here. This whole place is—"

He stopped talking, distracted by the rainbow-hued crocheted blanket—the one I'd grabbed from the chair and tossed over him like a net. While Marvin struggled to comprehend what was happening, my father reached out from his position on the floor, grabbed a corner of the loopy rainbow blanket, and yanked hard.

Marvin tried to escape, but his anger worked against him. The slim sword had passed through the wide, airy loops, and was now outside of the net. He couldn't cut his way free without risking cuts to himself. In his rage, he tore at the blanket, trying to rip his way out, but it was a strong yarn, strong enough to make dog collars and leashes. He only got himself more tangled.

With another tug from my father, Marvin lost his balance and started toppling over. I kicked the cane sword clear so he wouldn't hurt himself by falling on it—not that he didn't deserve it.

CHAPTER 35

ONCE WE HAD MARVIN safely under our own citizen's arrest, we called the police. Tony and Kyle showed up with what appeared to be the entire Misty Falls Police Department.

Marvin was still so tangled in the blanket that they left him in it, cuffed him through the loops, and led him away.

The paramedics tended to my father, who had some bruises but was otherwise okay, and to Logan, who would need stitches to close up the gash on his abdomen, but had escaped being disemboweled.

Jessica took Marcy to the spare bedroom to calm her friend. She'd told us most of what she knew about Marvin's actions. Her side of the story came out in a jumble of emotional outbursts, but still painted a very clear picture.

Marcy had suspected for a while that her husband had been having an affair, because he'd disappear for long walks with the dog. Stanley the Labradoodle couldn't talk, but the lack of snow clumps between his toes told the story of a much shorter walk, and a car ride.

It wasn't until a few days after Voula's murder that Marcy connected her husband's renewed interest in their marriage with the crime he'd committed.

She searched for evidence, and hit the jackpot when she found his tan shirt in the laundry hamper.

She couldn't test for gunshot residue, but she did find dark spots she suspected were blood, plus a button had been torn off at the cuff. She put the shirt in a plastic bag, then hid it in the attic, inside the box of Christmas decorations they'd just put away.

Marcy loved her husband enough that she tried covering for him, being his alibi without him knowing that she knew. It hadn't been easy, though. The stress had been causing hallucinations. She imagined she was being haunted by Voula's ghost.

As for why Marvin had shot Voula, our best guess was he'd found out she was using him, and didn't really love him.

I hoped for more information after the police questioned him, but I had high hopes for Dharma Lake coming back home to her husband, where she belonged.

Soon, things would be back to normal, or at least a new type of normal.

My father and Logan seemed to have bonded. I found out Logan had been nervous about the plan, and called my father as last-minute backup without telling me. On one hand, I'd been grateful to have my father there. On the other hand, he'd unwittingly supplied a very sharp weapon to our killer.

In all the chaos, we didn't get an opportunity to talk alone about what had happened, but we didn't need to. I could see everything I needed on his face. He kept smiling at me, looking like the proudest dad in the world. Regardless of whether or not he would continue being my mentor, I would have his support. He'd shown up for my crazy dinner party, after all.

It was hard to say whether or not my plan would have been successful without Finnegan Day. I tried not to think about it.

KYLE DEMPSEY CAME over to the living room window, where I'd been standing to stay out of the way.

"Fancy meeting you here, at another crime scene," Kyle said.

"At least there's no dead body, which is good, because this old wood floor already has enough stains."

"Do you have something for me?" He batted his thick, honey-colored eyelashes over his aquamarine-blue eyes. "A *little* something?"

I could feel my cheeks reddening. "Kyle, I'm not going to kiss you."

He grinned, deepening his adorable dimples. "I meant the evidence. Logan said you both had your phones recording the entire dinner, video and audio."

"Oh, *that* little something."

He leaned against the wall, his broad, muscled body blocking some of the noise from the chaos in my house. "Maybe there's somewhere more quiet you want to give that little something to me? A spare room, perhaps?"

"No need. Got it right here." I reached into my pocket for the external storage stick I'd transferred a copy of the recording onto already.

"I do like your house, by the way," he said. "Very comfortable. I should stop by for coffee more often."

"Dimples—I mean, Officer Dempsey—you and I can't see each other as more than friends."

"Stormy Day, you're not too old for me. Our age difference is *not* a big deal."

"Of course not. But I'm pursuing my private investigator's license, and I'll need your help from time to time. If you and I were romantically involved, I'd be taking advantage of you."

His smile got even bigger. "I *want* you to take advantage of me, Stormy Day."

Slowly, I placed the memory stick in his hand and closed his fingers around it. I bit my lower lip as I squeezed his hand. He had a beautiful hand, not too big, with an angelic haze of blond hair on his upper knuckles.

Then I forced myself to pull my hand away.

"Thanks, but no thanks, officer," I said.

"Whatever happens, it's my pleasure to serve and protect you, ma'am."

He nodded politely, then turned and walked away.

I allowed myself to look at his butt. Just once.

CHAPTER 36
FEBRUARY 14

"Will you be my valentine?"

I offered Jeffrey a heart-shaped satchel of catnip. He took it without so much as a thank-you, carried it over to the corner of the living room, and started enjoying a private catnip party.

"Is he okay?" Jessica asked. "He's breathing heavily, making a funny noise."

We both listened.

SNARF SNARF.

"Weird," I said. "I've heard him make that same snarf-snarf sound while rubbing his face on my father's dirty wool socks. Mr. Jeffrey Blue has eclectic tastes."

Jessica rested her head on my shoulder. "Hey, thanks again for letting me move in with you for a bit."

"Thanks for volunteering to scoop Jeffrey's litter box every day."

"That's funny. I don't remember seeing that detail on the lease."

I chuckled. "You should have read the fine print. You also have to make cinnamon buns for breakfast whenever I get a craving."

Jessica sighed dramatically. "I should have had my lawyer friend look over the contract."

On the floor in front of us, Jeffrey flung his catnip heart into the air, attacked and killed it, then resumed nuzzling the toy and making SNARF-SNARF noises.

Behind us, the movers brought in Jessica's dresser and took it down the hallway to the second bedroom. She had until the next day, the end of the fifteenth, to vacate her apartment, but we'd come up with the brilliant idea to book her moving date for the fourteenth, so we single girls had something to do on Valentine's Day.

When I'd first asked Jessica to move in, she refused, saying I was already too generous to her. It took me a while to convince her that she was doing me a favor, and not the other way around.

After all, it was me who'd invited her over for a dinner party that was just a ruse for confronting two murder suspects and having them turn on each other.

I should have known things might turn violent, and that sweet-as-a-peach, innocent, never-left-Misty-Falls Jessica could be traumatized. That night, she saw two of her friends at their worst.

Ever since then, Jessica had been making excuses to stay over at my place. When I gently confronted her, she confessed she'd been having nightmares and problems sleeping.

I felt beyond awful. Yes, I'd gotten Dharma free of prison, but there'd been a cost, and two of my friends had paid it. Logan would have a scar on his stomach, and Jessica was scarred as well, just not visibly.

Until Jessica healed, I felt better having her under my roof. As we got to work directing the movers and getting her clothes unpacked, I hoped that soon she would find comfort.

And also make cinnamon buns.

BY THE NEXT SATURDAY, Jessica seemed happy in her new surroundings—so happy, in fact, that she refused to leave her nest for dinner with me, Logan, and his former client, Dharma.

Truth be told, I wasn't that excited about the dinner, either, but I'd agreed to go.

In the month since the police arrested Marvin, I'd done a few more investigations for Logan. None of the cases had resulted in anyone getting skewered, but I did score another bruise on my rear end, slipping on ice while in pursuit of an adulterous spouse. On the bright side, I did get some crisp images of the cheaters exchanging more than kisses, up high in the bleachers at the skating rink.

Now that I was working for Logan, our relationship was evolving. We shared a roof, so it was easy to schedule meetings for dinnertime, then enjoy a casual meal while comparing case notes. Sometimes, one of us would show up at the other one's door with food, even when there was no new case information.

I wasn't unhappy with the comfortable place we were in, but there were times I longed for some passion in my life—and kisses from someone who didn't have cat whiskers.

For that night's dinner, I put on the stunning black and white dress I'd worn for New Year's Eve, then went next door to catch a ride with Logan.

He came out and started telling me about the stressful day he'd had, without even a glance at my dress.

In his truck on the way to the restaurant, I scrolled through messages on my phone and only half listened to him complaining about his high-maintenance legal clients.

AT THE RESTAURANT, Dharma greeted me with a warm hug, then stepped back and declared that I looked stunning *and* youthful. I returned the compliment, noting how beautiful her hair was in its natural snowy-white shade. She had gotten the dyed length trimmed off, so her hair was much shorter than my pixie cut, barely an inch long, but adorable.

The three of us took our seats, ordered some drinks, and settled in with some talk about the weather. Compared to how she'd been the night she turned herself in, Dharma was a whole different person, exuberant and charming. Her husband was doing well, managing his health issues, but didn't come along for dinner, because he preferred quiet nights in during the winter.

By the time our meals arrived, we were deep in conversation about the Voula Varga case. More information had been come to light, including the fact Marvin had been installing spyware on Misty Falls residents' computers. This malicious software gave him access to all sorts of things, including email and banking records. He'd shared information with Voula, so she could convince people she was tapped into a mystical, all-seeing psychic energy field.

The two of them had met when she purchased a refurbished laptop. The laptop had later been recovered at Misty Microchips, wiped as clean as a snowy mountaintop.

Once the police knew what they were looking for, it was easy to find the evidence. The crime lab found Marvin's hairs in Voula's laundry, and the police found an eyewitness—the black-haired girl with the

Corgi—who would testify that she'd seen Marvin leaving Voula's house several times.

Dharma's memory had returned. She remembered taking the gun from her uncle's mansion at Voula's urging. It was, in her words, a "stupid, childish" thing, but Voula had convinced her she was justified. Her uncle, Deiter Koenig, had been a miser to some family members, like her, but exceedingly generous with others. She wanted to invest in Voula's friend's movie, make her own fortune, and stop trying to suck up to her uncle at his horrible dinner parties.

She'd let jealousy and greed get the better of her, and it had nearly cost her everything.

As for the day of the murder, she'd left the gun with Voula, gone to her van to leave, and accidentally flooded the old thing by hitting the gas too hard. It happened frequently, and she knew the solution was to let the gas evaporate, so she waited.

She waited a good ten minutes, then leaned forward to floor the accelerator and try the engine. Before she'd turned the key, she heard a horrible bang.

The antique gun must have gone off by accident, she thought. She ran into the house to check on Voula. The ceiling squeaked with movements on the upper floor. She ran to the foot of the stairs, calling Voula's name.

Her friend didn't answer, but she thought she heard the radio. It was a man's voice, and he was talking about making someone a doll that looked like the only person they cared about.

She thought it was just another of the odd things the local radio DJ talked about in the afternoon, so she called out again for her friend, louder.

The house went quiet. She walked up the stairs slowly, entered the room, and saw the victim on the floor. Panic set in, making her decisive. There were no neighbors for miles, so she would drive into town to get help. Once the thought had come to her, she didn't even consider using the phone to call for help.

She ran outside, where the van started without flooding, and she raced toward town. That was when she ran me off the road—something she apologized for repeatedly—and then went on to crash into another vehicle on her way to the hospital to get help.

After our dinner, we ordered lemon mousse for dessert.

Logan gave me a sly smile when the bright yellow slices arrived at our table in a scented citrus cloud.

"I know this mousse," he said.

"But you didn't get any that night," I said. "It really was in the fridge, standing by to serve if I didn't get a confession from either Marcy or Marvin."

He lifted a forkful to his mouth, then closed his eyes and made a happy face. I really liked that look on him.

Dharma saw me watching him, and gave me a knowing look.

"Sorry you didn't get any lemon mousse that night," I said.

"That's okay. The sight of blood on my shirt would have ruined my appetite, if seeing your good friend *Tony* gobbling down the Golden Wok leftovers hadn't already killed it."

I let his comment go without correction. Captain Tony Milano hadn't eaten the Chinese food, at least not from what I'd seen, but he did pillage my refrigerator and "confiscate" the lemon mousse to serve to all the first responders who were on site. I think it was my father's idea. The two of them were in their glory, in the heart of chaos, celebrating the arrest.

Dharma set her napkin on the table, preparing to go. She'd already finished her lemon mousse, whereas I hadn't even started mine.

"My job here is done," she said.

"Wait," I said. "Your job? You're leaving already?"

"My husband's waiting at home, and it's our date night. Don't get up. You two stay. I've already ordered a special treat, and it'll be out any minute."

Logan and I exchanged a look, eyebrows raised. *Special treat?*

I turned to ask Dharma what she meant, but she was already gone.

The waiter appeared, and opened a bottle of *Veuve Clicquot* with a dramatic POP.

We sat in stunned silence as the waiter poured two flutes of champagne.

"I guess we're celebrating," Logan said.

I lifted my glass to clink it with his. "Cheers!"

"Wait," he said. "I want to do a proper toast."

"Okay." I set my glass back down and waited.

"First of all, you look beautiful tonight. That dress is my new favorite thing—not that I don't love your bathrobe, of course."

"Thanks, I think."

He gazed at me, his eyes as blue as the winter sky, and just as calm.

"You look beautiful every day," he said. "I've really enjoyed working with you these last few weeks, and getting to know you." He glanced down at the tablecloth bashfully, then back up at me. "What I'm trying to say is—"

He looked up, over my head, and frowned.

"Stormy, who's that guy, and why's he staring at us?"

I turned around in my chair and followed his gaze.

A man stood by the entryway to the dining area, at the hostess station. He straightened up with recognition when he met my gaze.

I turned back around slowly.

Uh-oh.

Dharma Lake had made a plan, and now her plan was going wrong.

"I'm so sorry about this, Logan," I said. "That guy staring at us is my former fiancé. It's Christopher."

THE END OF BOOK #2

TO BE CONTINUED...
IN STORMY DAY MYSTERY #3

DEATH OF A BATTY GENIUS

ANGELA PEPPER

www.angelapepper.com